WAKING OLIVIA

ELIZABETH O'ROARK

1

Olivia

I t's my first day at a new college and I'm dragging my feet like it's an execution. Which makes sense since the man I'll meet today has the ability to destroy my life.

I seek out the dining hall first, using the crappy, copied map the school sent me last month. Athletes are provided a dining plan whether they live on campus or not. Given that I've spent the past three months eating nothing but eggs and ramen, this is probably a good thing.

I get my food and sit alone with the exact breakfast I have every day during the school year: one scrambled egg, plain oatmeal, and one apple. I eat the apple first, praying I can hold it down.

I already know today's meeting can't possibly go well. After the incident at my last school, it was a shock that *any* team would have me, and I'm pretty sure my new coach is about to make his reservations clear. The best case scenario is a series of warnings and threats, and the worst is that he lays out conditions I can't possibly agree to. *They wanted you*, I remind myself. *They gave you a scholarship. It won't be that bad.*

But no matter how often I say it, my stomach continues to churn.

~

THE ATHLETIC DEPARTMENT is housed in a vast building that dwarfs almost any other on campus. It lets you know in no uncertain terms what matters most at East Colorado University. I suppose I should be grateful for this fact since it's the reason I've got a scholarship.

There's no wariness on the secretary's face when she tells me I can go in, which means she must be one of maybe ten people in the world of collegiate sports who don't know what I did. Most people watch me now as if I'm a rabid animal or that snake in Malaysia, the one whose bite is so deadly you collapse only a few feet from the site of the attack.

There's no doubt, as I enter the room, that the two men in front of me know *exactly* what happened. They're already looking at me sternly—narrowed eyes, arms folded—which means I'm already sort of pissed off.

I brace myself for the lecture I know is coming because I have no other choice. Peter McEwan, the coach in front of me, is the stuff of legends, and I *need* a legend right now. People used to call me a *gifted* runner. They spoke of my potential in awed voices. Now the only thing they talk about is how I evaded jail time.

But McEwan needs a legend too. ECU hasn't had a winning women's cross country team in nearly a decade, which is why they've incurred the vast risk of offering me a scholarship.

They need me to find that thing, whatever it is I've lost, almost as much as I do.

I'm willing to act contrite right now for a shot at working with McEwan. I'll even pretend I'm sorry. But only for McEwan, and not the guy beside him, who's barely older than me and looks like he should be posing for the cover of *Men's Fitness* instead of sitting there scowling. He leans back in his chair, blue eyes glittering like ice on his tan face, a smug lilt to his mouth that sets my teeth on edge. I'll let McEwan lecture me, but I'll be damned if I'm going to kiss this guy's ass. *Keep glaring at me, asshole. See how far that gets you.*

McEwan rises from his chair and greets me with a handshake. "This is my colleague, Will Langstrom," he says, motioning to the guy beside him. Langstrom rises too, but his eyes remain narrowed and unwelcoming. He towers over me, and between that and the fact that he's looking at me like I drown pets for fun, he feels like a threat. People either cower or lash out when threatened—I'll give you one guess what camp I belong to. I swallow hard. *Keep it together,* I warn myself, my stomach tightening. *You cannot afford to lose your shit today.*

"Olivia," he says.

"I go by Finn." I meet his eyes once, matching his belligerence. *I don't need your approval, dickhead.*

"Will is the coach for the women's cross country team," McEwan adds.

My stomach drops, and inside me there's such a combination of panic and anger and disappointment I can't tell one from the other. Mostly I'm mad at myself. Did I really think Peter McEwan was going to coach me personally? Talk about equal rights all you want, no school is wasting a revered coach on the women's team.

It also means I *do* need Langstrom's approval, and he's made it clear that isn't coming easily.

"You have two years until graduation," McEwan continues, "and whether we can make something of your ability before then is entirely in his hands and yours."

I shift uncomfortably. I can't say I love the phrase "make something of your ability." I still hold three course records.

Wasn't that something *made* of my ability? Am I going to have to keep proving myself for fucking ever?

"I don't feel we need to go over what happened between you and your former teammate," he intones. My spine relaxes, just a little. "I do, however, need to make sure you understand that it can't happen here." I nod again, hands clasped in my lap. *Contrite.* "And we're not going to wait until you've hospitalized someone before we kick you out of here," he warns. "We get even a hint of that temper and you're packing your bags. Understood?"

Not show a hint of temper? Impossible. You're on the verge of 'a hint' right now. I somehow manage to nod my agreement.

"The other thing is your *extracurricular activities*," he says. "According to the reports from your last coach, they had a huge impact on your ability to practice. That can't happen here, understand?"

I blow out a breath. He has no idea what my extracurricular activities really were. How they were so much worse than what he's imagining. How I couldn't stop them if I tried. And believe me, I've tried. "I understand," I say, grinding my teeth.

McEwan stands and says he'll give me and Langstrom time to chat. My throat grows dry watching him walk out the door, and only when it's closed do I reluctantly turn back to my new coach, who I already fucking hate.

"I don't want you here," he says flatly. "I'm not buying this whole good-girl-made-a-mistake crap. You nearly killed someone."

I stare at the floor, at anything but him, trying to rein myself in. I brace myself, tighten my thighs and my biceps, draw everything in so that I don't explode. *Fuck you fuck you fuck you.* Why should I have to listen to this guy anyway? He's tall and broad, the body of a swimmer or football player, not a runner. I wouldn't tell a mechanic how to change my oil, so why should this guy get to tell me how to run?

"I'm curious," he says. "Are you even sorry?"

My fists clench. People always ask me this, but they don't really want an answer. They simply want to remind me that I *should* be sorry. And I am. I'm sorry I lost my scholarship. I'm sorry I had to leave and that I'll never run for a Division I school again. But I'm not sorry I did it. When I think of Mark Bell, with his smug smile and that ugly thing behind his eyes, it's hard to feel much regret.

I'm going to try not to say that last bit out loud.

"I didn't mean to hurt him as badly as I did," I mutter. It's the one true statement I can offer that doesn't make me sound like a sociopath.

"That's not really the same thing as being sorry," he says.

No, it's not, asshole.

"Your running is crap," he continues. "You haven't placed better than third in nearly two years, and the last time you ran a 4:30 mile was three years ago. I think you've lost it."

These are words I hear in my own head daily. "I can get it back," I tell him. "I just need to apply myself."

He crosses his arms in front of his chest. He has particularly nice biceps, which would totally distract me if we were having a different conversation. "You're a liability and I don't feel like taking time away from really talented athletes so that you can 'apply' yourself, but Peter sees something in you. Claims you're a diamond in the rough."

The words console me, momentarily. Peter McEwan thinks I'm a diamond in the rough. That's got to be worth something.

His mouth goes to a flat line. "I disagree."

If I were a smarter girl, I'd pack my bags right now. Because one of us has to go, and I'm guessing it won't be him.

~

THREE GUYS SIT along a brick wall outside the athletics building as I walk out. "Hey, new girl!" one of them shouts. Athletes are cockier than the general population. They don't worry about being shot down as much as everyone else.

I stop, letting my dark hair swing over my shoulder as I turn my head toward them. It's soothing that no matter how much I fuck up, I still always have this one thing. Being attractive is the next best thing to a superpower. It's a get-out-of-jail-free card, causing men to overlook my many other terrible qualities. *And I have so, so many terrible qualities.*

"Yes?" I ask with an eyebrow raised.

They all grin like naughty children, and the boldest one saunters forward. He's hot. Broad, probably a football player. I like that. A skinny runner's build does nothing for me. "So you're new here?" he asks.

I raise a brow. "I thought we'd established that."

"I'm Landon," he says, and inwardly I flinch. Landon is a private school name, one of those kids who wears a pink collared polo shirt and beats up gay kids after class. But he's cute. The whole super-all-American boy thing isn't necessarily my type, but after a few beers I have a whole lot of types.

"Hi, Landon," I reply, but I keep walking because men love to chase. And he chases. Of course he does. They are all so fucking predictable.

"You didn't tell me your name," he says, catching up.

"You didn't ask."

He grins, not put off at all. "Okay, what's your name?"

I'm ready to end this conversation. "Finn," I reply without slowing.

He stops in his tracks and I keep walking. "That's a boy's name!" he shouts.

I laugh to myself. "I know."

"I want you to be my girlfriend, Finn!"

Yeah. I know that too.

2

Will

I don't want that girl on my team.

From the moment she walked through Peter's door, I knew it. The music from "Jaws" could have been playing and it wouldn't have felt more ominous.

It's mind-boggling that Peter brought her here at all. She took a bat to another member of her own team, for Christ's sake. Even if her talent could make up for that, she's hit-or-miss at best. Moments of brilliance followed by months and months of mediocrity.

"She's nothing but trouble," I tell him after she's gone. I try to make my voice neutral, try to disguise my vehemence because even I realize it exceeds anything close to reasonable.

"You need a frontrunner," Peter says. "Someone who's going to make your girls think they've got a shot. Someone they're going to work for."

I exhale wearily. Peter is the one who's been doing my job for twenty-five years, who's made a national—hell, an *international* name for himself. He could have left us for a Division I school decades ago. Peter is the expert.

But Jesus, this time he's just wrong.

"We've got Betsy," I say.

His snort of derision says it all: Everyone hates Betsy. She's arrogant, a bully, and only marginally faster than the other girls but acts like she's the star. Everyone's just too scared of her to point it out.

"Okay, but Finnegan?" I continue. "You think *she's* going to inspire loyalty? She makes Betsy look like Mother Teresa."

"Have you ever seen her run?" he asks.

I shake my head. I'd graduated from college two years before she entered. I heard her name a few years ago when she was a freshman and people thought she was the next big thing. And then the whispers faded and everyone forgot, including me. I wish I could have continued forgetting.

"She's unbelievable." He sounds slightly awestruck. "When she wants to be, she makes the rest of the field look like they're in slow motion."

I know he thinks she's ECU's chance to shine, and I'll admit it's vaguely possible. But I just don't want her here, end of story. "She hasn't been unbelievable in a long time," I counter, "and she sure as hell doesn't seem like the type who pulls people together."

Peter smiles. "Who better to teach her how to do it than you?"

I'm not interested in teaching her anything, particularly now that I've met her. That girl isn't just trouble of the not-a-team-player, not-a-reliable-runner variety. She's trouble of the devious, manipulative, too-fucking-hot-for-her-own good variety. Sashaying into Peter's office like a runway model, all long-legged and tan with big green eyes and a knowing smile. She's the kind of girl who causes trouble merely by existing, and then makes sure to cause more.

And the last thing I need right now is more trouble.

3

Olivia

I'm in the back of the car, and we're going too fast down a narrow street. There's a four-way stop at the end of every block, but we only slow at some of them. I watch my mother in the passenger seat, her shoulders stiff with terror. My brother, beside me, takes my hand and squeezes it once, hard, preparing me for pain.

And then I see the woman in the intersection. A navy blue dress and swollen ankles. Her eyes meet mine—stunned, horrified—and we both know what will happen next.

Her body flies up over the hood. The blood is there, on the windshield, a splatter of it like modern art, with such immediacy it almost seems like she must have been bleeding before we hit her. We slam on the brakes and she goes flying forward. And then the car lurches over the top of her like an oversized speed bump. I suck in air, trying to replace the terror in my chest with something else, gasping as if it's my lungs that just collapsed under the car's weight.

My mother turns to me then, her eyes wide with fear, sick with it. Suddenly we are in her room.

"Run," she whispers. "Hide in the woods." And though I feel almost paralyzed by that black, gasping terror, I do as she says. I run as hard as I possibly can, desperate and hopeless at once.

The woods, the woods, the woods. It's a single phrase burned into my brain.

Get to the woods.

I'm nothing but my desire to do what she's told me to do as if it can fix everything. I run and run, with my heart pounding in my ears, knowing he's behind me, knowing the blood pouring down my back is only the start.

Knowing I've done something very, very wrong, and when I stop it will all catch up with me.

I wake on a street I've never seen before, my heart still beating too fast, drenched in sweat, hands shaking. I'm still in the shorts and tank I fell asleep in, and barefoot because I never, ever manage to keep shoes on when I sleep. I have no idea where I am. The sun's not out yet but the sky has the promise of it, its black softened with expectation.

"Son of a bitch," I mutter as I fully wake up and realize what's happened. Now I've got to find my way home.

IT TAKES me over an hour to find my apartment because I'm not familiar with the area yet. I figure I only ran about three miles before I woke up, but I probably ran another four backtracking to find my neighborhood.

I arrive at the track a short time later, undoubtedly the only girl here who's already run seven miles. I stare off in the distance, trying to pretend I don't see the rest of the team around me whispering, shooting sly glances my way. They all know who I am. Most of them wish I weren't here. There's one girl in particular, taller than the rest, who makes no secret of her disdain. *Fuck.* I haven't even met my teammates yet and I already want to throw a punch.

Will Langstrom, my new coach and dickhead extraordinaire, walks toward us and every head snaps up. Now that I can observe him freely, I'm forced to admit that he's ridiculously hot. His tousled brown hair, the hollows under his cheekbones, the upper lip. Even his stride is sexy—*cocky*—and it only makes him more appealing. I sort of hate us both for that fact.

He grins. "Morning, ladies."

"Morning, Coach," they sing in unison. I remain silent. They're all looking at him like he's Prince Charming and Christian Grey rolled into one. He could pull down his pants right now and half of them would drop to their knees. *No wonder he's such a dick.*

"I assume you've all met your new teammates," he says, with a glance at me. They remain conspicuously silent, of course. He frowns and introduces the two freshmen before turning to me. "And this is our only transfer, Olivia Finnegan, who's come to us from the University of Texas."

Every girl on the team looks at me, delighting in the comeuppance I've clearly received, *the D1 girl sent back to the minors*, but not able to gloat too much, since I'm the only person here who can win them a title. Langstrom makes them all introduce themselves, but I don't pay a lot of attention to it. Betsy, the one giving me nasty looks, is the only one I remember. It's nice to put a name to the face I'm probably going to rub in the dirt.

"We're running the ten-mile loop this morning, and it's your lucky day because I'm running with you," he says to collective groans. "Hit the road and let's see how many of you slacked this summer."

I haven't slacked. I spent the whole summer giving riding lessons during the day and running morning and night. But that won't be reflected today.

Betsy takes off and we follow. She sets a decent pace. Nothing to write home about, but given that I barely had time to shower after my run this morning, I'm okay with that.

A nightmare like I had last night—and waking up nowhere near home—is not an unusual occurrence for me. It's been happening since I was a kid, usually when I'm under stress but sometimes for no discernible reason. There are other people out there like me. They have a forum online where they exchange stories, but I've never told mine, because even in a group of abnormal people, I'm the freak. Their stories involve running down a flight of stairs or maybe a block or two. Mine involve running miles, running through the woods, waking up bleeding and drenched in sweat—and potentially destroying my shot at a running career because I can't stop doing it.

Sometimes I don't feel it as much but today I do, that heaviness in my thighs as if I'm asking them to lift a weight with each step. It's not that I can't run seventeen miles in a day, it's just that I can't run them *fast*. I can't sprint them. And I must have sprinted this morning because my body has nothing left to push me forward. I manage, though. I have to. I can't fuck up here too.

There's a water stop at the halfway point, which is when I first take a good look at my teammates, covered in dust from the dry road kicking up, sweat streaking down their arms, creating tiny pathways through the dirt. I have a bad feeling about Betsy, the one who led. There's something arrogant, aggressive in the set of her shoulders, though I suppose the same could be said of me.

Will says nothing the entire time, and I have a begrudging respect for the fact that he can keep up with us at all. Every extra pound you carry, whether it's muscle or something else, is like carrying a few bricks along for the run. He probably outweighs me by eighty pounds. That's a lot of bricks.

It's a relief when I finally see campus looming in the distance. I kept up. I didn't embarrass myself on the first day. I've got that swimmy, unstable feeling that hits before I pass out, so it could have gone much worse. We reach the track and Will tells us he'll have notes for us at tomorrow's practice and sends us on in.

Well, almost all of us.

"Olivia," he says with an edge to his voice, "we need to talk."

I stiffen. It's clear this won't be a feel-good pep talk welcoming me to the team. Betsy, walking past, smirks.

"I go by Finn," I growl.

He acts as if I haven't spoken. "What the hell was that?" he demands. "I don't know what they did at your old school, but when I ask for ten miles, I want a little effort."

My jaw drops. *What the fuck? I about killed myself this morning and he's bitching at me?* "This is complete bullshit," I argue. "I kept up."

His blue eyes narrow. "You think we brought you on the team because we hoped you could *keep up*?" he asks. "We need a leader out there. You ambled down the road like a new mom trying to take off the baby weight."

My hands curl, nails digging into my palms. *God, he's such a dick.* "I was tired."

His arms fold across his chest. "You've done the exact same workout that everyone else here has, so you've got no reason to be tired," he says, "unless you've already violated Peter's rule about drinking the night before a practice."

I close my eyes, feeling cornered, as my pulse begins to race. The story I used at UT is not going to fly here, so I make the very questionable decision to go with the truth instead, something I've never found pays off.

"I ran a little this morning before I came out," I tell him quietly. People always say the truth will set you free, but right now it just makes me feel raw and small and weak, and there's nothing I hate more.

His mouth grows tighter. "And why *exactly* would you do that?"

For just a moment, a millisecond, I meet his eyes, though I

don't want to. There's a part of me that wants to beg him not to ask, not to question, not to try to take my secrets away from me. I look away because I refuse to beg him or anyone. "I ... I couldn't sleep."

He's silent for a moment, his jaw tense but his eyes uncertain. "You're on my watch now," he finally says. "You run when I tell you to run and that's it. Don't do it again."

He turns and walks away, and I remain behind, wondering how long I've got until he kicks me off the team. Because if I was capable of not doing it again, I wouldn't have wound up here in the first place.

I IGNORE everyone in the locker room. These people aren't my friends now, and they won't be my friends in two years. I've done all this before, and I know exactly where it got me.

"I'm Erin," says the girl changing beside me. She's extraordinarily wholesome looking—long blonde hair, scattered freckles and big cornflower-blue eyes. The kind of girl you'd see in an ad for milk or a church youth group. You can take one look at her and know she's never suffered. I shouldn't hate her for it, but I do.

I lean over my bag and grunt something in response, hoping it's sufficiently hostile to drive her away.

"So..." she says, wide-eyed and grinning like a loon, "is it true that you got kicked off the team for beating up Mark Bell?" My teeth grind together. The implosion of my entire life is just a juicy morsel of gossip for her. Funny how everyone looks down on me for what I did, but sees nothing wrong with the fucking *delight* they take in hearing about it.

"Yeah," I say, packing my bag. "So I've heard."

"So why did you do it?" she whispers as if this is some special "just us girls" moment of intimacy with half the team standing there with their ears cocked. "He must have done something to you, right?"

"Yes," I say, fixing a look on her along with the other little listeners, who no longer feign disinterest and are openly eavesdropping. I grab my bag and head for the door. "He asked me too many fucking questions."

4

Olivia

In the dining hall, I get a salad with grilled chicken, no cheese, no dressing, no bread. The world's leading female long-distance runners only have about fifteen percent body fat. Every pound you run with adds two seconds per mile, which might not sound like much, but an extra ten pounds over a six-mile course equals two full minutes, the difference between a win and a loss.

I watch the football players with envy as they load their trays with cheese fries and burgers and baked potatoes and pie. Just once in my freaking life I want to eat like a football player. I'm still watching them when Erin sits down across from me.

I groan quietly. This girl apparently cannot take a hint.

"I'm really sorry," she says, her big blue eyes full of remorse. "I feel awful. You were right, I was prying, and it was none of my business."

"Whatever." In truth, I'm too busy being fascinated by her tray to say anything else. Meat swimming in gravy, potatoes, bread, pie on the side and milk. She has at least two thousand calories on that tray. Just the sight of it alternately disgusts me and makes me ravenous in the same moment. I open my newspaper and pray she goes away.

"You aren't very friendly," she says, "you know that?"

"Yes." *Hint, fucking hint.* "I don't need friends."

"Everyone needs friends," she replies. "You're not going to scare me off, you know."

I sigh heavily. Fatigue is making my temper fray a little faster than normal, and I'm not exactly slow-tempered on the best of days. "Are you going to continue to babble while I try to read?"

"Yes," she chirps, digging into that disgusting pile of wet meat on her tray. I flinch, and yet I watch. "I've dealt with worse than you. You should see my brother. He's been in and out of rehab so many times it's like his second home. Maybe it's even his first home. And when he's using or coming down or detoxing, he's the biggest asshole you've ever met."

Okay, so I was wrong. A tiny bit of rain has fallen into Erin's perfect blonde world. I still don't care. "Fascinating," I mumble.

"He's great, thanks for asking," she replies dryly. As annoying as it is, my mouth twitches, and I would smile if it wouldn't encourage her. "He's in LA at the moment, exploring his 'craft.'" She rolls her eyes. "You're probably thinking LA isn't the greatest place for someone just out of rehab. Which is precisely what I told my parents, but they're so excited he's into something that they're trying to overlook it. Is that all you're going to eat?"

Jesus fucking Christ. This girl never stops talking. "Yes."

"You need food to build muscle," she argues. "You really ought to talk to the nutritionist. She'll tell you herself that's not healthy."

"I'm a nutrition major. I think I've got it under control."

"I still think that's not healthy."

I stifle another groan. I'm beginning to think I'd prefer Mark Bell to this girl. At least I could get *away* from him. "Do you always talk this much?"

She grins, wide-eyed. "I do. That's why we're perfect together.

You never speak and I never shut up. You're so lucky you found me."

I push the last bite of grilled chicken into my mouth and rise. *Dear God, I hope ECU has another cafeteria somewhere.*

IN THE AFTERNOON, I get on my bike and head toward the far side of campus, where the old Victorian houses give way to fields and woods, the kind of places where there will be no landmarks to tell me which direction might be home. I got lucky this morning, but I know from experience I'm not *always* lucky. It's bad enough to wake up and discover you're outside in the middle of the night, barefoot, defenseless, far from home, but multiply that by ten for the times when you wake up and have no idea where the hell you are. That means the more familiar I am with everything outside my apartment, the better.

I really have no other choice. I've tried sleeping with my cell phone tucked in my waistband, but it's useless. Half the time I throw the phone in my sleep, but even when I have it, the odds of getting a signal in the woods are zero-to-none, and who the hell would I call anyway? I don't have any friends.

I wander through the woods about three miles to the north of my apartment, trying to ignore the twisting in my stomach, the fear that something really bad will happen here. There's so much that could go wrong, and there was plenty that went wrong even when I *did* know where I was.

And it's all for nothing anyway: I came here solely to be coached by McEwan, thinking he might turn it around for me, and instead I'm being coached by some cocky asshole who probably didn't even run in *high school*.

I made a mistake taking a bat to Mark Bell, and I made a mistake coming here. Maybe staying will be the next big regret. In fact, I'm almost sure it will be.

5

Olivia

The next morning I'm ready to put Will Langstrom in his fucking place. His words from yesterday are still pissing me off almost twenty-four hours later. *Asshole*. I've had a full night's sleep, so let's see him try to complain about me now.

Everyone is chattering, the combination of nerves and dread making their noise a little more high-pitched and a lot more annoying—Erin in particular, whose breathless discourse is directed entirely toward me. Will eventually saunters up, and when he smiles that crooked smile they all titter like he's the lead singer of their favorite boy band. I guess if he weren't such a dick I'd be swooning too. Everything about him is perfect—the ice blue of his eyes, the slight curl of his hair, the ever-present hint of scruff, his mouth and the way his lip quirks upward when he's trying not to smile. I spy the edge of a tattoo peeking out from his shirt sleeve and wish I could see the whole thing.

"You're running six at race pace," he announces. "I marked the route earlier. I'm going to drive along today to assess. Everybody stop at the turn-around point and we'll reconvene there."

You're going to have to assess my ass from a distance. Get ready to eat your words, Langstrom.

When the time comes, I take off so fast and so hard that I don't see the other girls. I don't even hear them. I feel buoyant, as if I can fly. I'm crushing this, but what I love most is the freedom, the absolute freedom of not thinking or remembering or feeling anything at all.

I notice nothing but the hash marks he's left on the road, only vaguely aware of the miles ticking by. I get to the turn-around point and I keep running. Yeah, I know he said to stop, but I'm in my zone, my best place. *Fuck him.* He's not even a runner.

I don't look over when I hear an engine purring beside me until I realize it's Will shouting at me to stop. It's possible, based on how pissed off he is, that he's been shouting for a while. And now that he's yanked me from my happy place, I'm pissed too.

He pulls the car over to the side of the road and marches toward me. "When I tell you to stop you need to listen," he growls.

"I was *running*. That's what you do when you're not 'trying to lose the baby weight,'" I snap.

"Get your ass back to the turn-around point and stop showing off," he snarls, marching away.

I get back to the turn-around just as Betsy, the one who led yesterday, comes in. She is winded, the way she should be at the end, not the half. She leans down, hands on knees.

"You okay, Bets?" Will asks her.

"Yeah," she says, standing. Then she turns to me. "It's not a race, you know."

I laugh. "He said *race pace*. So yeah, it kind of was."

"Look," she snarls. "You're not DI anymore. You weren't DI material, so stop pretending you are."

Rage pulses in my veins. The unfortunate thing about a hard workout is that when someone pisses you off, the adrenaline is like a Greek chorus behind you, urging you to make things worse.

"Only one of us is breathing heavy," I say, stepping up so we are face-to-face, "so who's pretending?"

"That's enough," says Will, glaring at me. He places a hand on my shoulder and moves between us. "You two are on the same team. Try acting like it."

Unfuckingbelievable. He's blaming me, when *she's* the one who started it. I'm only two days into the season and I've already had it. I've had it with Betsy and her half-assed running, with the rest of them who are actually *slower* than Betsy, and with Will Langstrom, who is the single biggest asshole I've ever had to run for.

When he sends us back to campus, still scowling at me, I leave them both in the dust. I take all my anger and adrenaline and apply it to a single goal: leaving Betsy so far behind me that when this run is over, she will hate herself a little. At this very moment, as she makes a futile attempt to keep up with me, she feels useless, weak. I know because I've felt it too. I know she will come in angry at me and angrier at herself, and that the anger will fester, linger, for days, because this is what happens to me when I lose. I'm still mad, but it consoles me a little.

I get back to the track long before any of them. *Not Di material, my ass,* I think, just before I see Will stalking toward me. "You did that just to piss her off," he says.

My hands are shaking with anger and adrenaline once more. I put them on my hips to steady them. "What do you care? You wanted fast. You got fast."

"No," he says, jaw clenched tight. "What I want is a *team.* You can run to see yourself succeed, Olivia, but don't ever run to see someone else fail."

"I go by *Finn*," I hiss. He's just calling me Olivia to fuck with me at this point. "And she started it."

His arms fold across his chest. "And was it true? Are you here because you're not Di material?"

"No," I snap.

"Then act like it," he says in disgust, walking away.

Asshole. Asshole. Asshole. I just ran sub-fives for that prick and I get *nothing* but a fucking lecture? I watch Betsy coming in, gasping for air and glaring at me.

Sadly, she's no longer the person on the track I hate most.

I SHOWER QUICKLY and go to the cafeteria with Erin nipping at my heels like the world's most annoying dog. No matter what I do or how appallingly rude I am, this girl can't take a hint.

"That was crazy this morning," she says. "I mean, you're fast, you know? Like super fast."

I shrug. Am I supposed to feign modesty here? I *am* fast. I wouldn't be doing this if I weren't. But the truth is her words worry me. She's seen me run fast *once* and she's already got her hopes up. I could tell her right now that getting hopeful about me is a losing proposition, but I just open up my paper and ignore her instead.

But Erin is not, apparently, the only person on the team now expecting things of me. At that afternoon's practice, several of the girls stand near me while we wait for Will. "That was impressive this morning," says Nicole, who's the fastest girl on the team after me and Betsy.

"We totally have a chance at placing this year with you," agrees Erin.

I feel like I'm suffocating. I don't want them counting on me. God knows I can't even count on myself. "It was just one run," I reply.

Will is walking toward us in a fitted gray V-neck and shorts. It irritates me that I find him so freaking attractive. Knowing what a jerk he is should throw cold water on my hormones but it seems to do the opposite.

Nicole and Erin start to giggle, that kind of secretive girlish giggle I'm proud to say has never come from me. "We *love* the gray shirt," explains Erin with a lascivious grin.

When I roll my eyes, Nicole looks at me as if I've just denied evolution. "You don't think he's hot?" she asks.

"Maybe I'm just having a hard time seeing under that thick layer of dickhead he wears," I reply.

"He's not as bad as you think," Erin argues. "Off the track he's super nice. On the track too, actually."

"Not to me, he's not."

"He gives people what they need." She cocks her head, eyeing me somewhat warily. "No offense, Finn, but he seems to think you need discipline."

If it didn't piss me off so much, I'd probably agree.

I QUICKLY REALIZE I'm going to pay for my showboating this morning. Will has us doing speedwork, and though I no longer have that buzz of energy that kept me ahead of Betsy earlier, I'll be damned if I'm going to let her win. We are neck-and-neck during every 800, both of us destroyed during the recovery, and still going for broke when we start up again. But *I'm* the one Will calls out, of course.

He marches over to me with his ever-present glare. "What are you doing?" he demands.

I'm bent over my knees, trying to get air. I cock one brow at him. "Running 800s, like you said."

"Really? Because it looks to me like you're racing Betsy."

"Or maybe *she's* racing me. Why am I the one getting bitched at here?"

His arms cross. "Because I expect more of you."

Expect. That single word makes me feel like I can't breathe. I don't want him to expect anything from me, because God knows there's no guarantee I'll deliver.

"You shouldn't."

He looks at me. It's an honest look, not challenging or angry but *earnest* as if he's trying to see something in me that isn't there. "Yeah," he finally says, walking away. "You're probably right."

I've lowered his expectations. It's not the relief I thought it would be.

~

THE REMAINDER of the week passes with a few more lectures from Will and not a single compliment. I give him what he wants. I'm fast but I'm not too fast, and I don't race Betsy even though I'd like to pound her into the dirt and stomp on her remains, yet he stands there praising everyone but me. I scowl at him as I pass, but he doesn't even seem to notice. Probably because he assumes I'm not going to be his problem for much longer.

I guess I assume it too.

If he's not happy with me right now, then he's definitely not going to be happy when the real problems begin—when school starts in two weeks and our first meet looms. The stress will lead to nightmares, nightmares will lead to running, and running leads to meets where I perform about as well as a seventy-year-old trying out a treadmill for the first time.

I spend my time between our two practices mapping the town and combing the woods, which is where I almost always head during the dreams. I have no idea why I go there, and I don't really want to know.

Erin continues to follow me to lunch, despite the fact that I've told her I want to eat alone. At this point, her attempts at friendship are flat-out stalking.

"Seriously?" I groan when she sits at my table. "I think I need a restraining order."

"Restraining orders can only be issued if there's intent to harm," she quips cheerfully.

"I'm not at all surprised that you are so informed about restraining orders," I gripe.

She just laughs.

As if I was joking.

Will

"So how's it going so far?" asks Peter, but he can tell the answer by taking one look at my face. He chuckles. "You're just like your father, Will, incapable of hiding your thoughts."

It's taken the better part of two years for the mention of my father to stop hurting, and it will be a good two decades before I can appreciate the comparison. I did what he wanted. I gave up my career as a climber to take over the farm, but he wasn't alive to see it happen and it wouldn't have made a difference anyway. My father still would have found fault.

"It's okay," I sigh.

He nods slowly. "How's Finnegan?"

There are a million things I could tell him. That hostility comes off her in waves, that she looks at the rest of the team like she wants to stab them...and that she's troubled. Sure, she can run, but what was that her first day? What could possibly compel a girl to run before practice? I *need* to tell him this because if it continues it will spell disaster. She'll either go into shock or have a fucking heart attack right in the middle of a race. But for some reason, I think of how lost she looked when I asked her about it, young and lost and *destroyed.*

"She's going to be a lot of work," I reply. It's such an understatement it feels like a flat-out lie.

∾

FOLLOWING THE MEETING WITH PETER, I drive to my mother's farm. I can see five different peaks I've climbed on the way. I'm not sure if that's necessarily ironic, but it's definitely shitty. Fate's way of laughing in my face. Rubbing salt in the wound.

I climbed those peaks when I was younger and every single time it was against my father's wishes. Every single time it led to a fight. It took my desire to climb and transformed it, took something pure and made it angry and defiant. I look back on those climbs, how reckless they were, and realize they proved my dad right in a way. I did need to grow the fuck up. I just couldn't do it until it was too late for him to see it happen.

The farm is a full-time job, left in my unwilling hands when my father died. It was already failing when I inherited it. Coaching is part-time, covering my younger brother's tuition but not a lot else. Between two jobs and the debt my father left behind, there aren't enough hours in the day and there probably never will be, so my climbing days are over. I sometimes wonder if my dad is looking down and getting a good laugh out of the situation.

"Was Jackson even here this morning?" I grouse when I walk into my mother's house. We sold off some of the farm, but what's left is still too much for us and the part-time guys we've hired. "The stables look like shit. Probably because they were full, literally, of shit."

She sighs. "Yes, he was here. You know how that goes, Will."

Yeah, I know. No one is going to kill himself for a job that is seasonal or part-time. This is just a stop-gap until he finds something better.

"How's work?" she asks.

Troubling, I think, but it's nothing I'm going to tell my mom. She's got enough guilt about the fact that I'm here as it is. "Pretty good. This year's team looks okay."

"How are the new girls?"

"There's one with some promise." The words come out of my mouth before I can stop them. I don't know why but something about Finnegan makes me *want* to discuss her, and at the same time makes me want to pretend she doesn't exist.

She turns to the pot on the stove and gives it a stir. "Well, you've got four years to make something of her."

I lean over, bracing my forearms on the counter. "Only two. She's a transfer."

She nods. "That's right. Olivia, yes? Peter told me about her."

I raise a brow. Peter's been a friend of the family all my life, but I didn't know he discussed work with my mom. It's a little weird.

"She's fast, but she's unstable," I sigh. "That girl's got more problems than an entire psychiatric team could fix."

My mother smiles gently at me, the way she used to when I'd get mad as a kid. As if my irritation is childish and amusing. "Will, she just got here," she chides.

Yeah, she just got here with a goddamn three-inch binder of violations from her last school. "Did Peter tell you what she did at UT?"

"Yes," she says, "and I remember a time when you couldn't set foot outside this house without winding up in the back of a police cruiser. So maybe you shouldn't be so quick to judge."

Perhaps. But I never tried to *kill* someone.

Olivia

The next two weeks are basically a repeat of the first: Me, working my ass off, and Will, being a total dick about it. The twice-a-day workouts are so exhausting that I don't dream at all. I give him everything at practice, and while I don't deserve an award for it, I do deserve one for not telling him to go fuck himself. Actually, I deserve something better than an award for that. *Maybe a new car or a trip to Disney.*

Erin not only eats with me every day, but she gets my number off the team roster and starts *texting* me too. It's unbelievably annoying. I respond to her initial texts with one of my own.

Me: Stop texting me.

Erin: Aren't you cute? ;-) ;-)

Me: I hate emojis.

She replies with another emoji, of course. I'm not sure why I haven't just blocked her yet.

Soon it's not just her hounding me at lunch, either. Nicole joins us, followed by Meghan, whose dark curls are so big her head blocks half my view of the cafeteria. Then comes Hannah, blonde and quieter than the others, but not quiet enough.

Betsy and her small posse sit at a separate table. It feels as if we're two rival gangs, and I assume Erin and these girls are being nice to me solely because I'm faster than Betsy and add some clout to their side. Clearly it's not my winning personality attracting them. Each day I listen in surly silence as they chatter. Ten percent of the conversation is about running.

The rest is about boys.

"You'll see the guys' team at tomorrow's practice," Nicole tells me the week before school starts.

I couldn't care less about meeting the guys. Runners are too gangly for me. I prefer a build like Will's, though I want to take bleach to my brain the moment I hear that admission in my head.

"Mmmm, and Erin will get to see Brofton," Meghan teases.

"Dan Brofton is hands-down the hottest guy on the team," Erin informs me. "Aside from Will, that is."

There's a lot of sly giggling. "Will doesn't count. He's not on the team," Nicole objects.

"But if he were ..." Hannah sings, and there is more giggling. Coaches can't date students, and even if they could I can't imagine the appeal of an asshole like Will. Okay, that's a lie. I can totally imagine the appeal. But I refuse to let myself.

"Did you see the way his shirt clung to him at yesterday's practice?" asks Meghan.

"Wish his shorts had clung too," cackles Nicole.

I sort of wish that too, but I roll my eyes. "This is like listening to a bunch of horny teenage boys."

"Welcome to the team." Erin grins.

THE GUYS' team is waiting when we wrap up the next morning. I know who Brofton is immediately because he's the kind of good-looking that is universally appealing to everyone. Dark hair, knowing eyes, a little smirk on his face like he's imagining you naked, yet I remain unimpressed when he saunters over to me.

"You must be the D1 girl," he says.

"Wow," I deadpan. "Your psychic powers are top-notch."

"Fine." He grins, irritatingly unfazed by my bitchiness. "We've actually heard all about you."

My hands go to my hips. "And what exactly did you hear?"

He runs a hand through his hair. "That you put Mark Bell in the hospital."

I grab my water bottle and turn to go inside. "I hope that means you're all scared of me now."

He smiles again. "You don't look so scary, and I've met Mark a few times. He ran in my division in high school, and I know for a fact that he's a world-class prick, so I'm gonna guess he had it coming."

He definitely had it coming. But that's between me and Mark.

8

Will

I am on the south face of Denali. It's not necessarily the hardest climb, just steep as shit. The guys we're leading are already tired, which doesn't bode well since we've got at least three more hours before we hit the next camp.

"You got this?" I ask one of them. His name is Bob. He's from Beaufort, South Carolina, which sits below sea level, and this is his first major climb. Not sure Denali should be anyone's first major climb, but I don't choose our clients.

His mouth is pulling inward, stretched tight. He nods.

I asked. It's all I can do.

I look at the summit and the sun warms my face. It's cold as hell, cold enough that it's stripped everything inside of me. Any lingering uncertainty. Even the anger.

My father was wrong. He said mountain climbing was a hobby, not a profession, and that one day I'd be home with my tail between my legs. He was wrong, and I know it as I stand here. I know there's nothing else in the world I'm supposed to be doing. I know that even if this climb is my last—and no serious climber ever goes up without at *least acknowledging the possibility—it was worth it. I'd rather have had two good years with the sun on my face and the summit hovering above than a lifetime of working on the farm. Climbs like this are the only time, for as far back as I can recall, that I don't feel as if something is missing.*

~

I WAKE. I'm not at high camp or base camp. I know that the only climbs in my future are the ones I wedge into days and weekends that are already too full. I'll probably never summit Everest or Annapurna or any of the other ones on my bucket list. I'm going to live and die toiling on that farm, just like my dad did.

The only difference is that he had a choice.

There were things about climbing that sucked, that would have bothered me over time. It's hard to have a relationship when you're gone months at a time. I'd eventually have wanted kids, and it would have been hard to leave. But I was twenty-four. I didn't want commitment—I wanted convenience. And I had it. Sometimes I think if it had just been a little less perfect this wouldn't be as hard for me as it is right now.

There isn't a single afternoon, when practice is done, that a tiny voice doesn't suggest I go climbing. I hear it today, but I don't go. I never go. The sprayer's coming to do one last application of weed killer tomorrow and I've got to make sure the fields are ready first. Otherwise, I'll spend the next goddamn month fixing ruts he's put out there.

But the voice is still there, even as I head to the farm on the way home. *You've got four hours of light left,* it says. *You couldn't do much, but your gear is already in the car. You deserve just one.*

Sometimes I feel like an addict, except the only person my climbing ever hurt was my father. I'm sure as shit making amends for it now.

9

Olivia

School begins.

Between that and practice, I don't fall asleep at night... I collapse, which is ideal. Exhaustion tends to keep the dreams at bay.

I have fresh legs every day, not that Will is any less displeased. I'm running well, but he only seems to find fault. I am, *by far*, the fastest girl on the team, but every day he stands there looking for things to criticize, bitching about my turn-over rate and stride length, or making me stay after everyone else to run next to a metronome for Christ's sake. I'm doing every fucking thing he asks and he's still treating me like a burden, a charity case he's been forced to take on.

"Good job," he says to Erin and Betsy at the end of practice. I approach and his smile fades. "Your kick was off on the last lap."

For fuck's sake. "Well, I came in ahead of everyone else," I snap, "so maybe the rest of the team's kick was off too."

There's a small muscle at the corner of his jaw that pops

when he's mad. That muscle and I are practically family I know it so well.

"If you're not interested in improving," he says, "then stop taking up a spot that could be used by someone who is."

I swallow hard. I can't win with him, and I never will because he wants me off the team. He's always wanted me off the team and nothing is going to change it.

"Yeah, you'd love that, wouldn't you?" I retort. "I'm apparently the only person on this team who needs constant correction."

He pushes a frustrated hand through his hair. Even now, in the midst of his anger, I can't stop noticing things about him. His eyes are the brightest blue, like a postcard of the Caribbean. Especially when he's mad.

"Has it ever occurred to you that I ask more of you because I think you're capable of more?" he demands. "The rest of those girls are giving me everything they have, but you are not. Do you want me to just let you plod along and get through college having never taken first when you know you have the potential to?"

He's not lashing out and he's not lecturing. He's just being honest. And in response I feel this inexplicable urge to cry. I don't want that. I prefer anger. I don't know what to do with other feelings. "I'm going to shower now," I say, my voice slightly hoarse. He nods, looking unhappy and puzzled at the same time. Possibly even concerned.

I don't want his concern.

God knows it won't last.

～

ON THURSDAY, Hannah brings this massive box of stuff that her mother has sent, full of homemade cookies and peanut brittle and even rolls of quarters for the laundry.

"Ugh, snickerdoodles," says Hannah, throwing the bag into

the center of the table. "I'm already sick of snickerdoodles and school's only just begun."

"At least your mom sends you homemade stuff. My mom just sent me a bag of Oreos," says Nicole. "Like I couldn't go to the store and buy my own Oreos."

Hannah passes me the bag and I hand it on to Erin as if it's toxic, my stomach tight and my throat dry.

"Oh my God, Finn, live a little," gripes Erin. She takes a cookie from the bag and pushes it toward my mouth, but I avert my head.

"I don't like snickerdoodles," I tell her. It's a lie. What I don't want is the queasy feeling this whole discussion gives me. This tangible reminder of what other people have—a family who cares that they are gone.

"Saw Will's girlfriend heading to his office just before we left," Nicole says with a knowing grin. I never imagined him with a girlfriend and...I don't know. Better her than me, I guess. "Looks like someone's getting a little a.m. wake-up call."

"Not necessarily," counters Erin. "She works for the university. Maybe they're just meeting for breakfast. Is she hot?"

Nicole rolls her eyes. "She's dating *Will*. What do you think?"

What *I* think is that any girl who would date Will must have a big bag of stupid lodged in the area meant for white matter. I don't care how hot he is. Nothing is worth dealing with his bullshit.

10

Will

For some reason, after a relatively mild Colorado summer, it turns blazing hot on Wednesday. The girls were dragging this morning and, by afternoon, I'm not sure this practice can be technically classified as speedwork.

I'm half-tempted just to end practice early. God knows I have enough other things to do. As soon as I get out of here, I've got to mow the perimeter of the fields and spray the area between our farm and our neighbor's, which the sprayer didn't hit last week. I've got to start getting the grain bins ready, manually moving the last of it down since they're too light for gravity to do the job for me anymore. I'm stressing about that, about the team, about *everything*, when the men's team shows up at the track. Under the best of circumstances, I find them grating. We're only one week into sharing the track and I've already had it with the way they gawk at Olivia when she's running. The damn football team now has a *song* they sing when she passes. It's insane.

If I were being reasonable, I'd say I couldn't blame them. Olivia isn't just beautiful. Something compels you to look at her even when you don't want to. Like Medusa. The difference is that I realize Olivia *could* probably turn you to stone with her withering glare, while the rest of these idiots are completely blind to it.

"Looking good, Finn," Brofton says. Olivia rolls her eyes and keeps walking, but another kid, Piersal, stops staring at her chest just long enough to look at where the back of her singlet is gaping open.

"Jesus," he says. "What happened there?" He trails a finger over her skin and she jumps as if he's burned her.

"Nothing," she snaps.

Anyone who's even spent a modest amount of time around Olivia would know that tone means *leave me the fuck alone,* but Piersal is either clueless or has a death wish. "It doesn't look like nothing," he says. "How'd it happen?"

There's an expression on Olivia's face, a combination of panic and rage as everyone turns to watch. It worries me. I find myself crossing the track to reach her. "I don't know," she says through gritted teeth. She barks at the freshman to move and they scuttle.

"What do you mean you don't know?" He laughs. "You look like you got knifed! You *have* to know."

Before I can even process what the hell is happening, she's spun around and flung herself toward him, grabbing his shirt at the neck like she's going to kick his ass across the track, though he's at least six inches taller than she is.

"I told you I don't know," she snarls, pulling tighter at his shirt, starting to choke him. "Now ask me one more question so I can feed you your own balls."

I finally snap out of my shock and grab her, wrenching her away from him, and yelling at everyone to go on about their business. Once they've left, I round on her. "What the hell was that?"

She's red-faced, half anger, half embarrassment. She won't meet my eye. "He was fucking with me."

I stare at her, astonished she could have taken something relatively minor so seriously. "He just asked you a question."

"He *laughed*," she hisses. Her voice sounds strangled, anger and grief warring in her throat. "Did you not hear that part? A kid gets stabbed and it's just a big fucking joke to you people, isn't it?"

I freeze and am painfully slow to cover my surprise. Is she seriously saying someone *stabbed* her as a child? I don't even know how to respond to that. Who the hell could have stabbed her? "I'm sure he had no idea it was something that serious," I finally say.

She rolls her eyes. "Of course he didn't. Bad shit never happens to any of you. You all just stand around with your fucking care packages, salivating for a gory detail or two, and I get to be the bad guy for wanting some privacy."

I push both hands back into my hair. I could list a great many bad things that have happened to people other than her, but to be honest...it sounds like her story would still win. "You know, if you'd just answered the question that would have been the end of it."

"I *did* answer the question," she hisses, turning away from me. "How much do you remember from when you were little? And even if I did, it's no one's business but mine."

SOMEONE FUCKING *STABBED* HER.

I can't get past that fact. I want to forget it entirely because it causes this unfortunate pit of sympathy in my stomach and she's the kind of girl for whom feeling sympathy is dangerous. Feel bad and you start forgiving, making exceptions. The truth is that the odds of her getting through the next week without kicking Betsy's ass are slim. The odds of her making it through the season? Impossible. Getting attached to her in any way is futile at best. I want to not think about it and I want to not think about her. It's got to be the first time I'm actually grateful that I can go to the farm and throw myself into work.

"Did something happen at school?" my mom asks when I arrive. Sometimes my mother sees through me so easily that it's almost scary.

"Nothing I couldn't have predicted."

"What's the problem?"

I shake my head. "There's no problem." It's a lie, of course, but the truth is that I don't know what the problem is. I don't know why Olivia Finnegan seems to have taken over a small portion of my brain. The moment my attention isn't diverted, it seems to land right back on her.

I've been out in the fields for at least two hours when my mom takes the golf cart out to find me. "You left your phone inside," she says, handing it to me. "It's been ringing off the hook."

It's only then that I realize the sun is setting.

Crap.

The phone begins ringing again as I grab it. "Hey, Jess," I say, already preparing my apology. I really am the world's shittiest boyfriend. She puts up with a lot.

"I haven't heard from you all day," she says. "What time are you coming over? We're supposed to be at Cat's house by seven."

Shit. It's after six now, I'm drenched in sweat, and my mom's place is at least twenty minutes from Jessica's. "I'm gonna be a little late. I'm sorry. I was helping my mom and—"

"It's okay," she says immediately. "I know your mom comes first right now." In the time we've dated, Jessica's never once made me feel guilty about the farm, but I can picture her right now, twisting an auburn curl around her finger, her full mouth pouting slightly, and I feel bad. She deserves better than a boyfriend who forgot her all day long.

I'm going to try harder, I swear.

11

Olivia

That scar on my back is one small clue to a past I barely remember.

I had a brother once, I had parents once, but they all left me in quick succession, and now my memories of them are blurred and untrustworthy. I still think about them, though, no matter how badly I wish I didn't. Some days more than others.

Sunday is one of those days. Somewhere in the world, my brother is celebrating his twenty-fourth birthday. He ran away when he was eight, only three years older than me although, at the time, the difference seemed monumental. A year later, my parents ditched me and took off. I remember worrying that my brother might still try to return, like a lost dog, and discover we'd gone.

I wonder if he's alone like I am. Maybe leaving young like that gave him a head start. Maybe someone took him in. By now he's probably out of college. He liked to build things, elaborate towers made out of cans and sticks, a delicate suspension that would collapse at the first hint of a breeze, so maybe he's an engineer now, or an architect. Maybe he's married, or thinking about it.

I get a cupcake at dinner, which I won't eat, but I close my eyes and make a wish as if there's a candle, as if it's my wish to make, and my wish is that he wound up happier than me.

I WAKE SOMETIME BEFORE DAWN, standing in the middle of an unfamiliar road, drenched in sweat, my heart pounding in my ears.

My brother's birthday always triggers a nightmare, so I guess I should have expected it. I step forward and flinch in pain, lifting the sole of my foot to find a big piece of glass stuck in my heel.

"Why? Why can't you ever keep the fucking shoes on?" I groan to myself, wincing as I dig out the glass.

It's hardly the first time it's happened, but the cut is deep and it hurts like a bitch to return to my apartment in bare feet. I should just be grateful, I suppose, that it stopped me. Sometimes the injury becomes part of the dream, and a series of things underfoot just means fighting harder to get away from what's chasing me.

I get home in time to slap some gauze on it, hoping it's enough to get me through practice.

But it's not, of course.

"You're running like a six-year-old on Field Day," says Will a few hours later.

I exhale, feeling more weary than normal. "There's that voice of support I missed all weekend," I reply snidely. "And just for the record, I'm still faster than anyone out here."

He glares at me, his eyes the brightest blue. "I'm not coaching 'anyone out here' at the moment," he says. "I'm coaching you, and I want to know why your gait is off." His eyes are narrowed, his stare hard. He is sure I ran and I'm not about to tell him he's right.

"I broke a jar this morning and cut my foot," I tell him.

He glances down at my foot like he has X-ray vision. "Let me see."

I roll my eyes as I walk to a bench, not sure if this is actual concern on his part or suspicion. I take off my shoe and my sock and wiggle the ball of my foot at him. Blood has soaked through the gauze. "Happy?"

He scowls at me and then comes forward, grabbing my ankle to hold my foot aloft. He pulls the bandage off. "You need to go to the health center, Olivia. That needs to be stitched."

I shrug. "It'll be fine. It just needs a day."

He looks more carefully at it. "Why is your foot so cut up?"

"It's not," I say, jerking my ankle out of his grasp.

He groans loudly. "Do you have to argue about everything? I have eyes and I know what scars look like. Do you walk over broken glass daily?"

This is a conversation that can't go anywhere good. It'll either lead to a series of bizarre lies or—even worse—the truth. "Do you really expect me to answer that?"

"No," he says, crossing his arms the way he does when he's about to lecture me, which is *always*, "but I really expect you to go to the health center."

I shake my head. There's no fucking way I'm answering a battery of prying questions from a doctor. With my luck I'll find myself in some treatment program for cutters. "Despite your years of medical training, I'm gonna have to refuse."

For just a moment, fleeting sadness passes over his face. I have no idea why, but it makes me wish I hadn't spoken.

He sighs. "Go shower and wait in my office."

I freeze, wondering if I just took my refusal too far. Maybe I'm just going to get bitched out for not following his directions, or maybe I'm about to get kicked off the team. Either possibility seems fair. I refused to do what he asked. I ran when he told me not to. I was told no more temper and I nearly crushed a teammate's windpipe. I figured I'd lose my scholarship eventually, I just thought I'd get to go out with a bang.

WHEN I WALK IN, he looks at me with equal parts resignation and disdain, as if steeling himself to undertake a very unpleasant task.

"Take off your shoe," he sighs, going to his closet. He retrieves a small kit and pulls a chair up in front of mine and grabs my ankle.

"What are you doing?" I ask.

He shoots me an annoyed glance. "What does it look like I'm doing? You are obviously not going to the health center, since following even the smallest direction is impossible for you, so I'm fixing your foot."

I swallow. My heel is red and throbbing now after the run. This is not the time to let anyone push a needle in there to sew things up. "You don't have to. It doesn't hurt that much."

He shakes his head as he examines my heel. "I applaud your high pain tolerance, Olivia, but there's no way that doesn't hurt, and it affects your running, so for once stop arguing with me." He swabs it with alcohol, which hurts like a bitch though I refuse to show it, and then he pushes the needle into my skin. I suck in air and then freeze entirely, trying to think of something else while he works, stitching as deftly and assuredly as any surgeon.

"How'd you learn how to do that?" I ask.

He pauses, and his shoulders seem to sag a little. "I had some medic training at my last job."

His tone does not invite further questions, but I barrel on anyway. "You weren't always a coach?"

He shakes his head, still focused on my foot. "I was a guide," he finally says. "Mountain climbing."

After a moment of surprise, I realize how much sense that makes. It explains how cut he is and the tattoos hinting that he hasn't always been this goody-goody country boy. But it's more than that, even. There's something intense about him, something that demands complete immersion. He isn't a guy meant to stand on the sidelines and watch other people achieve.

"Did you climb any of the big ones?" I ask.

He doesn't look up. "Denali and K2."

He says it without inflection, without pride. Like a total badass. "Why the hell would you give that up to become a coach?" I ask.

His jaw sets. "My father died, so I came back and took over his farm."

I think back to the day I mouthed off about everyone with their perfect lives. I guess his isn't so perfect after all. "Did you even *want* to coach cross country?"

He ties a knot and cuts the thread. "It's a good job. I'm lucky to have gotten it."

"That didn't answer my question."

He closes the kit with an echoing snap. "Didn't it?"

I guess it did.

It's unusual for me to feel guilt, but I find it sitting in my chest right now, awkward and unwanted. I've been sort of a pain in the ass since I got here, and I've made so many assumptions about who he is that don't appear to be accurate. I sense that even the act of stitching my foot is reminding him of things he gave up. "You'd probably make a good doctor if you ever decided to leave the lucrative world of coaching," I tell him. "Not, mind you, a doctor who needs to be pleasant, like a pediatrician or something. But one of those doctors you expect to be an asshole."

"Is that right?" he drawls, trying not to smile.

I'm not sure I've ever made him smile before. I sort of like that I came close. "Yeah, I mean, can you imagine yourself as, say, an oncologist? I'm pretty sure saying things like 'your healing is crappy' and 'get better faster' wouldn't be as well-received by patients as it is by me." ·

He laughs. "Yes, it's so well-received when I say it to you."

I grin, feeling inexplicably pleased with myself and with him. Moments like this almost make me wish I were a better person. The kind who makes other people happy.

Or at least not the kind who makes them miserable.

12

Will

That girl.

I'm still kind of smiling when she leaves. When I realize this, I wipe it clean from my face. I cannot allow myself to get sucked in by Olivia Finnegan. She's already got half the men at this school watching her every move like she's a wet dream come to life. I refuse to join her cheering section.

I had to hide my shock when she took off her shoe. That cut was deep. I know a lot of tough guys, but none that would have run on a cut that deep unless their lives were at stake.

She's tough, but I'm not sure anyone is tough enough to overcome self-destructive tendencies as bad as hers. I know she's still running before practice, though she won't admit it. And why was her foot so cut up? I wasn't entirely kidding when I asked if she walked on broken glass every day.

What kills me is that she could be amazing if she'd stop doing whatever she's doing. She's capable of blinding, astonishing speed. She shouldn't just be running for a D1 school, she should be its star. At a different school, with a different coach, someone would be preparing her for the Olympic trials, not getting ready for a quiet local meet against four other D3 schools.

Which means she's capable of giving our team their first winning season in over a decade. But she didn't perform at UT, and I suspect that counting on Olivia Finnegan for anything is a losing proposition.

Peter walks in just after she leaves. "Saw Finnegan limping on the way out of the building?"

"She cut her foot," I reply, capping my pen. "Believe me, her foot is the least of our worries."

He takes the seat across from mine, watching me a little too carefully. "What do you mean?"

I wish I hadn't said it. "Nothing. She's just trouble."

"Trouble for you or trouble for the team?"

I tip back in my chair. "What do you mean? She's trouble for everyone."

He shrugs. "She seems to be working her ass off. But she's a very, very pretty girl. So when I hear you telling me she's trouble, I have to ask if you mean she's trouble as a runner, or for you personally."

I stare at him, dumbfounded. Peter's known me my entire life. I can't believe that he, of all people, would suggest something like that. "When have I ever been inappropriate with a student?"

He shakes his head. "Never. And I'm not implying you would be now. In fact, I know you wouldn't be, which is precisely why it might trouble you so much to have her around. Unnecessary temptation."

"Olivia Finnegan is the last person on earth who could be an unnecessary temptation."

He nods. He looks like he believes me. So I'm not sure why it feels like it was a lie.

13

Olivia

It's the week before our first meet.

Aside from Betsy, the entire freaking team is looking at me like I'm the second coming, and this is the week that every last one of them, *my coach in particular*, will discover I am not. I try not to think about this as I go to sleep. I try to think of happy things. I imagine floating on a raft on a peaceful sea, though it's something I've never actually done. I imagine, and I pray, that somehow this will keep me in bed tonight.

I find myself deep in the woods the next morning, gasping and drenched in sweat though the air is cool. I run back to my apartment, strip my running clothes off and pass out. An hour later, my alarm goes off. I'm still sweating when I meet the rest of the team at the track.

It happens again Tuesday morning, and then Wednesday, at which point Will loses his shit. "What the hell is going on, Olivia?" he demands. "Your running has been half-assed all week."

My throat feels tight. I can't keep lying, and I also can't tell him the truth. "I'm just tired from class," I reply, forcing myself to meet his eyes.

That muscle ticks in his jaw. "Is it that," he asks between his teeth, "or have you been running before we practice, even though I told you not to?"

I can't tell him the truth, now. He's made sure of that. "No, I'm just tired."

"If I catch you running before practice you're off this team," he says, holding my eye. "Do you understand?"

Fuck you, fuck you, fuck you.

I'm not allowed to say it, but I think it. My frustration clogs my throat, making my brain hazy. I want to scream at him. I want to tell him that I can't help it, that no one alive wishes it would stop more than me. But I've told people before. I know where it gets me, and I won't do it again.

At the end of Thursday's practice, Will gathers us in a circle and reminds us to take it easy on Friday, drink lots of water, no alcohol, extra protein, and carbs. The freshmen ask dumb questions because that's what freshmen do. He sends us off but stops me with a hand on my shoulder. "I shouldn't have to say this, but no running tomorrow. Got it?"

"I heard you the first time," I snarl, shaking out of his grip.

"I get the feeling you don't hear anyone but yourself," he mutters.

Of course I only listen to myself, asshole, I think. *I'm the only one of us who knows what's going on.*

And what I know is that there's only one thing that will keep me in bed on Friday night: exhaustion. So I run hard until it's dark, and slide beneath the sheets late, my chest tight with worry. Please, please, please let this work. I really need this to work.

I'm not sure exactly who I'm whispering this to because as far as I can tell, God hasn't looked out for or listened to me once my entire life.

WHEN MY EYES open again I'm in the middle of a field, barefoot, my legs cut to shit, an itchy trickle of blood down my ankle. My shirt is drenched and my heart is hammering as I gasp for breath. The gasping always happens, and I'm never sure if it's because I ran hard or because I was terrified.

I struggle for air and utter a slew of profanities. *Why?* Why the morning of our first meet? I'm doomed now. There's no way I'll perform. None.

The early morning air chills my damp skin, bringing goose bumps, and I know I've got to get moving. But where? At least if it were night, I'd be able to make out the lights, but right now I see nothing. Sure, I can tell which way is east based on where the sky is lightest. Doesn't do a damn bit of good unless you know what direction you went in the first place.

I jog back through the field for lack of a better idea. Eventually, I'll hit a road. Eventually, it will be daytime and someone can tell me where I am. But as the sky lightens, I realize I'm heading for more woods.

I double back and begin to run harder. It's probably between 5-5:30 right now and I'm supposed to be at school by 6:00 to catch the bus to our meet. With every step, I know I'm about to lose another scholarship.

By the time I find a road I'm desperate. I hear the rumble of an old muffler approaching. Hitchhiking is what's going to get me killed eventually. Today, though, it feels as if I've got no choice.

The guy pulls up alongside me, the roar of his truck drowning the silence. "Need a lift?" he asks, brow furrowed as he takes in my appearance. I'm dressed to run, aside from the missing shoes. I don't bother to assess his appearance. Even if he's got a machete on his front seat, I'm getting in the truck.

"Yes, please," I breathe. "I'm trying to get to campus."

"You ran here all the way from campus?" he asks.

I nod.

"Now why'd you do something like that?"

I'd really love to stop this game of twenty questions and push his foot to the accelerator, but I have to play nice. "I was out running, and I got lost, and I think I just got more and more lost," I reply. It's not entirely untrue.

"Well, damn, girl, you belong on a track team. We got to be seven miles from campus at least."

Oh shit.

We start driving. He's blathering on about something, but all I can think is that I'm completely fucked. I probably ran nine miles this morning all together. There's not a chance I'll perform. There's not a chance I won't be the slowest girl on the field. How the hell am I going to explain it?

"You got a boyfriend?" he asks.

I glance at him warily. I dislike the eager glint in his eye as he waits for my answer. "Yeah."

He laughs. "Can't be much of one if you're jumping out of his bed to go running this early in the morning." He tells me he has a son who's eight, but he only sees him about once a month. He tells me he has a boat. "You like being out on the water?" he asks.

I nod, though I've never been.

"I'll take you out on my boat sometime, then. Write down your cell," he says, pushing a receipt toward me. I make up a number and hand it back, directing him to a sorority house on the other side of campus. No fucking way is this guy finding out where I live.

Once he's out of sight, I bolt across campus to my apartment and get home with just enough time to change before I have to run back across campus to the track, and I'm still late. Betsy's smirk is so wide I'm surprised it doesn't crack her face.

Will never even glances at me as I climb on the bus, which feels intentional somehow. The girls talk, anxiety making them extra annoying. Some of them have parents coming to the event, which I suppose is an extra layer of excitement if you actually have parents you'd want attending.

I chug my water bottle, but there's no way I can drink enough to make up for the fact that I ran as much as I did this morning. Today it's that loose-limbed weakness that comes after a long, hard run. It's the kind of weakness that no effort on my part can overcome. I can't think of a time in my life when I ran that far and stayed asleep. I'm going to fuck this meet up as badly as I've ever fucked up anything.

"Are your parents coming, Finn?" asks Nicole.

I shake my head. "They're traveling." It's easier than telling the truth, and less embarrassing too.

"Where'd they go?"

"Your guess is as good as mine." And this is entirely true. As far as I know, they've been traveling for the fourteen years since they dumped me with our neighbors and took off.

Will listens to our exchange, still stony-faced. I get this sick feeling in my stomach, watching him, that he already knows what I did.

"What crawled up his ass?" whispers Erin as we climb off the bus.

I shrug. Whatever it is, it will be a hell of a lot worse after we don't place today. I get in line for the port-a-potties, and the moment I've gone, I feel like I have to go again.

Will tells us to try to stay ahead of Denton, our biggest rival, to block them out in the last mile. But he doesn't direct a single word of this to me, as if I'm not going to be in the race at all. It's a fair assumption.

We line up and the weakness overwhelms me. I have to pull it together. I have to at least stay with the team. I need to pee again, but it's too late. The gun goes off and from my very first steps I know how this will go. Some days you feel weak and it turns out that it was transient, nerves or just some shallow weakness with a deep reserve beneath it.

This is not one of those days.

For the first mile, I run with Erin, noting her curious glances. I've never stayed back with her before, and she probably thinks this is strategy on my part.

It's not. I'm running with her because it's all I'm capable of.

At the second mile, it gets tough. I'm breathing heavy, and sweat rests thick on my back, bristling against my skin like something alive. My stomach is churning and I think that water I drank coming here might be about to make a return trip.

On the third mile, I'm still with Erin, but barely. She's all that is keeping me going. My vision has begun to dim on the sides as if I've got a flashlight pointed on her in a dark room.

The circle of the flashlight narrows...

Narrows...

Narrows...

~

WHEN I COME TO, I'm in the back of an ambulance. We're not moving, so I assume we're still on the field.

Will is there, hovering behind the paramedics. He looks vaguely concerned but mostly he looks pissed off as if I fainted on purpose. Even now, looking angry, something about his face draws me in, makes me long to run my index finger over the rise of his lip, his cheekbone...

Stop, I command myself. It's inappropriate in so many ways. Mainly because Will is an asshole. They've already started the IV. "I don't need this," I mutter.

"I must have missed the part where you got a medical degree," snaps Will, his tone drawing surprised stares from the paramedics and me.

My jaw drops. Will is an asshole, but I expected a little sympathy in the back of a freaking ambulance. I scowl openly at him. "I'm not dehydrated, and even if I am, I'm fine now. I can drink it myself. I don't want to hold everyone up."

"Oh, so *now* you're worried about the rest of the team?" he scoffs. "I think your worry is coming a little late, don't you?"

"Dude ..." says the aghast paramedic to my right. "Seriously? She just passed out."

"I'm sorry if we didn't place," I tell Will between clenched teeth, hating him in an altogether new way. "I don't know what happened. I think I'm just coming down with something."

"That's interesting," he says, looking me dead in the eye. "Because you looked pretty healthy running across campus this morning."

THE RIDE back to school is the longest of my life. No one seems to blame me for the loss—Will hasn't told them precisely how much of it is my fault—but no one's happy either. And Will ...

He doesn't say a word to anyone.

"My office," he hisses as we exit the bus. "Now."

I almost refuse. He's going to kick me off the team anyway. Why allow him to bitch me out first? It's a testament to how badly I want to stay that I follow him upstairs, his face so cold and so still as we walk that it could be chiseled in stone. I walk into his office and he slams the door behind me. "Explain," he demands.

My brain frantically searches for an excuse. I'm not telling him what happened. I doubt he'd believe me anyway. "About this morning?" I ask, forcing myself to smirk. "You've heard of the walk of shame, right?"

He narrows his eyes. "Dressed in running clothes?" he demands. "No shoes? Drenched in sweat?"

I grin. "You're probably not aware of this, but when sex lasts more than thirty seconds, the girl can get sweaty too."

His piercing blue eyes focus on me, freezing me in place. "Cut the shit, Olivia. I want the truth, and you'd better not lie when I ask it. Did you go running this morning before the meet?"

Resignation hits me at long last, a weight so heavy I feel like I can barely sit up straight. I have nothing to lose at this point. He's probably going to kick me off the team no matter what. "Yes."

His hands are clasped and his head is bowed, as if he's waiting for a guilty verdict. "How far did you go?"

My eyes drop to my lap. "About nine miles." My voice is nearly a whisper.

"You must be out of your mind," he growls. "On the morning of a race you ran nine miles? Why?"

I say nothing. I mean, he's right, isn't he? I'm definitely out of my mind. I don't think that idea is even in dispute at this point.

"That wasn't a rhetorical question," he snaps. "I expect an answer. I specifically told you to stop running before practice but you did it anyway. Unless you can offer a compelling reason for it, you're off the team. You're nothing but a liability."

"You don't know that," I retort. "It was only the first meet."

His head lifts and he holds my eye. "I know how fast you are, Olivia. We should have placed today. So yeah, I do know you're a liability. You're incapable of taking direction and we all paid the price for it today."

I push my hands through my hair. "I can't control it!"

He gives me a weary and very unhappy laugh. "Is someone forcing you at gunpoint? I must have missed that this morning."

"I do it in my sleep, okay?" I snarl. "Like sleepwalking, except I run."

I'm not sure what's more horrifying, that he wants to kick me out of the program already or that I just told him the truth. I don't know why I told him. I've only admitted it once in my adult life, and it really didn't work out for me.

He stills for a moment, and then he rolls his eyes. "That's the stupidest thing I've ever heard, and I've heard a lot of stupid things."

I should have expected his reaction, but it still hurts. "Fine. Don't believe me. Kick me off the team." I jump to my feet. "You know what? Don't bother. I fucking quit."

I slam his door and run across campus, back to the shitty apartment I'm only in so I can attend a school I never wanted to be at in the first place. I really wish I could cry. I'd like to right now.

I just ruined everything.

14

Will

The door slams shut and I sit in shock.

Her story sounded so far-fetched. It never occurred to me for a minute it could be real. Not until she jumped to her feet, her eyes wide and hurt.

It can't possibly be true, though. People don't sleep *run*.

This is just one of Olivia's many talents—the ability to tell a ridiculous lie and make you want to believe it. The minute those big green eyes of hers go even the slightest bit vulnerable I want to hand her my keys and sign over my paycheck. God help the man she ends up with.

It's for the best that she's gone. She's been nothing but trouble since day one, and she's no longer my problem. But I have a curiously empty feeling as I drive out to the farm.

"How'd the meet go?" my mom asks.

Fucking terribly. And team morale is in the toilet now, and I can't blame it entirely on Olivia. I was so fucking pissed on the way there, and even more pissed on the way home. "Bad question," I grumble. "I'm gonna go check the horses."

She gives me one of those smiles that makes me feel like I'm a little kid again, doing something I'm not supposed to. "The horses are fine," she clucks. "Sit down and I'll make you some lunch."

"I don't have time for lunch. I have a shitload of work to get done and Jessica expects me by seven."

She pushes me into a chair. "One quick sandwich and I'll leave you alone," she promises.

Once she's got a sandwich and chips in front of me, she slowly drags out the story of my intensely frustrating morning. "So, in a nutshell," I conclude, "we lost because she wouldn't listen, which I told Peter would happen from the start."

"It sounds," she says gently, "like you'd have lost with or without her?"

My tongue pokes inside my cheek. "But we could have placed if she just didn't go running this morning. That's the whole point. And then she tells me the most preposterous lie to get out of it."

My mom tips her head. "Are you sure it's a lie?" I have no idea why she's always in Olivia's court when she's never even met her.

"Of *course* it's a lie. You don't know this girl. She's made of lies. People do not *run* in their sleep."

"And you're sure of that?" she asks. "If I asked you to stake your life on the fact that it's a lie, you would?"

"Yes," I reply, less certainly. I guess I'm not actually sure at all. But no, this is just Olivia's influence again, and God knows I'm lucky to be separating myself from it. "She's been trouble since the start, so she can go be trouble for someone else."

I shove the plate away. I've suddenly got no appetite.

I GO out to the fields, but I can't seem to move on with my day. Olivia is like this small, insistent wound in my side. Always there, making itself known every time I bend one direction or the other. Even now, when she's no longer my problem, I'm still seeing that lost look on her face and feeling as if I just kicked something small and defenseless. That look stays with me. I see it as I turn on the tractor. I see it when I should be inspecting the fields. I see it when I'm fixing the water. I see it as I drive away, and find myself heading not toward Jessica's at all but back to my office.

"I can't believe I'm doing this," I grumble as I go online. Sleep running does not exist. I'm angry at myself for even checking. I'm angry at her for having the pull over me that she does.

Except seconds after I type the words into the search bar, results fill the page.

One link after another about sleep running. And it's at this moment I realize how badly I wanted to find nothing. How badly I wanted to believe she was willfully destroying her running career, rather than having it destroyed by something she can't control.

I don't want to feel sorry for her. I don't want to feel *anything* for her. And I think the problem is that I already do. I already care about her outcome, and it feels dangerous for no reason I can pinpoint.

There is website after website devoted to sleep running and forums for people who do it. It explains so much. Her exhaustion, the fact that her college career has been a long series of disappointments. I pull up her file from UT. They must have known, but how could they have just let it go on the way they did? I find nothing. The notes discuss only her performance and that she seems to implode under stress. The underlying implication is that drugs or alcohol are the culprit, but it's unclear to me how they really could have believed that. She often shows up exhausted, but I've never once seen her show up hungover.

I go through her academic file and it is similarly unrevealing. She gets good grades and she keeps to herself. But then I find three notes written shortly after she'd arrived at UT.

The first: 3:42 a.m. *Student was running through lobby, attempting to leave dormitory. Student was informed that she could not leave premises, but was hysterical and broke free of officer in charge. Student was later identified by security officer and informed that disciplinary action would be taken in event of further incidents. Student claimed to have no knowledge of incident.*

The second came only two weeks later: 2:19 a.m. *Student ran through lobby and did not respond to commands to stop. Campus security was alerted and found student running barefoot toward southern end of campus. Several officers were required to restrain student, who resisted and did not appear oriented to time or place. Medical personnel called to scene. Student taken to UMC by paramedics. Patient's next-of-kin could not be reached.*

The only other note comes a week later: *Due to psychological distress caused by close living environment, student has requested and been granted a stipend in lieu of remaining in the residence halls.*

My stomach feels as if it's dropped to my feet. Olivia's been keeping secrets for years, and today, when she finally opened up to someone—to *me*—I laughed in her face and told her I was kicking her off the team. I bury my head in my hands. Jesus. Why did I doubt her so much? Why did I refuse to give her any credit? She works her ass off at practice every damn day. She has been doing everything else I asked perfectly, so why was I so hell-bent on getting rid of her, on seeing the worst? I'm not sure I want to look too closely at it all, but I know it needs to be fixed.

SHE LIVES in the worst possible section of town. Her apartment complex looks like it was built in the 70s, and was last maintained then too. Once we sort out what's going on with her running, I need to get her back into the dorms. Even *I* don't feel safe on this end of town.

I knock and she opens the door without unchaining the lock. "Yes?" she asks, her eyes empty.

"Can I come in?"

She bites her lip. "I'll come out," she finally says.

She unchains the door and opens it as little as possible in order to get out. I get the distinct impression she doesn't want me to see what or who is in her apartment.

"Am I interrupting something?" I ask, nodding at her door.

She gives me a dirty look. "Yeah. Me, packing my shit."

Some small piece of me is tempted to laugh. She isn't going to make this easy. No surprises there, I guess. I turn to face her. "I'm sorry about earlier," I say, pinching the bridge of my nose. "I shouldn't have implied you were lying."

Something surprised and soft, almost vulnerable, passes over her face until she blinks it away. She takes a seat on the curb and I follow. "Why the sudden change of heart?" she asks sourly. "You realized I'm your only chance of winning in two weeks?"

"You really think as piss-poor as your performance has been so far that I'm putting my hopes on you?" I demand. It's harsh but true, and I know she's the kind of person who responds more to candor than flattery. I could tell her that I think it's possible she could win it for us, that I see in her the kind of untapped potential that makes almost *anything* possible, but I don't. She wouldn't believe me anyway. "I'm here because it appears possible that I was wrong."

"That's big of you," she snarls, climbing to her feet. "The way you're conceding it's *possible* I'm not lying. Thanks for stopping by. Come back if you'd like to tell me you think it's also possible that I don't deal drugs or poison children, and in the meantime, go fuck yourself."

"Sit," I bark, pointing at the curb. "And stop being a pain in the ass." She pauses, arms across her chest, scowling but not going inside either.

I bite my lip, not even sure where to start. "How long have you been doing it?"

Her jaw shifts. It's a conversation she's dying to avoid. "Since I was little," she says with a tiny, defiant shrug. As if it's meaning-less when it appears to have defined her life for years and years.

"*Why* does it happen?" I ask. This, I suppose, is the most important question, because it will tell us how to make it *stop* happening.

"How should I know?" she asks, but she finally lowers herself beside me on the curb.

Her legs are crisscrossed with small scratches. The para-medics had mentioned it earlier, but at the time I was too pissed about her early morning run to care. I feel a little sick thinking about it. Now that I know what's going on, there will never be a time when I see a scratch on her, or see her limping or exhausted, that I won't worry about what occurred the night before.

"What happened to your legs?"

Her jaw grinds. "I assume I ran through some brush," she says quietly. "It wouldn't be the first time."

"It doesn't wake you up?" I ask.

She shrugs. "If it hurts enough."

I sigh heavily. I don't know what to do with this girl. That she hasn't been badly injured is a miracle. "Have you seen anyone? A specialist?"

"When I was a kid," she says, "but it just made things worse."

I glance at her, hard-pressed to see how this situation could possibly get *worse*. "How?"

She shakes her head again. Apparently even on this day of self-disclosure, there are things she isn't ready for me to know. That's okay. I can wait. I haven't been worthy of her trust until now, but that's going to change.

"You can't keep doing this," I tell her. "You've got to stop."

"You think I don't want to?" she asks with a miserable laugh. "Do you know how humiliating it is to be hitchhiking barefoot at five a.m.? To walk up to a stranger's door and tell them you have no idea where you are or how you got there?"

"Jesus Christ," I exhale. "Whatever you do, don't hitchhike."

"I had to! I wasn't going to make it in time for the meet otherwise."

"You're going to get hurt. That's far worse than missing a meet. You've probably already *gotten* hurt at some point."

She closes her eyes. I'm beginning to decipher Olivia-speak. Anything that isn't flat-out argument is unwilling agreement. She has gotten hurt, and I'm guessing it was bad.

"There's got to be some kind of sleeping pill they can give you," I insist.

"Yeah, and it'd make me comatose the next day. You think my run today was shitty? Watch me the morning after I take the drugs."

How could she possibly think her running matters so much that it's worth risking her life for? "There are things that matter more than running."

She looks at me like I'm insane. "Not for me."

This girl. This stupid, stupid girl. Does she not realize how badly she could be hurt? How in a moment's time it could all just disappear?

"What about your *life*?" I ask. "Isn't that more important than running?"

She turns to me with a single brow raised, her eyes bleak and unapologetic. Nothing's more important to her than this. It's an answer I understand all too well. That's exactly how I felt about climbing.

THE NEXT FEW days are uneventful. She's on time without a single scowl or acid-laced barb. She gives me exactly what I ask for, bearing my adjustments to her form in silence, but she also avoids my gaze entirely. She puts on a good act, but I'm beginning to suspect that tough shell of hers is there for a reason. That perhaps it's hiding something so fragile she's not sure it could survive out in the open.

It's not until Friday that she's done it again. That she can't keep up, and ends up hanging back with the slowest girls on the team. I almost tell her to stop. When they come back to the track, I see her hands and legs jerking, the muscles spasming, and she clasps her arms around her waist to hide it as best she can. Still not meeting my gaze.

"Good practice, ladies," I call. "Head in and I'll see you Monday. Enjoy your last free Friday for a while." She turns to follow them and I stop her. "Hang on, Olivia."

She nods but stares at the ground, her legs knocking together. It's hard to watch. How much must she drive herself in order to keep up on the days when there's nothing left?

I tell her to sit and hand her a drink. "What are we going to do about this?"

Her glance at me is both panicked and angry, shooting quickly toward me and then away. "I don't know. If I knew, I'd do it."

"What makes it better? What makes it worse?"

"Exhaustion," she says. "Exhaustion makes it better. Stress makes it worse."

I look out over the track as I let this sink in. What this tells me is that races create the perfect storm for her. Not enough of a workout to tire her the day before and tons of stress on top of it. And me there, acting like she's going to lose her scholarship the minute she messes up. Coaching a runner isn't rocket science, and yet I'm at a loss as to how I can help her.

"Your parents must have had a way to stop you, though," I say. "They couldn't have allowed a kid to just run out in the middle of the night."

She looks at me again, that small wounded thing inside her making only the briefest appearance before it goes away. She shakes her head. "Nothing stopped me."

God, the idea of her out running like that unnerves me. She thinks she's tough, but the truth is that she's 5'7" and about 110 pounds. A large child could probably take her down. The idea of her hitchhiking to get home ...

It sits in my stomach like a stone.

"You know if you get too far from campus you can call me, right?" I finally ask. "Or if you just need a ride when you wake up? For Christ's sake, don't hitchhike, anyway."

She almost smiles, but not quite. "How am I going to do that, Will? I don't stop to grab my phone on the way out the door."

Jesus. She's right. She's absolutely right. I can't stand the idea of her taking the risks she must take when it happens. "You need to go to counseling."

"It won't do any good," she says flatly.

"I said that wrong. What I meant is you *are* going to counseling. This is not a negotiation." She glares at me and I laugh. "You're giving me that look like you wish I were dead again, so at least things are back to normal."

Her mouth twitches. All of the trouble she's caused me so far feels worth it the moment I see her almost-smile.

15

Olivia

This is going to go so poorly.

Will, I'm sure, thinks I'm going to go in to see this counselor, and by the end of the session I'll be crying about how I never felt loved or how my mom skipped my ballet recital when I was five or whatever it is normal people cry about. And then I'm going to pop out of my chair, healed and ready to move on. Except I'm not normal. I'm so far from normal that I doubt even the psychologists have seen one of me before. I have experience with this. I have so much experience with this that I swear to God I could switch chairs and counsel myself.

It doesn't work.

The therapist's name is Ms. Daniels. She's small and chunky and has a big, fake smile on her face. I hate her on sight, which seems like a bad omen.

She has a whispery little baby voice and sings her words to me like I'm a toddler. "Olivia?" she hums. I don't bother correcting the name because I already know I'm not coming back. "I'm so happy to meet you," she coos as we sit in her office. She still has that eager smile on her face as if I'm here to plan a trip to Bali and she's on commission. "Why don't you tell me what brings you in today?"

This is bullshit. She knows exactly why I'm here. Why should school funds pay for her to sit there and listen to me recount something she can read for herself? "Isn't it already in my file?" I ask.

"I saw a few things," she sings, "but I want to know why *you* want to be here." She continues to smile. It's freaky. I didn't come in here because I just won the lottery, so why the fuck is she smiling?

I tell her I'm only here because my coach forced me to be. "If you'd read my file you'd know that," I add. That gets her. I watch her eyes blink a little extra. She's growing nervous.

"Well, then we can talk about why you don't want to be here."

"Because I've done this before. It just doesn't work."

"Not all therapists are the same," she says, eyes brightening. "Maybe your last one just wasn't a good fit."

"No, I mean that I don't think it works for anyone," I reply. "Did you know psychiatrists commit suicide more than any other profession?"

Her mouth twitches again. "I don't think that's true."

"Look it up."

"I don't need to look it up, Olivia," she says, growing flushed. "This session is for you to talk about your feelings."

"My feeling is that you're scared to look it up." I almost feel sorry for her, but not quite. If she wants to position herself as the expert, then she should freaking be an expert.

She glances at the wall behind me. No doubt she has a clock there and is trying to gauge exactly how many more minutes this will drag out. And it will drag out, believe me, because I plan to make this every bit as unpleasant for her as it is for me.

It's one of the very few things I'm good at.

16

Will

On Tuesday afternoon, I tell the team that there will be a time trial the next morning. The top three runners will fly to Oregon in early December for the Cooper Invitational. I don't want to look at Olivia's face, but I do, and I regret it. She's scared. I can see it in her eyes. She deserves one of those three spots. Hell, she deserves all of them. She's the best runner this school has seen in a decade, if not more. But that fear I see is only going to feed on itself, ensuring that she runs tonight. I feel powerless as I send her off. I hate the feeling, and I hate that it's probably how she feels almost all of the time.

That night, Jessica and I have an early dinner. I walk her to her door, but I don't come inside. "You're not staying?" she asks, looking at me beneath long lashes, arching her limber frame so her chest brushes mine. She has the kind of body few men can say *no* to, and she's well aware of it.

"I'm sorry, I've got to be up early tomorrow." She knows I don't sleep well at her place. It's nothing personal, but I inevitably wind up on her couch because I can't fall asleep next to someone. I've never been able to, but that has nothing to do with why I'm not staying tonight.

"I have alarms here, you know," she says, tucking her hand into the waistband of my jeans before she starts to tug at my belt. I place my hand over hers.

"I would love to stay, but you're slightly too distracting, and I've got work to do."

"Work? Will, it's 10 p.m. What work can't wait until tomorrow?"

And that's the question I can't answer.

There's no way to make what I'm about to do sound reasonable, or ethical. But I think about the possibility of stopping Olivia, and how spectacular she might be at a meet on a full night's rest, and I just don't care.

As I head to Olivia's apartment, though, I remember Peter asking me if she was unnecessary temptation. I shut the conversation down at the time, but now I have to reopen it. Am I really here because I want to see her succeed, or am I here for another reason? Olivia Finnegan is so pretty that you feel compelled to look at her even when you don't want to. You want to memorize the delicate structure of her face, her full rosebud mouth. She's so pretty that pretty isn't even the word for it. It's something that makes me feel like I can't breathe on the rare occasions I see her smile.

It's that last part that worries me.

I watch her apartment. I see her shadow moving back and forth behind the window, and when her lights finally go off, I sit on her steps. I'd rather stay in the car, but I'm drowsy enough at this point that I'd pass out and never even notice her racing past.

It's almost 2:30 when I'm startled awake. A thump from inside her apartment. My heart is beating hard, as if I'm about to cross a line, but then again, I'm sitting outside a student's apartment in the middle of the night.

I guess that line is already crossed.

17

Olivia

T here's a storm coming. Something bad. The sun is out, but my mom is like a tornado, running from room to room.

"Mommy?" I ask. "Are we okay?" The possibility of disaster always exists in this house.

She spins on her heel to look at me, running her hands through her dark hair like she's fixing to yank it all out. I shouldn't have stopped her.

"No!" she screams. It's her angry-sad scream, the one that brims over with the tears she's holding back. Her sadness makes her want to lash out, and when she does the guilt will make her sad all over again. "Just give me five minutes in peace, Olivia, please!"

I nod and back away. She drops to her knees and begins crying hard, holding out her arms for me. "I'm sorry, baby," she whispers into my hair. "Mommy is just a little stressed."

She tells me we're going on a trip, but we have to leave really fast. She asks me to run to the basement and grab a few toys, and then go to my room and get the white dress I wore on my last day of school.

I run to the basement and pick a doll I don't even play with, don't even like really, so when I look at her, it won't make me feel sad for what I've left behind. I go back upstairs but haven't reached my room yet when I hear a car door slam outside. My mother comes to a dead stop, a violent shudder running over her skin.

There's a storm coming. A storm that is outside but rushing at us fast.

She squats in front of me. "Run out the back door. Run as hard as you can and don't stop until you get to the woods. And whatever you do, don't come back."

No. She is where safety lays. Not outside in the open, where anything can happen.

"I want to stay with you," I beg.

That's when we hear the front door open, the heavy tread on the first step, and I know the storm has caught us. And when a storm is inside your house, it's too late to run.

She shoves me into the closet. She tells me to stay and hide and not to make a sound until she comes for me, not a sound. Her words are threatening but her face is so, so sad. "Don't watch," she says. "And if he finds you, run."

Then she shuts the door.

I peer through the crack. Darkness fills the house, clouds rumble overhead, and his shadow stretches long and thin across the room, reaching from doorway to bed, where she sits with her hands in her lap. I can feel her fear. It fills the room, slides under the closet door and then it fills me too. She will not fight him because there are things in this world too large, too terrible to fight, and he is one of them.

Suddenly I'm running, hard like she told me to.

Down toward the high corn where I am small and he is big and only I can hide. But then he has me, grabbing me from behind, his arms wrapped around me like a straightjacket, immovable. I fight but it's useless. I wait for the pain to come, the pain I know is coming again, the sharp heat in my back and the wet feel of my shirt sticking and the blood on his hands. I know all this will come.

But there is nothing.

He tells me to calm down, begs me to calm down, but it's not the monster's voice. It's a soothing one, one that rolls over me and through me like a drug. A voice that tells me I'm safe, which can't be true but he says it again.

I give way.

I believe him.

I stop fighting and let the world grow black.

∾

"Liv. It's time to get up."

I open my eyes slowly. I'm not in my room, and it's daylight. In a flash, my grogginess gives way to panic. If I'm not in my own room, I've done something very wrong. I've run or I've passed out again and I'm in a hospital or somewhere worse.

The time trial. I've missed it or I'm about to.

I sit up, blinking at the bright sunlight, at the unfamiliar room. The first thing I see is Will. For a fraction of a moment I see something on his face I haven't seen before, something that isn't disdain or even concern, and then he squeezes his eyes shut.

"Jesus, Olivia," he groans. "Cover up."

Oh God. I look down and then look over the bed, where at some point in the night I flung my tank. This is getting worse and worse.

I yank the sheet up, but he's already turned away and leaving the room.

"Where am I?" I ask.

"I'll talk to you when your clothes are on," he rasps, his voice sounding a little strangled.

I bury my head in my hands. *Oh my God, Olivia, what have you done now? And why did you do it with him of all people?* I don't mind getting naked. I'll strip down in front of almost anyone. But not *him.* My tank is still the tiniest bit damp, and I shiver as I slide it over my head. I must have run and, par for the course, stripped it off at some point. But how exactly did I end up stripping it off *here*? And why don't I remember any of it?

When I walk out, he's in the kitchen pouring coffee, his shoulders rigid as if he's angry. He seems to be making a point of not looking over at me. "Where am I?" I ask.

"My apartment," he replies. He glances up as he hands me a cup of coffee, and then storms out of the room.

I've clearly done something terrible. I try to recall the evening before. Large quantities of alcohol would explain both why I am here and why I stripped off my clothes, but I don't remember anything.

He returns, handing me a T-shirt, again without looking at me. "Put that on," he says. "You're practically naked."

I look down. Between the fit and the dampness of the shirt, I guess it doesn't leave much to the imagination. There is only one logical explanation for why I'd be in his apartment with no memory of it. "Why am I here?" I ask. "Did we...?"

"No," he gapes, with an insulting mix of shock and disgust. "Of course we didn't."

"You don't need to act like it's so repulsive," I snap. "You could do a lot worse than me."

His hand pushes through his hair and holds there, giving me a distracting glimpse of one very nice, tattooed bicep. "You don't remember *anything*?"

It's humiliating, and humiliation—like everything else— pisses me off. I scowl at him. "Isn't that somewhat obvious?"

"I caught you trying to run from your apartment," he says, leaning one hand on the counter. "You were asleep or ... I don't know what you were. I stopped you and you just kind of passed out."

I close my eyes and feel dread wash over me. I'd prefer that he'd seen me drunk. I'd prefer him seeing me naked. At least I'd have some idea who I was then, but the running episodes are a mystery to me. I'm scared of who I am in those nightmares, and I'm scared of who I am when I'm running away from them.

"Did I, um, do anything?" I ask. The words are so quiet I'm not sure if he's heard me.

"You took a swing at me," he says with a low laugh. "But I kind of deserved it, under the circumstances."

"Sorry," I murmur with a quick glance at his face, assessing him for damage. "Did I hurt you?"

His mouth curves upward. "No, I sort of knew what I was getting into. You're hardly known for your even temper."

I roll my eyes, and then force myself to ask the thing I dread most. "Did I talk?" I don't want to know what I said, so God knows I don't want *him* to know what I said.

"A little." He hesitates, and my stomach drops. "You were really upset. You kept saying something like 'I left' over and over, but I couldn't understand it. Then you just sort of collapsed."

I steel myself to look at him and find the exact emotion on his face that I don't want to see.

Pity.

I'm inclined to just walk out of his apartment right this minute, except I'm barefoot and I have no idea what part of town I'm in. "Jesus, this is humiliating," I whisper, staring at the counter. "Why were you there?"

His shoulders sag. "I shouldn't have been. I knew you'd be stressed out about the time trial and would run, so I waited. I just thought if I saw it firsthand ..." he sighs, shaking his head. "I don't know what I thought. I didn't expect anything so extreme. Do you know what the dream was about?"

"No," I whisper. I stare at my hands, gripping the coffee cup so hard that they are drained of color.

"Maybe you should try to remember. Maybe that's the key to ending all this," he says. "Did you talk to the counselor?"

My eyes roll again. He seems to bring it out in me. "She was a moron."

I get a small flash of his half-smile, high on one side. "I'm guessing you say that about most people you meet."

"Well, it's true of most people I meet." I bite my lip. "How did I, uh, end up here?"

His smile fades. "Your door was locked. I could have woken you, but I was scared you'd freak out. I didn't know where else to take you, so I put you in my room and I slept on the couch." He sets his coffee down and braces himself against the counter. "But this is bad. You absolutely should not be here. I could get fired for this."

For the first time I realize how much he risked, doing this. For me. I don't like it. "It's not like anything happened," I argue.

"No one is going to believe that, Olivia," he sighs, turning away. "Not with you."

My jaw drops. I had a reputation at UT—wholly undeserved, by the way—but *this* is bullshit. I haven't even been out with anyone in a year. "Just because a few guys on the team ask me out doesn't make me the team slut," I snap.

He rubs his eyes. "I wasn't trying to imply you were," he groans. "You're attractive. That's all I was saying."

A tiny warmth weaves its way through me. It shouldn't. I shouldn't care what he thinks. "I'm attractive, huh?"

He walks away. "Don't worry, your personality ruins it. Let's go. You're gonna make us both late."

MY EYES SLIDE toward him as he drives me to my apartment. It's almost unfair how pretty he is, with that jaw and that hollow under his cheekbones, the ruggedness of his face contrasting with his soft mouth.

"Oh, shit," he says as we pull up. "I forgot you're locked out."

"I keep a key under the flowerpot to the right. Just in case you ever happen to be stalking again."

"I wasn't stalking," he growls.

I wonder how long he sat outside my apartment on the off chance I might run. I'm astonished by it all over again. He probably could have gotten fired for that *alone*.

"I guess I never thanked you," I say reluctantly, "so, um, thanks."

"I can't keep you from doing what you're going to do," he says quietly, staring straight ahead, "but if you tell anyone, I'll probably lose my job."

I'm annoyed he'd even think it, but I guess I haven't given him much reason to expect the best from me. "I would *never* tell anyone." I start to remove his T-shirt and he stops me.

"Just keep it," he says. "Being seen leaving my car is bad. Leaving it half-naked would be worse."

I climb out. "Thanks again."

"Olivia," he says. I glance back at him. The uncertain, guilty, anxious version of him is gone. Coach Will is back, stern and no bullshit. "Show everyone what you can do today."

I swallow and nod. I could give two shits about *everyone*. But for *him*, I will.

18

Olivia

Thirty minutes later, Will and I are both on the track, avoiding each other's gaze. He's in a shitty mood and barking at almost everyone as we warm up. Everyone but me. "Higher kick, Olivia," is all he says and even that is muted. As if I'm damaged.

"You can't do that," I tell him quietly.

He seems to actually *look* at me for the first time since I got here. "Can't do what?"

"Don't start treating me differently. Don't act like I'm fragile, because I'm not. Nothing you've seen is new for me."

"You're normally crying about how hard I am on you," he sighs. "I can't win, can I?"

"A, I don't cry, and B, I like Asshole Will. He's a known commodity."

"If I'm such a known commodity," he says, his mouth lifting on one side, "you'd know not to refer to me as 'Asshole Will.'"

I walk away, wanting to laugh and yet feeling unsettled. I

know how to be angry at him, but I don't know how to feel *this*. Or even what, exactly, *this* is.

AFTER THE WARM-UPS, Peter comes down to the track with the men's team following him. They'll do their time trial first. I wish it were us. My stomach dropped the moment he walked down here, and it's going to remain swimming and nervous until this is done.

"You're pale," says Erin, sitting beside me in the grass. "You can't be nervous, you're the fastest girl here. You're the only one who *shouldn't* be nervous."

"Things go wrong." My voice is tense, and for some reason even talking seems to rock the uneasy thing in my stomach and make it feel less stable.

"I can't believe I'm saying this," she replies with a small smile, "because you sure don't seem to think a lot of things through, but you need to think less."

I scowl at her.

"I'm serious. Let your mind go blank. Say it with me." She crosses her legs and puts her hands in the lotus position. "Ommmm."

"Please shut up, Erin."

She laughs. "That's super un-Buddhist of you."

"You know what else is un-Buddhist?" I warn. "Punching someone in the face. So stop talking." Erin doesn't tend to get scared off by me the way she should, and I doubt I've scared her now, but she does, for once, stop yammering.

Will motions us to the starting line, looking oddly anxious given that he just has to stand there looking pretty. It's not until we're lined up and I catch his quick glance that I realize he's anxious for *me*. I hate that. I don't want anyone anxious for me or wanting things for me. It's bad enough when I only disappoint myself.

The gun goes off. I stop thinking. My body takes over, pulling me through as if directed by some outside entity. My legs pump and I feel that rasp in my chest that warns me I've gone out too fast and I don't care. I ignore it because I want this. I want to show Will I'm worth his effort. Over the past five weeks, in his own abrasive way, he's done more for me than anyone I've ever known.

I see him standing by the bleachers, watching, and I don't look around me. I don't even look at the finish line. I pass it, and I am first, and the whole time he is the only thing I see.

19

Will

She was brilliant.

She was absolutely fucking brilliant.

And the truth is I'm not surprised. I need to get out to my mom's, but seeing Olivia's performance today has given me tunnel vision. I want to solve this for her so she can become what she's *capable* of being. I realize it's naïve—her family has probably spent the last decade trying to fix it, so there's no reason to think I'll be any more successful, but I have to at least try.

I go to my office and pull up her student records again. Will she be pissed that I've called her parents? Undoubtedly. Do I give a shit? Not really. The nightmares have to stop. I think about her wandering that neighborhood in the middle of the night *asleep* and I feel sick to my stomach. It's just a matter of time until she gets hurt.

There is no listing for her parents anywhere in her file. I know she said they were traveling but if they are still legally responsible for her they'd be in here somewhere. Instead I find her grand-mother's name and number. If she was raised by her grandmother, why doesn't she just say so? The more I try to solve the mystery of Olivia Finnegan, the more mysterious she becomes.

I dial her grandmother's number. The chipper voice on the other end informs me that I've reached Sunset Springs Assisted Living. For a moment, I think I've dialed wrong.

I ask for her grandmother by name. "I'm her granddaughter's coach," I explain, "and she's listed as the next of kin."

"I'm sorry, sir," she says briskly, "but we have instructions to only pass calls through to Miss Anya from family."

I grip the phone tight, trying hard to rein in my impatience. "Look, this is kind of important. I need to get in touch with someone and she's the only contact number we have."

"I doubt she'd be much help anyway. Alzheimer's," the woman says, her voice dropping to a whisper. "I'm not supposed to tell you that, but hers is pretty advanced. She doesn't remember anybody these days."

Olivia's emergency contact is a woman with advanced Alzheimer's disease.

Which can only mean she has no one else.

"How long has she been with you?"

"Well, I'm not supposed to release that kind of information either," she says, and then her voice drops to a whisper again. "But it's been a little over four years."

I rub at my chest, at this ache that's sprung up there over the course of this call. Olivia wasn't even out of high school yet. So who was raising her all those years? And where are her parents?

I'm DISTRACTED through dinner at Jessica's that night. The minute I think I'm beginning to grasp what Olivia's been through, it just gets worse.

"What kind of work did you have to do last night anyway?" Jessica asks, pulling my attention back to her.

My intentions were completely innocent with Olivia. And had it all stayed that way I'd probably tell Jessica the truth.

Except it didn't, because something changed in me when I caught her last night. And then it changed again, in a far more dangerous way, this morning. When I saw her asleep in my bed, her back bare, her breathing even, her hair spread over the pillow...

I've tried a hundred times to block the image. And the one that followed, when she sat up and the sheet slid to her waist.

I can't.

It's pretty much all I've thought about all day, despite my best efforts. It's left me feeling as if a small crack has formed, a fault line, one that could grow into something unmanageable.

It's the first time in the months we've dated that I tell Jessica a lie.

20

Olivia

I run hard for him the next day.

I follow his every command to the letter. In the end, when he has not a single criticism to offer, I feign shock.

"Wow. Nothing shitty to say?" I ask, wide-eyed. "Does that mean you were actually *pleased*?"

"You know you did well," he says. "Don't fish for compliments."

I roll my eyes. "I'm pretty sure it's the only way to get them out of you."

"Try running like that in the meet and the compliments will flow freely."

I was on the *cusp* of finding him bearable and now he's ruined it. My mouth goes into a hard line. "Awesome. So basically, as soon as I'm able to stop doing something in my sleep I don't even know I'm doing, *that's* when you'll be pleased."

He sighs, pinching his nose between his thumb and forefinger. I know his moods now, his tells. He does this when he's frustrated, and when he's about to face something he doesn't want to face.

"Go shower and come to my office," he says, turning away from me.

I can't imagine what he thinks a talk in his office will accomplish. He's probably going to send me back to that idiotic counselor, who will send me off with some stupid fucking homework. Last time, I was supposed to list things that make me happy. "Like bubble baths," she'd said. "Doesn't a nice bubble bath make you happy?" I told her a bubble bath would make me feel like I was wasting valuable time, which still makes me laugh although she didn't seem to appreciate that much.

I shower quickly and head to his office, where he's already waiting with a particularly grim expression on his face.

I sink into the chair across from him. "I'm not going back to the counselor if that's what this is about."

He almost smiles. "Yes, you've made your feelings about her known."

I sigh. "Look, I'll try to stay awake all night. It usually fails but maybe it'll work. Or sometimes if I do a hard run before bed, I'm tired enough—"

"No," he says, cutting me off. "I want you fresh, and that'll just give me some version of the half-assed running you give me when you've had a nightmare."

I slump in my seat, struggling not to bark at him. "So what's your magic solution then?"

He leans forward, looking grimly determined as he meets my eye. "You're going to stay with my mom."

My mouth falls open, and for a moment I'm frozen by the sheer stupidity of this idea. "With your *mom*?" I finally manage. "Are you crazy? I punched you! What would I do to her? And how could she possibly stop me?"

His shoulders sag a little and he releases a heavy sigh. "I'll be there too," he says. "It still looks bad, but no one needs to know I was there. I'll sleep on the couch so you can't get by without me hearing."

The effort he is making causes something to tighten and twist in my chest, a small pain that radiates outward and makes me long to walk away from this whole conversation. "You shouldn't have to do all that," I mumble.

"I want to."

When I reluctantly meet his gaze, I see how badly he wants me to succeed—not for him, but for me. The pain in my chest gets worse, and I look away. "Okay," I whisper. A single word that doesn't begin to express what I am feeling. No one has ever made an effort for me until now.

I'm not sure why it hurts that he is.

He's outside my apartment Friday evening.

"This is embarrassing," I mutter like a sullen teen, climbing into the passenger seat.

He arches one brow. "What's embarrassing?"

I swallow. "Your mom is going to think I'm some kind of freak."

"And she'd be wrong to think that because ...?" he asks with a grin.

I give him my most menacing look, which he seems to now be impervious to, annoyingly enough.

"She's not going to think you're a freak," he continues. "My brother used to sleepwalk when he was little. It's not that different."

"It's really fucking different," I sigh, "but okay."

"She'll have put a lot of work into dinner so be nice about it," he warns.

I am not at all interested in sitting down to some awkward-ass meal with Will and his *mother*. God only knows what we'd talk about. "I already ate."

"What did you have?"

"Oatmeal and an apple," I reply. "I would have eaten on campus but there wasn't time."

"It's the night before a meet," he grumbles. "You can't possibly think that's enough food, not after what happened last time."

I shrug. "Last time was sort of an anomaly."

He gives a short, unhappy laugh. "You *are* aware that 'anomaly' means 'an unusual occurrence,' right?"

"That's why I said 'sort of' an anomaly," I argue.

He cuts me a glance. "And that's why you're 'sort of' going to eat dinner at my mom's house."

Argh. I'm clearly not going to win this argument. I'm not sure I win *any* arguments with him. I turn toward the window, watching campus recede into the distance. It's surprising how quickly the town becomes rural, and reminds me of where my grandmother lived, the endless roads with nothing but farmland and forest on either side. He soon pulls onto a bumpy gravel road littered with potholes that send me bouncing toward the ceiling of his truck. In the distance I see a small house and a substantial barn.

"This is where you grew up?" I ask.

"Yes," he says with a sigh. "I suppose you have some smart-ass comment about it?"

I *did*, but now that he's called me on it I'm inclined to keep it to myself. "No," I say huffily. "I was going to say it looks nice."

"Right." He stops in front of the house and jumps out, leaving me to follow. I enter tentatively, surprised by how much larger it seems on the inside than it did from the outside, like some kind of *Alice in Wonderland* trick of perception. There's a big living room with a kitchen on the right, bedrooms to the left.

His mom comes out of the kitchen. "You must be Olivia," she says, hugging me with so much enthusiasm I feel certain Will has kept a number of details about me to himself. "I'm Dorothy."

I disengage myself with an awkward smile.

"It's still a while til dinner," she says. "Why don't you take Olivia for a quick ride, Will?"

His lip curls at the very idea. "I don't think so."

I huff in exasperation. *He's* the one making me do this. He doesn't need to act like I'm some gross clingy girl he wants to avoid. "Am I really that awful?" I demand. "You're acting like she just asked you to give me both kidneys."

"It's the night before a meet. You might get sore."

"I spent the whole summer riding horses," I argue. "I'll be fine."

"Okay, Olivia," he says with just a touch of acid to his voice. "Would you care to go horseback riding?"

"I'll go on my own," I tell him. "I don't need a chaperone." I walk out the front door and he's on my heels.

"Where the hell are you going?" he demands. "Do you even know how to saddle a horse?"

I groan loudly. "Do you really think I'd just jump on bareback and take off?"

"Right, how silly of me," he replies. "You have such a reputation for restraint and good judgment."

I march toward the stables, trying to ignore him. The smell hits me first. It is, without a doubt, unpleasant—hay and manure and grass baked in sunshine, the faint smell of leather beneath it —but the memories it brings back are good ones. I spent summers as a girl cleaning out the stables down the road from my grandmother's house. I got to ride in the afternoons when I was done, worth far more to me than the crappy pay I got for doing it.

He leads me to Trixie, who looks so docile I'm not sure she'll even wake up long enough to be ridden. Once she's saddled, I climb on but he grabs the pommel to hold me in place.

"Don't even think about going faster than a trot," he warns.

I roll my eyes. "I doubt this horse is *able* to trot."

He's saddled a much better horse for himself, I notice. He

climbs on and we ride side-by-side while he assesses my seat. The only sign of approval I get is his eventual decision to ride ahead.

And I might not enjoy his company, but I'd be lying if I said I didn't enjoy the view. He looks good riding a horse. *Really* good. He wears the hell out of a pair of jeans on his worst day, and even twenty feet behind him I can see the definition of his arms. I picture sneaking up behind him and pressing my nose to the nape of his neck, just below where his hair is shaved close. A small shiver brushes over my arms at the thought.

I don't want him.

I don't.

I don't want his bossiness and his bad temper and the way his upper lip curls when he's mad at me. Half the time I'd just as soon kick him in the balls as fuck him. I need to focus on the part of me that wants to watch him writhe in pain because right now, at this precise moment...the other part seems to be winning.

We get to the crest of the hill and a lake comes into view. "I assumed it was all woods down here," I tell him.

He frowns. "My dad built it for my brother and me."

I cast a suspicious glance at him. It's not a pond. It's a lake the size of a football field. "He *built* it? How the hell do you build a lake?"

Will shrugs. "Engineering background and a lot of persistence, I guess. We used to swim in it all year long. It's built over a hot spring, so it stays warm for the most part."

"Why?" My voice is quiet and uncertain, and I'm embarrassed by the question.

"Why does it stay warm?"

"No." I swallow. "Why would he build it for you?"

Will cocks his head, looking at me as if he's trying to understand something. "Because he loved us. Why else would he do it?"

I don't answer, but the truth is that I can't imagine someone caring about his children that much. I can't imagine anyone caring about anyone that much. It's something I'd rather not think about. "I'm ready to head back," I tell him, turning toward the barn.

It's time anyway, since the sun is starting to set. The air feels crisp, a hint of fall at last.

"So what was the deal with you and Mark Bell?" he asks, coming up beside me.

I stiffen. Mark Bell is a topic I discuss with no one. "What do you mean?"

"It takes a whole lot of rage to take a baseball bat to another human being. I figured he must have cheated on you or something."

A small, choked laugh escapes my throat. "No, we weren't dating. I don't date." And I sure as fuck wouldn't have dated *Mark*.

"What do you mean you don't date?" His tone suggests astonishment, as if I just told him I don't breathe. "*Ever?*"

I shrug. "If I want to sleep with someone, I don't need him texting me all the time and pretending he actually likes me as a person in order to do it."

His jaw falls open. It's possible he looks even more dumbfounded than he did the day I told him about the sleep running. "*Jesus*, Olivia," he says. "Then wait for someone who actually *does* like you as a person. And how do you know they're pretending?"

My hands tighten on the reins. "I know my strengths, Will. Likeability isn't high on the list. You'd be the first to attest to it."

"I never said you were unlikeable," he protests.

"You don't have to. It's written all over your face every time you look at me." I sigh, tiring of this whole conversation. Thank God the ride is ending so I can escape it. "Don't worry. I'm used to it."

He grabs my reins and stops us both. "Olivia, there are guys out there who would actually like you. There are actually men in the world who mean well."

He's wrong. There are guys who convince themselves they

like the whole package when they actually just like the box it comes in, but even they'd figure it out soon enough.

"When I'm looking for someone to hook up with," I reply, pulling the reins from him, "the last thing I want is someone who *means well*. Nothing's less exciting than a guy who's too nice." In that one area of my life, I want a guy who isn't scared to take charge. Who's a little bossy and knows exactly what he wants. Someone like...*no, I'm not even going to think it.*

We get to the stables at last, unsaddle the horses and start heading back to the house.

"Race you?" I challenge, assuming he'll refuse.

"Your funeral," he says, to my utter shock, and takes off. I'm so stunned that it takes me a second to even start running myself.

"No fair!" I shout from behind. He slows just enough to let me catch up and then we are flying.

It's my favorite kind of run. The kind where the breeze is warm and blowing at your back and you feel so light and so strong it seems possible you'll take flight. At the very last minute he pulls ahead to win and we both crash into the front porch, laughing.

"You cheated!" I protest.

"How was that cheating?" he demands.

"Because I didn't know you were that fast!" I shout. "I'd never have challenged you if I thought I might lose."

Dorothy is standing at the door. "Will, did you never mention to this poor girl that you ran cross country at ECU too?"

"*You?*" I gasp, following him inside. "*You* ran cross country?"

He shrugs. "You don't have to sound so shocked."

My mouth is still hanging open. "It's just that you're big," I protest. "I mean, you're not just tall but you know, you're broad shouldered ..." I begin stammering because all of a sudden it sounds like I'm describing him to a teen magazine. "I just meant you're muscular," *dammit I'm just making it worse,* "and so you carry a lot of weight." It's a relief to finally conclude on a note that doesn't sound semi-pornographic.

He gives me a half-smile. "Broad shouldered and muscular," he says, heading for the table. "Those are the only words I heard." He points me toward a chair.

"I raised you better than that," his mother chides. "Pull her chair out."

Will gives a loud sigh. "Mom, this isn't a date. I'm not pulling her chair out."

"She is a lady," his mother says, "and you always pull out a lady's chair."

He smirks. "I think even Olivia would agree that calling her a *lady* is a stretch." He yanks the chair out from his seated position. "There you go, princess."

I sit and survey the table. Dorothy's made enough food for the entire damn team, and it smells unbelievable. I'd probably even cut myself a little slack tonight, except I really can't eat before races. If I do it'll be sitting there in my stomach tomorrow like a twenty-pound dumbbell.

I take a little of everything and Will glares at my plate.

"More, Olivia," he says.

"I'm going to get sick," I argue.

"Not as sick as you will if you don't eat enough," he says. "Do I need to remind you what happened last time?"

Dorothy doesn't look surprised by this, so apparently she knows I passed out. I wonder what else she knows. I take more food, glaring at him the whole time. The joke will be on him when I can't run tomorrow because I'm carrying an extra pound of pasta in my stomach.

In spite of my worries about this meal, it turns out to be sort of fun. Dorothy clearly adores Will and his younger brother— away at school—but has no problem calling Will on his shit. It's about time someone did.

When the meal is over, Will and I clear the table. I've just finished drying a bowl when he walks into the kitchen and tells me to go sit. I ignore him, holding the bowl aloft. "Where does this go?" I ask.

"Top cabinet," he says.

I'm on my tiptoes trying to reach up there when he comes up behind me. "I got it," he says, sliding it onto the shelf. I turn just as his arms come down and find myself facing him, our chests touching, his arm brushing mine as it descends.

I feel a snap of desire in my abdomen, and suddenly it's as if the part of my brain that has any common sense has shut down. What remains is the part that notices the smell of his skin, the tiny scar on the bridge of his nose—and the look in his eye, vanquished as quickly as it appears, that is different from anything I've ever seen from him before.

For a single moment, I think his brain shut down too.

AFTER I'VE PUT on the running clothes I sleep in, there's a knock on the door. Dorothy pops her head in and smiles. "Just making sure you didn't need anything. I used to make Will drink a glass of warm milk the night before a meet. Would you like one?"

I feel a pang of envy and joy simultaneously. "No, thank you," I say, stumbling over my words a little. "I'm fine."

"Okay." She grins. "Sleep tight."

I lie down and turn the lamp off. I imagine Will here once upon a time, getting tucked in. A part of me is jealous, but I'm glad he had this growing up. Even if I could take this memory, make it my own instead of his, I wouldn't.

I feel peaceful, imagining him here, and it makes me feel safe knowing he's on the other side of the door. It seems possible that tonight I won't even dream.

21

Will

I exhale with a groan when she finally goes to bed.

I've spent the last hour pretending to not be completely freaked out by what happened in the kitchen. When she turned and I found her pressed against me like that, looking up at me with those big eyes and that mouth of hers, a mouth which could inspire unwelcome thoughts at any hour of the day—*and has*—I didn't just *think* about kissing her. I planned on it. Some baser part of me took charge and demanded a hundred different things it wanted before I came to my senses.

I must have been out of my mind.

She does that to me. She does that to everyone as far as I can tell, but it's only me I'm worried about. It's not just that I'd lose my job. It's that it's *wrong*. She trusts me. She's counting on me to help her with this, make her the runner she is capable of being, and there I was not just imagining kissing her but fully intending to do it.

She can't stay here again. I'll explain the situation to Peter in

the morning, the way I should have when I first found out.
Knowing about her issues means the school is liable if something
happens, and it's possible he'll take her off the team...which is the
reason I haven't told him until now. But maybe he can come up
with another solution. Maybe if she agrees to counseling he can
find some female chaperone on nights before meets. All I know is
it can't be me, ever again.

IT TAKES me a while to fall asleep on the couch. I wake with a jolt
in the middle of the night, realizing slightly too late that it's Olivia
I heard, and that in the time it's taken me to realize it she's
already out the door. I vault over the couch, jump from the top of
the porch to the ground and bypass the steps entirely. She's
flying, halfway to the stables by the time I hit the ground. I
struggle to catch her and when I do it's not pretty, more of a football tackle than a rescue, and we both end up face first on the
ground. She scrambles to get up as I roll off her, but my arm is
around her and she can't get far. She screams, begs, fights. It's
unintelligible and heartbreaking. Wherever she is right now, she's
begging for her life and she sounds very, very young.

I pull her against me, heedless of the dirt and grass underfoot,
binding her with my arms so she can't flail. "It's okay, Olivia," I
plead. "I promise. It's okay. No one's going to hurt you. It's just
a dream."

I tell her these things again and again until the fight leaves
her, until her eyes close, until it's the two of us lying in the middle
of the open field late at night, one of us sound asleep. Gingerly, I
lift her. Her face at rest is perhaps the sweetest thing I've ever
seen in my life. As pretty as she is by day, what I see right now is a
thousand times more compelling: Olivia—vulnerable for once,
and trusting. Trusting me of all people not to hurt her, to help her

through this. I look at that face and know I'm not telling Peter anything tomorrow. I'll find a way to deal with my own demons.

Right now all I care about in the entire world is making sure we deal with hers.

22

Olivia

There's a knock on the door early in the morning, and Dorothy peeks in again.

"Rise and shine!" she sings. She is just too fucking cheerful for this hour of the day, equal parts irritating and endearing. "It's your big day!"

That's when I realize I'm still in bed. I sit up, looking at her in astonishment. "I didn't run?"

Dorothy comes toward me, frowning, and pulls a leaf out of my hair. "What's all over your shirt?" she asks.

I peel the covers back and look down. I'm covered in grass stains and dirt, head-to-foot.

Will comes to the doorway. He glances at my knees, which got the worst of it, and winces. "Sorry," he says. "I, um, sort of ended up tackling you in the grass."

I bury my head in my hands. For a moment there I'd really hoped I hadn't done it. It's bad enough on my own, but this—having witnesses—is so much worse. Dorothy silently retreats as Will takes her place next to the bed.

"Are you okay?" he asks.

I nod. "Just embarrassed," I sigh.

He perches on the mattress, hands clasped between his knees. "There's nothing to be embarrassed about."

"Sure. It's completely normal to need your coach to tackle you in the middle of the night to keep you from losing your scholarship. Did I hurt you?"

"No, but I landed on you pretty hard. I was more worried about you."

I swallow. *Please, God, let this be all there is to it.* "Did I say or do anything ... stupid?"

He frowns. "I don't know why you're so worried about that. No one is going to hold you responsible for what you do when you're not even aware you're doing it." Which doesn't really answer my question.

"I just ... I don't like having this piece of me out there that even I don't know," I explain. "I do enough stupid shit when I'm conscious."

He rises from the bed. "You don't do anything stupid," he says. "In fact, you're a lot more lovable asleep than you are awake."

"So you think I'm lovable?" I tease.

He scrubs a hand at the back of his neck. "Everyone is lovable. Some of us more so than others," he grumbles. "Get dressed. We're leaving in ten."

I take a quick shower, change into my uniform and go to the door, where Dorothy and Will both wait.

"Thank you for having me," I tell her, wondering if I'm supposed to shake her hand or something.

She pulls me in for a hug so fierce I'm almost disabled by my surprise. "I loved having you here, Olivia," she says. "Come anytime."

She actually seems to mean it, and stands at the door waving until we are out of sight.

"Your mom is a nice woman," I say, looking back at the farm. "How'd you turn out to be such an asshole?"

He rolls his eyes, but I can tell he wants to smile. "No one thinks that but you."

"You sure about that?"

He laughs. "No, not entirely."

~

ON THE BUS ride to the meet, my serenity slowly drains away. I got a good night's sleep, but I still don't feel good. We arrive and discover the course is muddy, so we're wearing long spikes, which I dislike. My teeth begin to grind and I press my hands to my stomach, pacing back and forth, wishing I could escape the chaos of my team and the crowd here to watch us.

It's bad. This is bad. It's a new course. I'm in new spikes. I ate last night. God, why did I let Will talk me into eating?

The course is a one-mile repeating loop. We jog one loop slowly to get familiar with it, and my limbs feel heavy, weighted. When we're done, Peter comes over to talk to us. Despite my initial chagrin at being coached by Will, I've begun to suspect that, for me, he's a better fit. Peter's advice is generic: don't go out too fast, hug the corners, and don't get cocky when you're ahead. It's the same advice every coach has given since the sport began.

When he finishes, all the parents and friends and significant others who've come out for the meet surround us, making me feel like I can't breathe. Their excitement just makes this thing in my stomach worse. Nicole introduces me to her parents and asks if mine are still traveling. Will's head turns toward us.

"Yeah," I say, wondering why he's listening. "They'll be gone the whole season."

"Must be nice," Nicole says, turning to her father. "Finn's parents have been traveling for *weeks*. Why don't you guys do that?"

Her father grumbles something about having to pay for her frequent trips to Macy's and I extricate myself, breaking from the group and heading toward the field behind us.

I begin to pace, holding my stomach. I thought escaping would make the anxiety better, but it doesn't. I slept last night and this should be an incredible day, a perfect run, but it won't be. I feel it in my bones. I've now had every benefit I've been denied at past meets and I'm still going to implode, and then what happens to this unfounded belief I had in my potential?

"This is all fucked up," I whisper to myself again and again. "This is all fucked up."

Will walks out to find me. "You look sick," he says. "Are you okay?"

I shake my head. "I have a bad feeling. You shouldn't have made me eat. God, why did I listen to you? I'm going to tank."

He laughs. "Liv, everyone has a bad feeling before a race. It's called nerves."

I shake my head again. He's wrong. Today is going to be a disaster. I can feel it. I *know.*

"Listen to me." He holds his hand to my shoulder, forcing me to meet his eye. "You. Have. This. You do. Just go out and run your own race. I know Peter told you to stay near the top runners until the very end, but I'm telling you different. Get cocky. Go ahead and separate from the pack when you're ready. And blow it out in the last mile. You always have something leftover when we're done. Today, leave it all on the field."

I meet his eye and feel this small crack in my anxiety. A tiny opening inside me, allowing for the possibility that he's right. That, just maybe, he knows more than me this once.

We walk together to the start, and I get in position. Erin punches my arm. "You've got this, my friend."

I glance at her. It's her race too and she's worrying about me. That sliver of light in my chest? It expands a little more. "Thanks," I whisper. "Good luck."

The gun goes off. There's a flurry of movement, all of us too close, dirt flying into my face from the girl ahead of me and someone's elbow in my side.

I try to focus on what Will said to me, but instead hear my own ranting.

I feel weak.

I shouldn't have eaten.

The spikes are throwing me off. They don't feel right. I should have trained in them more than I did.

It shouldn't feel this hard in the first mile.

Except Will, who has been right every time he's told me I can do something, who's been right every time he's told me my stride is off or my kick is short, believes I have this. I hold onto his words. *You have this.*

I let go of my own voice and I cling to his instead. And I fly. Down the field, into the curve of the woods. It's only been me and two other girls for a while, and when we get our one-mile split, I realize that we are *blazing*. It felt hard because we just ran a fast first mile, which means that no matter how bad I thought I felt, I'm performing as if I'm good.

I have it today. Whatever it is I need, I have. And the moment I realize it, I break ahead and forget about everyone behind me. They're not my competition. *I am.* I'm competing against my desire to slow, against the burn in my legs, the rasp in my chest. With one mile left, I blow it out. I'm sprinting and I'm still *fine* when I see the finish line in the distance, when I come around the curve and hear the clang of cowbells and the shouts. That's when I know that I'm really going to do it. I blow through and the first person I look for is Will. He's already running toward me, exultant, and I feel something in my chest that pulls me toward him as well, as if we are tethered. He comes at me fast and then stops himself short, clapping me on the shoulder.

"You did it," he says, his smile wider than I've ever seen it. "You broke the course record."

I smile back at him, wishing I could say something or do something that I can't do. I want to thank him for believing in me. I want to wrap my arms around his neck and hug him the way his mother hugged me.

Instead, I stand here speechless, gratitude caught somewhere in my throat.

23

Will

I told Jessica that I'd head to her place after the meet, but I drive to the farm instead, almost surprised to find myself there when I pull up.

As always, my mother smiles wide when I walk in. I hate how lonely it must be for her out here—she went from a full house to living alone in three years' time. "Didn't expect to see you again today," she says.

"Thought I'd just stop by for a second and check on the horses," I say.

My mother knows me well. And she knows this is what I do when I need to work something out in my head. At one time, I'd used climbing to accomplish this, but it feels self-indulgent now, with so much to be done here.

"How did Olivia do?" she asks.

I can't stop my smile from spreading, creeping out from the corners of my mouth. I was pretty much restraining that smile the whole bus ride back to campus. "She broke the course record."

"I'm glad. I really liked her," she says.

This I knew. Olivia brought out the maternal in my mother the way a newborn would. She was one step away from putting Olivia in a high chair and spoon-feeding her. "No accounting for taste," I reply.

She clucks her tongue. "Now what kind of thing is that to say? She was lovely."

For some reason, agreeing with her in any way on the subject of Olivia feels...dangerous. "She's a nuisance."

My mother glares at me in a way I haven't seen in a long time. "In what *possible* way is she a nuisance?"

"She just is." Except...she wasn't. Sure, she still didn't listen for shit about anything—the horses or the dishes or even the eating, because for all her complaints she ate maybe half of what she should have. But it was oddly...easy, her being here, unexpectedly so. Comfortable. And perhaps that's what made me let my guard down, allowing that moment in the kitchen to happen. I remember the feel of her pressed against me, that mouth of hers, ripe and waiting, and I flinch.

Disliking Olivia is a hell of a lot safer than the alternative.

My mother tilts her head, studying me a little too closely. "How are things with Jessica these days?"

I sigh. Yes, Jessica, my *girlfriend,* the one I completely forgot existed several times last night. "It's fine. It's good."

"You've dated her for a while now," my mother says. "Don't you think it ought to be better than 'fine'?"

"What are you getting at?" I ask tersely.

She shrugs. "I just think that Jessica is a little more serious about this whole thing than you are."

This is something I have no desire to discuss with anyone, particularly not my mom. "We've only dated for a little while and we're both young. I've already told her I'm not getting married for a good long time."

"Just because you've said it," my mother warns, "doesn't mean she believes it."

I go to the stables, suddenly feeling like there are now too many things I have to avoid thinking about. All of them female.

I throw myself into mucking out the stables. By the time I emerge from my worry and begin to feel steady again, the sun is setting.

Which means I am very, very late.

JESSICA MADE DINNER. It's cold.

I apologize and tell her I had to go to my mom's, which isn't technically true, but I can't exactly explain that going to the farm makes me feel peaceful, and coming to her apartment does not.

"It's okay," she says. "I'll just warm it up."

I feel guilty, and resent that I feel guilty which only makes me feel worse. Jessica deserves someone a lot more invested than I am. "You didn't have to do all this," I tell her. "I thought we were eating out."

"We can't eat out all the time," she tsks. "You ought to let me take care of you more."

I feel a tick of anxiety at the base of my chest. There's something a little pointed about Jessica's domesticity these days. She even offered to do my laundry a few weeks back, though I refused. I've told her so many times that I don't want to settle down. I've even implied that I'm not sure I *ever* want that.

I worry, for the first time, that my mom might have been right.

24

Olivia

I can tell something has changed when I get to the track on Monday.

It's the women's first win in over five years, and there's this buzz in all of us, a renewed dedication. Everyone works hard, pulls from a reserve we never guessed was there. It's not until practice ends, as we go to gather around Will, that all that good feeling dissipates, at least for me.

"Finn, if you take first again next week we will totally place," gushes Nicole.

My stomach tightens. I guess everyone was thinking it anyway, but now it's out there and official. They all need me to take first and if I don't, they'll be disappointed. It's entirely on me, and I don't want it to be. She's right of course, and it's probably *because* she's right that it bothers me as much as it does.

"There's a fifty percent chance she'll just pass out in the middle of the course instead," snorts Betsy.

I snap, my anxiety going straight to rage, as always. "If that happens you could pick up the slack, right, Bets?" I ask. "Oh ... No, wait, you've never placed, have you?"

"That's enough, you two," Will says. "Olivia, I'd like to speak to you for a moment. *Now*."

If Betsy were a smarter girl, she'd wipe that smug smile off her face before I do it for her.

My fists clench while everyone walks away, nails digging into my palms to keep me from exploding. The moment they're out of earshot I round on him. "You *always* blame me. She started it. You heard her."

He meets my eye, completely unmoved by my outburst. "Yeah, I heard her."

"So why am *I* the one over here?"

"Because you're the only one who's off the team if there's another incident, remember? If you're going to lead this team, you're going to have to do better. And maybe that starts with realizing that Betsy's jealous and giving her a pass."

My hands go to the top of my head, frustrated anew. "I don't want to lead this team," I reply. "I want them to stop depending on me."

"I know you do," he sighs, "but it's only because you're not sure they should. But *I'm* sure, Olivia. I'm sure they should. And if I do anything this season, it's going to be making you believe that yourself."

My shoulders sag. It's hard to stay pissed off when he says it like that. "You could at least *suggest* that she shut the fuck up occasionally."

He gives me half a smile. "Go take a shower. Try not to beat anyone up."

～

THE NEXT FRIDAY Will once again picks me up to go to his mother's. "You're sure this is okay?" I ask as he takes my overnight bag from my hand.

He holds the door for me. It's almost like he's forgotten I'm a burden he's taken on and is thinking of me as a female instead. "Why wouldn't it be?"

I hesitate. "Because it's a lot ... Your mom can't be fired up about having me there again so soon."

"Get in the car," he says. "My mother likes you. She's excited you're coming today."

I glance up at him in surprise. Will doesn't lie—I know he doesn't—but this seems hard to believe.

He shrugs. "It's as much a mystery to me as it is you."

WHEN WE ARRIVE, there's a beat-up Honda Civic in the driveway I don't recognize. I look over at Will.

"Brendan," he says, his jaw clenched. "My brother."

From the little I've heard, Brendan sounds like a bit more of a wild card than Will, but then who *isn't* more of a wild card than Will? I've seen pictures of him as a little boy—a cute kid with a kind of impish smile. I get the sense that the impishness is still there, and that while Dorothy enjoys it, it's an irritant to Will.

As am I. So maybe Brendan and I will get along just fine.

I don't have to wait long to meet him. The man himself comes running out of the house and tackles his completely unaware older brother while I look on. Brendan is a rangier version of Will. He has the same ice blue eyes, the same light tan, the same wide mouth, but there's something boyish about him that no longer exists in Will.

Brendan jumps up and whoops, then runs in a circle shouting, "Vic-tor-y! Vic-tor-y!"

"Brendan," sighs Will, climbing to his feet, "stop being an idiot and say hi to Olivia."

Brendan blinks, focusing on me for the first time. "Oh. Holy shit. I mean, hi." He laughs at himself. "Sorry, I wasn't expecting you. I mean, I knew Will was bringing a student home. I just didn't know it would ... Wow. I'm sorry. I'm gonna stop talking now."

"Good plan, jackass," says Will, picking my bag up and slinging it hard at Brendan, who staggers backward.

"Hey!" I object. "Don't use my bag as a weapon. What if it had been full of priceless glass objects?"

"Yeah," smirks Will, "you seem just like the type who'd collect priceless glass objects."

"*I* can totally see you collecting priceless glass objects, Olivia," says Brendan with the kind of smile that probably gets him laid non-stop. Like his brother, Brendan is insanely hot. Also like his brother, he seems well aware of it.

"More the type to beat up priceless glass objects," mutters Will. "Put her bag in my room."

Brendan raises a brow. "*Wow.* Being a coach isn't as dreary as I thought."

"It's not like that, dickhead," says Will, pushing me inside.

Brendan tosses my bag into the bedroom and saunters back out. "I'm going to Jimmy's, this bar in town," Brendan says to me, ignoring Will entirely. "Have you been?"

"She's not going drinking the night before a meet," snarls Will. I feel a flash of irritation. It's not like I was going to agree. When's he going to start giving me a little credit?

Brendan glances over at me, giving me another of those sly half-smiles. "I don't have to leave right away," he says to his mom. "Maybe I'll stay in tonight. At least for dinner."

"I was going to hold dinner so Olivia could go riding first," says Dorothy.

"Cool," says Brendan. "I'll go with her."

Will's face has gone, over the course of this conversation, from its standard stern look to something far more grim. Right now he's giving Brendan a scowl I thought he'd reserved only for me.

"You hate horseback riding," he says.

Brendan grins. "Under the right circumstances I don't."

25

Will

I can't remember the last time I wanted to hit my brother as much as I do right now.

I've certainly had better reasons for wanting to hit him. Technically, he's not doing anything wrong, but my brother runs through pretty girls the way Starbucks runs through coffee, and he loves a challenge. And right now he's looking at Olivia like a mountain climber staring at Everest from its base.

He not only invites her out, but when she refuses (okay, I guess I actually refused on her behalf) he starts waffling about whether or not he's going to go out *at all*, when he just drove three fucking hours to see his friends, proving he still does ninety percent of his thinking with his dick.

"Let's go for a walk," I tell him between clenched teeth.

"Walk?" he asks, meeting my eye. "Don't you think we should stay back and make sure our guest is comfortable?"

I swear to fucking God I am going to knock his ass out.

"Brendan," my mother sighs unhappily, "go with your brother."

I walk outside and he follows. I'm quiet for a minute, trying to pull my thoughts together. Brendan will mess with her solely to piss me off, so I need to make sure I handle this the right way. Diplomatically. I can't forbid him to do anything—I just need to calmly explain the situation, make him understand how fragile she actually is.

"Jesus Christ she's hot," says Brendan, walking up beside me. "That's one hell of a job perk."

I round on him, any hope of diplomacy abandoned. "She's off limits."

"Why?" he taunts. "Saving her for yourself?"

I refuse to even consider what he just said. Brendan's an immature asshole, so I shouldn't have expected him to see it any other way. It doesn't mean he's right. "I'm her coach, remember?"

"Exactly," he replies. "So if she wants to go out with me, the road is clear, right? And it's also none of your fucking business."

"Leave her alone," I hiss, grabbing his collar and yanking him toward me before I'm even aware I've done it. The two of us stare at each other in shock. It's the first time since we were kids that I've even come close to threatening him, and both of us know it. Our entire lives it was me who protected him from our father, and suddenly I'm the problem. I have no idea why I've gotten so carried away, why the idea of him with her makes me feel crazy.

I drop my hands and back away from him. "I'm sorry. It's just ... she's been through a lot, okay? She seems tough but she isn't, not at all, and you know how you are."

His jaw goes up. "What's that supposed to mean?"

"It means that you tend to tire of people pretty quickly."

"Trust me," he says, smirking, "it would take a long, *long* time for me to tire of that girl."

The desire to hit him overwhelms me. I've always had Brendan's back. I've covered for him too many times to count over the years, but it's about to end here. "Lay a finger on her and I tell Mom you got busted for possession last year."

He freezes, stunned. "You've got to be shitting me."

Am I in the wrong? Probably. Do I care? Not at all. "Go inside, say goodbye to Mom and Olivia, and get the fuck out of here. And I'd better not see your face again until Olivia is gone."

"Seriously, bro," Brendan says, shaking his head. "What's going on with you and that girl?"

"Nothing, but she's our first shot at a title in over a decade, and I don't want anything messing that up."

He looks like he doesn't believe me. I'm not sure I believe it myself.

I DON'T RETURN to the house until I see Brendan drive off. I ignore the strange look from my mother and ask Olivia if she wants to go riding. I'd sworn to myself that this time would be strictly professional, that I'd eat dinner with her but have no other interaction, but the thing with Brendan got me riled up, so fuck it. I want to go riding, and for some bizarre reason, I want her to be there too.

"So that was Brendan, huh?" she asks as we walk to the stables. "You two always get along that well?"

I shrug. "We used to be close. It's been a little tense since my dad died, I guess."

She looks over at me with her tongue in her cheek. "What changed?"

"Not him, that's for damn sure," I mutter. My life ended when my dad died, but Brendan is still doing his thing. Hanging with his bros, getting high, sleeping with everything that moves, doing just enough work in college to avoid getting kicked out. I had to become an adult, while it's looking like he never will.

"That didn't answer my question," she says quietly.

I sigh. Jessica has asked about this too, and I've always brushed her off. Maybe it's just because Olivia trusted me with some of her burdens that I feel okay sharing mine. "My dad left a ton of debt when he died. The farm was failing and none of us knew it, so we had to give up a lot of things. I guess I resent the fact that I'm the only one who had to give anything up."

"Did you guys ever think about selling it?" she asks.

"We did sell part of it. We had to. But it's my mother's only source of revenue, and she's lived here her entire adult life. I can't take that away from her. Even if she sold it, I can't make enough as a guide or as a coach to support myself and her, plus cover Brendan's tuition. Not to mention that it will take years to pay off the second mortgage my dad took out."

"And you think Brendan should have dropped out of school to help?"

I shake my head. "It's just that now he's talking about all this bullshit. Auditioning for some reality TV show when he graduates, maybe going to Europe for a year. He doesn't have a single actual goal, but he's still not planning to come back and help."

"While you had a goal and had to abandon it," she says, holding my eye. "It seems like he ought to come back."

Except my dad never wanted Brendan to take over the farm. He wanted me to. It's caused this rift between me and Brendan, this bitterness I can't seem to escape. Even in death, my dad is still causing me trouble.

∼

ONCE AGAIN THAT NIGHT, Olivia picks at her food, pushing it around her plate as if that's going to convince anyone over the age of five that she's actually eaten.

"You aren't eating much," my mother frets. "Is everything okay?"

"It's delicious," Olivia says. For whatever reason, that hostility that seems to mark Olivia's every interaction is completely absent when she deals with my mom. "I'm just nervous about tomorrow."

"There's nothing to be nervous about, honey," my mother soothes. "You go out and run your own race, and what happens, happens."

"That's not the way the rest of the team sees it," Olivia says. "They're looking at me like I'm about to cure cancer."

"You don't need to worry about what they think or want," my mother says. "Tell them if they're so desperate to go to regionals, then they should run faster."

I laugh quietly. "That's awesome, Mom. Just what Olivia needs —advice on standing up for herself. Maybe you can teach her some new fighting techniques next."

My mother scowls at me but Olivia's mouth twitches with the desire to laugh.

"Are your parents coming to the meet?" my mother asks her.

Olivia stiffens and I grow still, waiting for her answer. "Uh, no," she says, staring at her plate. "We aren't close."

I look over at her. "I thought you said they were traveling."

Her eyes narrow but I see a touch of fear alongside the anger. "Yes, and their travel plans don't include a visit to me."

She's lying. She's been lying all along. And now both of us know it.

THAT NIGHT, while Olivia is in the shower, my mother calls me to the porch. "What was that today?" she asks. "The thing with Brendan."

It's an effort to make my voice sound neutral. "You saw the way he was looking at her."

"She's a beautiful girl, Will. I imagine that's how most men look at her."

I heave a sigh, collapsing into the rocker beside hers. "He wasn't just looking, though. You heard him. He was gonna change his plans so he could sit here and hit on her all night."

She sighs. "I don't see the harm. That's just Brendan being Brendan."

"Well, he can go 'be Brendan' around some other girl. Olivia doesn't need that shit. She has enough going on right now without adding him to the mix."

My mother opens her mouth as if to argue, but then leans her head back and closes her eyes. "Maybe it's time you told Peter what's going on with her."

I lean forward, staring at my hands. It's the same thing I've said to myself so many times I'm tired of saying it, but the answer is always the same. "I can't. If Peter knows, then the school is liable if something happens to her. They'll kick her off the team."

She nods, but she's still frowning. "It just seems like this is too much for you to deal with."

"I don't know why you'd say that. I was able to stop her last weekend. I'll be able to stop her tonight."

She stands and kisses my cheek. "Honey," she says, turning to go inside, "I think we both know I'm not talking about the running."

26

Olivia

When Will wakes me up the next morning, he can't quite seem to meet my eye. It's almost as if he's scared of me. "Fuck," I sigh. "Something bad must have happened last night. What did I do?"

"Nothing," he replies. "I caught you before you even made it to the door." Even as he says it, though, there's something muted, reserved in his tone.

"And that's all?" I ask.

"That's all."

I still don't believe him.

~

THE SECOND MEET is in many ways a repeat of the first, but my fears are different. This is a more difficult course than last week's. I'm positive I haven't trained for it properly. Once again, Will is there, talking me through it, convincing me to ignore my fears and just run.

"All of this you're feeling," he says, "it's like a person running beside you, shouting shit in your ear to tear you down. But it can only change the way you run if you choose to believe it."

I'm not sure why but, this time, I listen. Maybe it's because he was right last time, or maybe it's something that goes deeper than that. If Will told me I could jump off a skyscraper and survive, I might even believe that too.

The gun goes off, and I let his words drown out my own. I outrun her, the nasty person who tells me I will fail, who is convinced disaster lies around every corner. And when the finish line approaches, I realize that in outrunning her, I've managed to outrun the competition too.

Peter reaches me first, swooping me up in a hug. "You're gonna put our program back on the map, young lady," he crows.

Will comes up a moment behind him, smiling with quiet pleasure, but there is worry on his face too. It sucks a lot of the joy from the moment. Whatever happened last night...it was bad. And he's keeping his distance from me because of it.

Everyone on the bus is jubilant. Erin asks me to go to lunch, and I might even be inclined to say yes if I wasn't so determined to talk to Will.

He's gathering his stuff when I arrive at his office. He looks surprised—and not entirely pleased—to see me.

I swallow hard. Knowing is better than not knowing, I remind myself. "What happened last night?" I demand. "You're being super weird about it, so please just tell me the truth. Did I hit on you or something?"

He laughs. "*That's* what you're worried about?" His smile fades. "It wasn't a big deal."

"Then just tell me."

He exhales and runs a hand over his head. His triceps pop when he does it, which is almost enough to make me forget what I asked. "You ... cried."

I stare at him for a moment. And then I laugh. "I don't *cry*," I retort. I can't remember crying once, not in my entire life. I'm *unable* to cry. There have been plenty of times when I've wanted to and I just *can't.*

He isn't laughing. His face is sadder than I've ever seen it. "You cried so hard I could barely understand you."

I sink into the chair behind me, gripping its handles with a force that could splinter lesser materials. In a way, I want to leave this room and forget the conversation ever occurred, but I can't stand having him know something about me that I don't.

"What did I say?"

He hesitates. "It was kind of like last time. You repeated 'I shouldn't have left' again and again. Whenever I catch you, you're terrified. You're running from someone. But you also seem to feel guilty about it. And I've heard you telling people your parents are traveling for the last two months, but your grandmother is the only contact we have on file for you. Did something happen? Did you run away from home?"

My heart begins to hammer in my throat and it feels as if it's constricting me, making it impossible to take deep breaths. Somehow he knows too much, as if all the parts of me are escaping and I'm helpless to stop them.

I'm torn between a desire to flee from this conversation and a desire to fight.

Naturally, I choose option two.

"I'm allowed to keep some shit to myself," I snarl. "That's why I tell everyone they're traveling. I have no idea why everyone thinks it's okay to go around asking about my parents all the time anyway. And I didn't fucking run away from anything."

"Then where are your parents?" he demands, refusing to back down.

My jaw grinds and I stare at my lap, unable to meet his eye. "They ditched me when I was six," I admit, "and I never saw them again." I hate them for it, and hate myself for it too. If I'd been a different kid, if I'd been sweet, like Erin, maybe it would have been different.

"No siblings?"

Of all the things in the world I don't want to discuss, my brother is first. "You're no better as a therapist than that chick at the health center was if that's where you're going with this."

He doesn't move a muscle, and he doesn't let it go either. "You didn't answer the question."

"I had an older brother. He ran away when he was eight."

"You mean he ran away *permanently*? For good? They never found him?"

My heart is beating rapidly now, too rapidly. I need to get out of here. I need some air. "I gotta go," I reply, jumping to my feet.

"Olivia, wait." He stands. "I'm sorry."

"Don't be," I say through clenched teeth. "They were shitty parents and they did me a favor, so save your sad face for something serious."

"You don't think any of that has to do with your nightmares?" he asks.

The idea makes me feel helpless, and feeling helpless enrages me. I roll my eyes as I turn to walk out. "How could it possibly matter?" I ask. "Even if they're responsible, it doesn't look like they're coming back to fix it."

I BARELY REMEMBER MY PARENTS.

My father is a dark shadow on the periphery of my early childhood, a thing that hung in the background as a threat more than a real person. He took me fishing once, but mostly he had a bad temper, and I stayed out of his way, relieved when he left town. At some point, he was gone permanently, and soon thereafter, my mom was gone too.

I don't remember being left with my neighbors. I don't

remember anything, really. Small snapshots of early childhood, that transition without explanation into another life, the one under my grandmother's roof.

My grandmother didn't want me. I guess I can't blame her. Who'd want some kid who wakes screaming and flailing in the middle of the night, who bolts out of the house without warning?

Her mind was already slipping, even then. She couldn't remember the word for ice cream. She'd call me Alicia, my mother's name. If I corrected her she'd usually get angry, but sometimes she would cry instead—a heartbroken sound I was desperate to avoid so I eventually stopped correcting her. She got worse, of course, and I couldn't help but wonder if it was me—the running, the nightmares, the fights at school—that had made it so. It's probably not a coincidence that all the people in my life decided to leave in one way or another.

I storm out of Will's office, all my earlier goodwill toward him gone. These thoughts are always in my head, but he's brought them front and center today and God, I wish he hadn't. I go to campus for dinner, feeling edgy and looking for a distraction. Landon, the guy I met on my first day here, slams his tray down beside mine.

"Party tonight, future girlfriend. You in?"

It seems like a bad idea.

"Yeah," I reply. "I'm in."

~

THREE HOURS LATER, the world is a much easier place to exist. With enough liquor in my system, everyone seems entertaining, and right now, everyone seems entertaining as hell. If Landon and his buddy, Jason, would stop fucking following me, I'd say tonight was almost perfect.

"Stop talking to him," says Landon the moment Jason leaves my side. "I'm the one who brought you here."

"This isn't a date, Landon," I sigh. "I can talk to anyone I want."

"I'm gonna beat his ass if he keeps hitting on you," he replies. I laugh. Men are so stupid. There's not a chance in hell I'm going home with either one of them.

Time passes quickly, a blur of faces I don't know but am now best friends with. Being that social is a sure sign it's time to stop drinking, but I bravely plow on. My talk with Will is still in there, a poisonous thing in my chest, and I will continue to drink until it's forgotten entirely.

Jason appears out of nowhere. "Let's dance," he says. Somewhere in the back of my head, a voice tells me that Landon will be pissed, but it's silenced by a louder voice saying that's not my problem.

He takes my cup and puts it on the counter before he grabs both of my hands and pulls me onto the dance floor. For such a big guy he's a surprisingly good dancer, and for such a drunk girl I'm staying surprisingly upright. I don't really object to the way our dance turns into more of a grind within a song or two. It's not like everyone else on the dance floor—which is actually just someone's living room—isn't doing the same thing.

And then I'm knocked backward, falling into other dancers, and Landon is on top of Jason. I regain my balance and watch, surprised and mildly amused, as Landon and the other idiot beat the shit out of each other.

"Do you always start this much trouble?" says the guy behind me. He's hot. Way hotter than either Landon or Jason.

I grin at him over my shoulder. "Always."

"C'mon," he says, pressing his hand to the small of my back. He leads me into the yard, grabbing us more beer on the way.

His name is Evan, and I find something about him specifically appealing. He's tall and well-built—too muscular to run cross country but too lean to play football. Sort of like Will.

One minute we're in the backyard talking and the next we're

in someone's room. I guess I've had more to drink than I thought, but that's okay. It's time I get this over with, time I face my worst memory of UT and replace it with a better one. Evan kisses me and I feel nothing. His hand slides under my shirt, into my bra, and I wait for it to end, like sitting through a movie you really aren't enjoying. My satisfaction only comes from how much progress we've made, how close it is to being over. And then his hand moves to my jeans and I fly off the bed, panicked.

"I'm sorry," he says, his eyes wide with surprise. "I thought it was okay."

"I can't," I gasp. "I'm sorry. I thought I could, but I can't."

He climbs off the bed, handing me my shirt. "It's okay, Olivia," he says. "Seriously, it's fine."

He's so much nicer than Mark Bell would have been under the same circumstances. But then Mark didn't ask.

And he didn't stop until I made him.

27

Will

I can't shake what Olivia told me after the meet. How could her parents have done that to a six-year-old? I'm furious at people I've never met because they created the mess she's in now. *It's their fault* she's having these nightmares, that she's putting her life at risk when she has one. *It's their fault* she's forced to survive off stipends and loans, hoping to God she can hold on to her scholarship.

Jessica and I go out to dinner then watch TV after. "You're distracted," she says. "Is everything okay?"

"Yeah," I lie. "Just a long day."

But that's not really it. I'm pissed off on Olivia's behalf, but it's more than that. I feel oddly unsatisfied tonight. Jessica and I went to a restaurant I chose and are now watching a movie I've been wanting to see. She never argues with me, always does exactly what I want, but it feels empty, like a meal that can't satisfy me no matter how much I consume.

And it wasn't like that last night.

I bickered with Olivia while we watched a TV show I didn't

want to watch in the first place, and when it was time to go to sleep, I wished it wasn't. But right now, with my girlfriend, I just want the night to be over.

"Let's go to bed," Jessica suggests.

A part of me wants to make an excuse, wants to get out of here, but why? Because I'm lusting after a twenty-one-year-old student who is a constant pain in my ass and has problems I can't begin to understand? Leaving seems like giving into it, and that's something I will not do.

I let Jess pull me into the bedroom, watch as she pulls off her clothes and begins to remove mine. *Focus*, I say to myself. It's harder than it sounds.

She's beneath me but all I see when I close my eyes is Olivia, so I try to keep them open. I picture Olivia anyway. Asleep face down in my bed, her hair spread over my pillow, the sheet twisted around her waist, one long leg breaking free of it, her back bare. The moment she sat up, the sheet sliding to her waist...

That last image appears unbidden and I finish with a hoarse cry of surprise, ashamed of myself even as it happens.

Jessica curls up against my side, and I squeeze my eyes shut, wishing I wanted to be here. Thinking instead of holding Olivia last night while she cried.

Because I wanted to stay.

And right now, with Jessica, I'm counting the seconds until I can leave. The same way I always do.

AFTER PRACTICE ON MONDAY, I get a text from Jeff Jordan, one of the assistant football coaches. He needs to "chat". *Fuck*. A meeting with one of the football coaches is never good. They never want to give you anything, and they're often looking to take something away. And the sad truth is that at this school—at almost any school—football trumps everything else.

"We had a fight this weekend," he tells me instead. "Two players. Our defensive end is out the rest of the season with a broken hand."

"Yeah?" I'm still not seeing what this could possibly have to do with me, which of our meager resources he's going to ask us to give up to fix this.

"Apparently it was over one of your girls."

My pulse begins to rise. Before he's said another word, I know *exactly* which girl he's talking about.

He tells me the version he's heard from members of the team: Olivia, bouncing back and forth between a running back and a defensive end, laughing when they got mad at each other, dirty dancing with the one who *wasn't* her date. Then leaving with a third guy. For some reason, it's that last bit that's got me seeing red.

"Just keep her away from my team, okay?" Jeff asks. "I have no idea who this girl is or what's so magical about her, but I don't need any more of my guys on the bench this season."

If this were about any other girl on the team I'd be pointing out that he should blame the drunk assholes who did the fighting. But instead I'm fucking enraged at Olivia myself, and I'm pretty sure it's not for the right reasons.

28

Olivia

I'm summoned to Will's office on Monday afternoon, which can't possibly be a good thing.

"I've been hearing some stories," he begins, leaning back in his chair. "Big fight this weekend. Over a girl."

I roll my eyes. "I wasn't fighting over a girl if that's what you're accusing me of. I don't swing that way."

"I'm glad you find this so amusing, Olivia," he says, his eyes glittering. "Because the story I'm hearing is this girl sees the problem and does nothing whatsoever to discourage it, and then *leaves* with someone else. So I hear this story and the first thing I think—*the very first thing*—is 'please don't let Olivia be the girl.'"

"Seems sort of unfair, the way you assume the girl was me."

"The girl *was* you, Olivia."

I slouch in my seat. "I didn't *tell* them to fight," I mutter. "And if you ask me, this is all pretty misogynistic on your part. Two grown men decide to pummel the shit out of each other over some girl who isn't interested in either of them and she's the one at fault?"

"I'm not saying you're at fault, but you sure weren't trying to help the situation either, were you? And by the way, maybe it's not a great idea to get trashed with a bunch of guys who are twice your weight."

Maybe he's right but Saturday night was hard on me too and I don't want to hear it. "I can take care of myself."

"Yeah? And how did taking care of yourself work out for you at your last school?"

My whole body tightens like it will implode if I don't brace myself. I hate the decisions I make sometimes, how stupid and unjustifiable they are, and I hate him even more for calling me on them. "You've made your point. Are we done here?"

"Olivia, you're going to do what you're going to do. But I'd better not hear another 'Olivia was so fucked up' story for the rest of your tenure here."

I stand and walk out without saying a word because, just like the nightmares, there's not a chance in the world I can make him a promise like that.

～

FOR THE REST of the week, Will is unreasonably rude to me. He's angry and critical and doesn't smile at me once. I think he'd like me to just disappear.

I just want to put it all behind me, but on Friday morning, a tray slides next to mine in the cafeteria and I find Evan sitting there. Sure, he was nice about everything that night but it's awkward. I'm embarrassed by the way I freaked out if nothing else.

"I've been looking for you," he says. I thought maybe my memory of his looks was beer-influenced, but it wasn't. He's every bit as cute as I thought. Black hair cut almost military short, nice mouth, mischievous eyes.

I continue to eat. "Why?" I ask without interest.

He grins, not dissuaded at all by my chilly reception. "You're much nicer when you've had a bunch of beer."

"Everyone is nicer when they've had a bunch of beer," I retort, returning to my newspaper. "What do you want?"

"I want to take you out," he says.

I sigh, rubbing the bridge of my nose. "You seem like a nice enough guy, but the truth of the matter is that you're only here because you're hoping if you buy me dinner I'll sleep with you, and I'm not going to, so let's just stop while we're ahead."

"Wrong," he says, and I have to admit he looks a little offended. "How about this: go out with me, on a real date, and I won't even try to kiss you at the end of it."

I raise a brow at him. "What would you get out of it?" I ask.

"You're hot, and you're pretty fun when you're not trying to scare me off. That's what I'd get out of it."

"I don't really date."

"You don't like food?" he asks. "You don't like movies? Going to see a band?"

I shrug. "Yes, I like those things."

"And tomorrow night, for instance, would you have more fun making ramen noodles in your apartment and watching *Project Runway* than you would going to a restaurant with me?"

"I don't watch *Project Runway*."

He laughs. "You're avoiding the question."

I almost smile. "I'll have to think about it."

He starts eating. "You think. I'm just gonna eat my breakfast."

"I didn't mean I was going to think about it *now*," I argue. "It's not a snap decision."

"Well, I'm still going to eat here. So just pretend I'm your buddy. Your super-hot buddy who you secretly want to date."

I allow myself a small laugh. I'm not going out with him. *I'm not.* But I can't say it's the worst offer I've ever heard.

29

Will

I was out of line. My anger, my reaction ...
It was entirely wrong.
I know this because I've forced myself to imagine it, and if it were Betsy or Hannah or any other girl on the team who got drunk and caused a fight, I know I'd have put the blame squarely where it lies: with the two idiots who fought. But it wasn't Betsy or Hannah, it was Olivia, who seems to do something to me that no one else does. If I'm being honest, the part that angered me most didn't involve the fight. It involved her leaving with someone.

I know I need to pull back, and I spend the rest of the week doing just that. I don't speak to her unless I have to. I don't even *look* at her unless I have to. Maybe I'm doing her a disservice as her coach, but I'm doing her a greater disservice by getting invested in the wrong way.

By the next week, however, she makes sure I can't ignore her anymore.

On Tuesday afternoon, I can tell she's off. She gets through four 800s but she's weary in a way she normally isn't. There's a look on her face on days like this—grim determination, like she'd die before she'd give up, but she's barely hanging on.

At the end of the fifth 800, I can no longer stand to watch. I call out to her, and I know by the panicked look in her eyes as they meet mine that she's going to pass out. I'm sprinting toward her before she's even begun to fall, but she's on the ground before I reach her.

I was worried the last time this happened, but now it's a different sort of thing, bordering on panic, because I care a little more than I should. The whole team is hovering around her when she finally opens her eyes.

"Olivia, do you know where you are?"

"Yes," she groans. "I'm fine. Let me up."

I put Betsy in charge and take Olivia to my office so I can clean off her cuts.

"You're having a bad week," I tell her as I tape off her knee. "What's up? Are you stressed about the meet?"

She sighs, staring out the window over my shoulder. "Everyone assumes I'll take first now."

I'd like to tell her she's wrong, but she's not. Olivia's accomplishments are no longer a surprise, a thrill. They're expected, and as hostile as she tends to be, I know that she doesn't like disappointing people.

"Is that it? Or are you worried because you won't be at my mom's?" Our next meet is too far for a day trip, which means that we'll be in a hotel the night before, away from the safety of my mother's house.

Everything about her posture is tense as she answers, as if she's trying to compress the truth inside herself. "A little."

"What normally happens when you're in a hotel? You must have dealt with this before. It's not like you can stay up all night when you're sharing a room."

A flush ghosts her cheekbones, which surprises me. I didn't

think she was capable of being embarrassed. "I usually tell whoever I'm rooming with that I'm sneaking out."

My next question sounds angrier than it should. "To do *what*?"

"To go serve food to the homeless," she snaps. "What do you think? I let them think I'm staying with one of the guys."

"And do you?"

"What good would that do? You think I'm any less likely to run from a guy's room than I am from my own?"

A tightness I wasn't even aware of seems to release in that moment, just a little. "So what do you do?"

"I go outside and walk to keep myself awake. If I can find a place that's open all night, I'll go there and hang out. When I start to fall asleep, I start walking again."

"Olivia, walking all night isn't much better before a meet than a six-mile run. You can't do that this weekend."

She sinks back in her seat. "So what's your grand plan, Will?" she scoffs. "You gonna tie me to the bed? Because I'll warn you in advance I really, really like that."

Thank God I'm sitting behind a desk right now because there's definitely a part of me that reacts to that as if I'm not her coach and she's not off limits.

"No," I say, closing my eyes and trying to push the image from my brain. "Better. You're going to room with my mom."

30

Olivia

At first, I refuse. The idea of Dorothy being the victim of my craziness when I'm not even aware it's happening horrifies me. Eventually, he convinces me by promising that he'll be in the adjoining room and his mother will make no effort to stop me. I appreciate what they're doing for me, I really do, but it still blows to have the rest of the team think I'm rooming with Dorothy because of my bad reputation.

We climb on the bus for New Mexico Friday afternoon, and Brofton plants his cocky ass beside me.

"Heard you're staying with Will's mom," he says, smirking. "So we'll need to be really quiet when I come to your room."

I laugh. "If you were in my room, I guarantee I'd be quiet. I'd probably sleep right through it."

"Keep giving me something to prove, Finn," he says with his wide grin. "It's just going to make it that much better when you're screaming my name."

"Only thing I'd be screaming for with you is a magnifying glass," I reply. Everyone around us cracks up, but Will's shoulders tense, which tells me he's listening and he's not happy. Fuck him. I'm not a nun. I didn't take an oath of celibacy to be on this team.

The conversation turns to room placements, and how many people will stay with their parents instead. I tune it out, staring out the window at the mountains in the distance. And then I hear Betsy. Fucking Betsy, being intentionally loud, making sure I hear. "Why do your parents never come, Finn? I guess they must like you about as much as everyone else does."

"I'm surprised your parents bother," I retort. "Seeing as how you've never placed."

"That's enough," Will intones without ever turning his head. I don't appreciate him intervening like he's our fucking dad, but at least he let me get in the last word.

WHEN WE ARRIVE, Erin's parents are waiting with their wide smiles and their bright eyes. I want to resent it, but oddly I don't. I like Erin. I'm jealous, yes, but I still wouldn't want to take this away from her. I know that somewhere deep inside I've looked at these situations and felt that something was taken from me, as if every set of proud, involved parents could have been mine if they didn't belong to someone else, as ridiculous as that is. But even if it were true, I would never want Erin to be on her own the way I am. She's too sweet, too soft. If one of us had to draw a short straw, I'm glad that it was me.

Her parents invite me out to dinner with them. I agree, feeling oddly chagrined that I won't be eating with Dorothy and Will, which makes absolutely no sense. Why would I *want* to eat with my dickhead coach and his mother for Christ's sake? I shower and blow out my hair, put on a little makeup, skinny jeans, and my favorite royal blue blouse.

"Don't you look cute?" Dorothy smiles. "Where are you off to?"

Just then, Will knocks on the door. His face seems to empty, go blank, for a moment, as he looks at me, as if he didn't expect to find me here at all. "You guys ready to go to dinner?" he asks.

"Erin invited me to go out to eat with her and her parents."

His mouth goes into a tight line. "Not happening."

"What do you mean?"

"I mean I don't trust you enough to let you go to dinner with Erin."

"Seriously?" I snap. "How much trouble do you think I can get into between here and Erin's room?"

"Plenty," he retorts, "but that's not what I'm concerned about. I don't trust you to eat."

"I'll eat. I don't need a babysitter."

"I had to force feed you *last week*. But suddenly you've got it all under control?"

"If I'm telling you I'll eat, I'll eat."

"Fine, I'll give you two choices. One, you tell Erin I said you couldn't go. Or two, you write down every bite of food you put in your mouth and Erin's parents come here personally and vouch for the fact that it's true."

"Will," his mother says softly.

"No, Mom," he snaps. "Do *not* take her side. I've had to watch her pass out one too many times and I'm not watching it tomorrow too."

When the door slams behind him I turn, jaw agape, to Dorothy who—to my surprise—has a small smile on her face, the kind people get when they're looking at a puppy or a newborn.

"You *support* this?" I demand. "He's being completely unreasonable! You can't possibly think he's right?"

"No," she says, "but I think he cares. And it's been a long time since I've seen my boy care about anything."

Something seems to flip in my stomach at her words, nauseating and hopeful at once, but I cling to my anger instead. I know well enough that feeling hopeful about anything is always a dead end.

31

Will

I'm not sure why I did it. I guess I just assumed she'd be eating with us. And when I saw her all dressed up and discovered she had other plans, I was weirdly–I don't know exactly what it was. Angry? Disappointed?

Whatever it was, it was illogical and I should have gone about it another way. I could have insisted that she eat a decent breakfast, or even have a snack when she came back to the room, but instead I behaved like a controlling dick, which has led us to the present moment: a dinner where Peter and my mother chitchat away while Olivia and I scowl at each other across the table in silence.

I stop her before she goes into my mother's room when the meal is over. "I'm sorry," I tell her. "I was out of line about dinner and I should have handled it better."

Her eyes flutter open in surprise, and then her mouth turns down at the corners unhappily and she looks away. Her awkwardness is something I could easily have predicted. When she feels threatened or mistreated, no one is more sure on their feet than

Olivia, but apologize or show her the smallest amount of kindness and it's as if she's on a foreign planet.

My mom goes to bed early, so despite the rules I let Olivia come to my room to watch TV. She stretches out on the double bed beside mine, clad in a T-shirt and shorts, offering me an unfortunate view of long, tan legs, no matter how hard I try to avoid looking her way. We watch the last forty-five minutes of some movie I'm completely incapable of focusing on. Every time she moves I grow aware of her to the exclusion of all else. And then she moves, and her T-shirt rides up, revealing a swath of toned stomach and I have to stifle a groan.

I had it pretty easy in high school and college. If I wanted something from a girl, I almost always got it. This must be my karmic payback, because I don't think I've ever wanted something quite this much, yet I'm *absolutely* not allowed to have it.

When the movie ends, a trivia show comes on. The guy walks away with over $500,000, even though Olivia and I answered the questions before he did.

"We totally could've taken him," she says sleepily, rolling over on the pillow to face me. Her shirt rides up again and it takes almost superhuman restraint not to look.

"What would you do if you won that money?" I ask.

"Spend it all on hookers and blow."

I laugh. "No, seriously, what would you do? Would you stay in school? Would you keep running?"

She's quiet for so long that I begin to think she won't answer. "I'd find my brother," she finally says.

Her words take my insides and twist them in a tight grip. I don't want to know this. I don't want to know anything more about the soft side of Olivia than I do at the moment. I already know far too much.

"You realize you could probably find him just by going online," I tell her.

She shakes her head. "He could've found me if he'd wanted to."

"So why do you need the money?" I ask.

"He probably hasn't had an easy life," she says quietly. "I'd just want to make sure he has what he needs."

My chest aches, listening to her. "Do you really believe he's still alive?" I ask.

She looks away from me, her voice growing hard and intent. "My brother is crazy smart. And crafty. And he was fast. He could outrun anyone. That's how I know he got away."

She jumps to her feet and says she's going to bed before I can ask her what he was getting away from. But I wonder if it's the same thing that chases her in dreams.

I turn off the light but struggle to fall asleep. Her insistence that her brother is okay haunts me. The way she clings to the idea feels desperate, perhaps even childlike. If I were to guess, I'd say that the reason she hasn't looked for him has nothing to do with the fact that he doesn't want her.

I give up on sleep and flip on my light so I can read. A few minutes later my mother comes to the door.

"Why are you still up?" she asks.

"Worried," I reply.

"She's a sweet girl," my mother sighs. "And she's the only one who doesn't realize it."

She's right. Olivia seems to see only the worst things in herself. She believes she deserves nothing from anyone, yet something about her makes me want to give her everything.

"I wish I could fix things for her," I tell my mother. I wish I could fix every single wrong that's been done to her. Get her out of that God-awful neighborhood, make the nightmares end, protect her from all the bad things that might lie in wait for her.

"You're doing your best," she replies. "But for now you really need to get some sleep."

"I can't. I'm too worried I won't hear her from here if she runs."

My mother hesitates, then comes into the room. "Take my bed," she says. "And I'll take yours."

"I don't know," I answer. "I realize I'm already breaking rules, but that seems so ..."

"You have her best interests at heart," she says. "I wouldn't suggest it if I thought for a moment it was truly wrong."

I go into the other room and lie down in the bed across from Olivia. I'm just dozing off when she begins to talk. Unintelligible words that sound young and distraught. The minute she flings the covers off I'm out of bed and beside her, my arm anchoring her while I do my best to convince her she's okay. I shush her again and again, promising her she's safe.

"It's just a dream," I whisper. "You're okay."

And something miraculous happens. She doesn't fight me. She jolts for a moment as if she's been shocked, and then she curls into me, her head pressed to my chest, her hands fisted tightly in my shirt as she cries, still sound asleep.

I hold her until her tears slow and then cease, and then something slightly less miraculous but still surprising happens.

I fall asleep too.

32

Olivia

Holy shit.

Holy shit, holy shit, holy shit.

Will Langstrom is standing in front of me, shirtless.

I'm gawking, and that probably needs to stop. It's not like I didn't *assume* he'd look fan-freaking-tastic without a shirt, but he exceeds anything I was previously capable of imagining. Yeah, fine, I admit it, I occasionally imagine things with him, and they're usually R-rated. Except when I imagine him there isn't an alarm going off in the background and he doesn't have a pillow clutched to his stomach or a panicked look on his face like he has right now.

"Why are you in my room?" I ask.

His expression grows surly. "Waking your ass up," he growls.

"Good morning to you too," I snap, rolling over and putting the pillow over my head. "And I've seen you in shorts before, dummy. What's with the sudden modesty?"

He makes a testy noise that I ignore and heads toward his room.

"Did she run?" asks Dorothy, passing Will as she comes in.

"She never left the bed," he replies without coming into view. There's something about his phrasing that I find suspect, but I let it go. I didn't run. Before a big meet. Before a meet I was sick with nerves over. It's a freaking miracle.

"Wait. Why were you just coming in from Will's room?" I ask Dorothy. "Did you sleep in there?"

Her eyes widen. "He was worried about you, so he took my bed and I took his."

Somewhere in the recesses of my mind, I remember the feel of his arms around me, of curling into a warm chest in the middle of the night.

Maybe another dream ...or maybe not.

WHEN WE ARRIVE on the course, Will walks with me through the back field and gives me his standard pep talk, which, being tailored to me, is less "pep" and more "stop being insane." He does this despite the fact that at this very moment he has a thousand other things to do and people to deal with, despite the fact that a young male coach wandering off with one particular female student is bound to draw suspicion.

I know it looks bad that he spends so much time with me. I know he's put his job on the line again and again when I've done nothing but give him grief in return.

Today I want to give him the only thing I'm capable of giving. I'm going to win.

I take off too fast at the sound of the gun, feel that itching in my chest far too early, yet I keep going. I will win for him if it kills me. That voice in the back of my head tells me I'm going to lose if

I keep going like this, that I'll never make it, but I silently tell her to shut the fuck up.

I cross the finish line going so fast that I run an extra twenty feet trying to stop, like a car with bad brakes. This time it's him, not Peter, who catches me, holding me by the shoulders so I don't collapse. "Another record, Liv," he whispers, just as Peter runs over.

I'm happy, but this time my happiness is entirely for him.

A TEAM TAKES FIRST by weighting the scores of its runners. Today we manage to place, coming in second for the first time in a decade. Everyone is ecstatic. Brofton picks me up on his shoulder and spins me around and I actually laugh without threatening to hit him. He sets me down as we line up to climb on the bus, and I'm so dizzy I stumble into Erin.

"Watch it," she says to Brofton. "She's our ticket to regionals. I want you treating her like a delicate flower from now on."

"Yeah," I laugh, "that's me. A fragile little flower."

Betsy pushes forward, looking oddly annoyed given that we just placed. "If *someone* hadn't come in sixteenth," she sneers at Erin, "we might have taken first today."

I hate the way her words have leached all the joy from Erin's face. "We'd have won if you'd placed better too," I snap.

What happens next occurs so quickly that I have little memory of it. One minute I'm speaking, and the next she's pushed me so hard that when my face hits the side of the bus, I'm blinded momentarily by the pain. And then I'm on the ground, with Betsy pinned beneath me. There's blood pouring from her nose and someone's arms are tight around me from behind, a straitjacket.

"Liv!" shouts Will. "Stop!"

I realize, suddenly, what I've done, but the time between my face hitting the bus and now remain a complete blank, as if it never occurred. Will's arms are around me, holding me back as he pulls me off Betsy. She gets off the ground while all my teammates, and Peter, look at us in shock.

It's Mark Bell all over again.

"She assaulted me!" screams Betsy. "You said she got one chance and she just blew it!"

"It was self-defense," Brofton interrupts. "I saw the whole thing. Betsy slammed Finn's head into the side of the bus."

"Finn was just defending me," Erin tells Will rapidly, "but she shouldn't have bothered. Everyone knows you're just jealous, Betsy."

I can see the fear in all of their faces, and my stomach sinks. I had my one shot, and now I've blown it. Hannah, Nicole, Erin— they look at me with some mixture of desperation and resignation, wanting to fix it and knowing it's too late.

"You promised she wouldn't hurt anybody," Betsy argues, holding her shirt to her nose.

"Everyone on the bus," Will says. "We'll discuss this when we get back."

It's a silent, painful ride home. Betsy sitting there, playing up her injury but giving me a smirk every time no one's looking, Erin, wan and worried.

I feel completely empty, depleted. It's not that I don't care that I'm about to lose my scholarship. It's that I care so much I can't stand to think about it. I have a backup plan. I can make my way to Seattle, and train there. The idea once even appealed to me, but now I can't seem to feel anything about it at all.

By the time we get back to campus, I'm as broken and weary as I've ever felt, while Betsy is jubilant and not even trying to hide it. The two of us follow Will to his office, and he takes Betsy in first. When she walks back out, she shoots me a nastily triumphant look. No matter what they did to her, I'll get worse.

I go in. Will's got his head in his hands and looks beaten,

which makes me feel slightly ill. He did so much for me. This is how I repaid him.

"I'm sorry," I whisper, folding myself into the chair across from him.

He raises his head. "You're a smart girl," he says. "Don't you see through her? She's trying to get you kicked out. She's been pissed off and jealous since you arrived. You've got to be smarter."

I freeze. "You're not kicking me off the team?" I ask, nearly mute with shock.

"No," he sighs wearily. "But it can't happen again. You can't let her bait you."

"She wasn't trying to bait me," I argue. "She was just being a bitch to Erin."

He laughs unhappily. "Yes, because she knew she'd get a response from *you* by going after Erin. I can justify this one as self-defense, but next time something happens, even if she hits you, you've got to hold back."

I exhale. When I first got here I was willing to blindly promise him and Peter anything they wanted to hear, but I don't feel like I can lie to him about this. Not when he might be the one to pay the price for it. I stare at the ground, my hands clasped. "I don't know what I did today," I whisper. "I don't remember anything from the moment she pushed me until the moment you were pulling me off of her. None of it. I don't even know how I got her on the ground. I saw her bleeding and didn't even realize I was the one who'd done it until you yelled at me. And I don't want to promise you it won't happen again because I have no control over it."

I finally meet his gaze. He's staring at me like the psycho I am. "Jesus, Liv," he breathes. "So has this happened before?"

I nod. It's happened plenty. It's a wonder I haven't killed anyone.

"Mark Bell," he says. Not a question, a statement.

I sigh. "Sort of. I remember fighting him and I remember seeing the bat. I don't remember the rest."

Will's face grows still, wary. "What did he do to you?"

I bite down on the inside of my cheek. What happened with Mark Bell isn't something I need to share. It's not like anyone would believe me anyway. "Nothing I couldn't handle."

"That's not what I asked you," he says between clenched teeth. "I want to know exactly what he did."

I roll my eyes as if it doesn't matter. But the truth is that it does matter, to me, and he'll be the only person alive to whom I've told the truth. "He found out about the nightmares. He offered to stay with me the night before a meet to keep me from running."

Will's face has fallen just a little. Anyone can see where this story is going. Anyone could have seen it then too, aside from me. It was so fucking stupid to trust Mark, and I'm not sure why I did. Maybe because I just wanted, so badly, to think there was a solution. To think someone alive was willing to help me. "I'm sure you can figure out the rest," I sigh.

His mouth opens and it takes a second for any words to emerge. "He *raped* you?"

"He *tried*," I reply. "That's where the bat came in." The asshole had the gall to press charges against me, which he only dropped when I told him I'd gone to the hospital that night and had everything documented. I didn't really go, of course. A few bruises and some torn clothes weren't proof of anything, but he didn't know that.

"Olivia," he groans, putting his head in his hands. "Did you tell the school that?"

I laugh, but it's a miserable sound, the kind that might turn to tears if I was capable of it. "I was sleeping in his apartment and had the worst reputation in the history of the school's cross country team. Who the hell would believe it was rape? I could have had the whole thing on film and no one would've sided with me."

He sits back in his seat, looking helpless and stunned. "This is insane. All of it. You should still be there, and that asshole should be in prison."

I sigh. The difference between us is that he doesn't expect bad things to happen, and thinks there's a fix for it when they do. I know better. "I wasn't going to be there in any case. No way was I getting another year out of that scholarship."

"But that's not the point!" he cries. "You left there letting hundreds of people think you're some sociopath who goes around swinging a bat!"

"I *am* a sociopath who goes around swinging a bat, Will," I retort. "I don't remember *anything* after I saw that bat in the corner, so why shouldn't they think it?"

He slumps in his chair. "That's what this is really about then," he says. "You hate that you did it. You feel guilty it went as far as it did and this is how you're trying to pay for it."

There's something in what he's saying that stings and I don't like it. "If you're done with the analysis, Dr. Langstrom, I think I'm gonna take off."

"You need to get your cheek checked out."

I shrug. "I think it's okay."

"Right," he says with a hint of a smirk. "I forgot about that medical degree of yours." He gets up and kneels in front of me. "This might hurt a little," he warns. "Let me just make sure it's not broken."

I close my eyes because he's too near. His warm mouth and the curves of his face and his ungiving jaw make me feel slightly unhinged when he's this close. The pad of his thumb presses to my skin. He stops when I wince in pain, holding his hand there, waiting for me. He continues, and just the brush of his skin against mine awakens other things. Things I'm not supposed to feel. My eyes open of their own accord and lock with his. His hand holds my face, his mouth slightly ajar as he looks at mine, both of us breathing quickly. I want him to kiss me. I want him to kiss me so badly that my blood starts to sing, and all logic goes rushing from my brain. It sits between us, quicksand that drags us under so fast that fighting it seems impossible. He leans toward me, for just a second, before his hand falls away suddenly and he practically jumps backward.

"Nothing is broken," he says roughly. "Just ice it over the weekend, okay?"

I practically run from the office. The idea of losing my scholarship was scary, but whatever just transpired between Will and me is a thousand times more terrifying.

33

Will

I refuse to think about what just happened.

Nothing happened, nothing at all.

We had a talk, I checked out her cheekbone, she left to spend her weekend however she sees fit and I am doing the same.

Nothing happened.

Yeah, the nothing that happened maybe leads me to work a little extra at the farm, leads me to be late getting to Jessica's again, makes me so distracted that I can barely carry on a conversation all weekend ... but that doesn't change the fact that *nothing happened.*

I've been with plenty of pretty girls. Jessica was hands-down the best-looking girl at my high school. But all of them felt ... *replaceable.* Olivia, in my office, wasn't replaceable. The need for her was sharp, urgent, painful, unlike anything I'd ever felt. At that moment, there was nothing in the entire damn world I wanted more than her. And it felt like there was nothing else I would *ever* want. It was insane and I'm taking it for the warning it was.

I need to stay away from her.

I IGNORE HER ON MONDAY. It's the best thing for everyone. I'll ignore her, and she'll get pissed off and things will feel totally normal again. I just hope it happens sooner rather than later because all I can think about is her mouth inches from mine and the surprise of discovering there were a thousand things I wanted to take and do, and I only wanted those things from her.

I send them out on a six-mile run and try not to think about it. I will fix this somehow. Next weekend, when she's staying at my mom's, I'll ... I don't know what I'll do. I have five days to figure it out, but I *can't* be alone with her again.

I'm just about to head out after the team when I get a call from Peter's secretary.

The police are here.

For Olivia. Who else?

34

Olivia

I take off for my run on Monday with Will treating me like a communicable disease, as if the shit in his office was entirely my doing, and when I return he's wary...but it's a different kind of wary.

"There are police in Peter's office," he says. "They're waiting to talk to you. Do you have any idea why?"

My stomach is instantly in knots. It seems unlikely I'd have done something *illegal* in my sleep, but I'd also have sworn I never cried in my sleep and look how wrong I was there. Mark Bell could be pressing charges after all. *Betsy* could be pressing charges. It could be anything. "No," I reply quietly.

"I don't want to be blindsided, Olivia," he says. "If you've done something, please tell me now."

My temper flares. I was already hurt by the way he acted this morning and now he's treating me like a criminal. "Maybe it's that counterfeiting operation I run out of my bedroom," I say, rolling my eyes. "I'm not on *parole*, Will. I don't routinely go around committing crimes."

I take a quick shower and go up to Peter's office. When I enter, what unnerves me most is not that the police are here—it's the look on Will's face. There's something raw and shocked there that doesn't bode well. What the hell could I possibly have done? I take the seat next to Will's, feeling chilled to the bone, suddenly.

"Olivia, these men are here to talk to you about your brother," Peter says.

Immediately my heart rate picks up and I begin to sweat. I think about walking out, which Will seems to sense. He places a warning hand on my arm, telling me to stay where I am.

"As you know, your brother was presumed dead—" one of the officers begins.

"No," I say, cutting him off. They don't get to claim this just because they didn't do their fucking jobs. "He wasn't *found*. That doesn't mean he's dead."

"There's been a new development in the case," the other one says.

My breath stops in my throat. Whatever he's about to say, I don't want to know. I want to plug my ears and sing to block him. I want to flee.

"Last month," he says, "a child's remains were found buried in the woods about a mile from your old home."

My ears begin to ring and I can't get a full breath. I jump to my feet, but Will blocks me, gripping my arms and holding me in place.

"Olivia," he says. "You need to hear them out."

"No, I don't," I insist, trying to wrestle free. I can feel the panic slipping into my blood, and that's never a good thing. "I don't know who they found, but it isn't my brother."

"Miss Finnegan," the officer says gently, "we ran a DNA test. It's been confirmed."

The sweat turns to ice. I'm leaving. I'm not listening to another word of this. I will my feet to move, toward the door, out of this office, but they don't respond.

"An autopsy was performed," one of them says.

"Stop," I whisper. "Stop talking." Why can't I move? Oh my God, I need to get out of here as badly as I've ever needed anything. "Please make them stop," I beg Will, but I know by the pained look on his face that he will not.

"Miss Finnegan, we could really use your cooperation here. Someone snapped his neck."

I need to go.

I need to go.

I need to go.

I need to go.

I take one step forward and then there is nothing but black. A long dark tunnel and I'm falling into it ...

~

THE FIRST THING I see is Will's face. It's October, but he's still tan. He has beautiful eyes. So pale against his skin that they seem to glow.

"I called 911," says a woman's voice.

"No," I whisper. "I don't want help."

The woman starts to argue and Will cuts her off, still looking at me. It feels as if I'm drowning and his eyes are the only thing keeping me from going under. "She's okay. She doesn't want help."

He raises his head and looks to the police officers. "I think you should go now. Everyone out. She just needs a minute."

There's the click of the door and then there is silence. I sit up and he moves back, just enough, still crouched in front of me.

I wish I could cry. There's a sadness in me, so infinite and boundless that it seems as if I shouldn't be able to do anything else.

"Can you make them leave? The police? I don't want to see them."

I squeeze my eyes shut. My brother ... I can't think about it. But I'm picturing him in spite of it, how little he was, how fragile. "I'm gonna be sick," I whisper, and I lean over and throw up in Peter's trashcan. Will holds my hair back while I empty the contents of my stomach.

When it's done I sit up again, with my head between my knees.

"Is there anywhere you have to be?" he asks.

"I have astronomy, but I'm not going."

"Then come on," he says gently, pulling me up by my hand. "I'm taking you to the farm. I'm not letting you sit in that apartment alone all afternoon thinking about this."

This tight ball in my chest, this vacuum in my stomach ... they are never going away, whether I'm alone or not. "You don't have to do that. I'll be fine."

"Don't pretend around me," he says. His hand, resting at the small of my back, is a comfort.

We walk out and the police say they have questions and Peter urges me to return to the office and for once I don't have to defend myself, I don't have to tell anyone to leave me alone.

Will does it for me.

35

Will

There's something frighteningly vacant in Olivia's face. For the first time during her waking hours she seems fragile, the way she does in her sleep. We leave straight for my car and she walks beside me blindly. I'm not sure she's even aware that we're moving and that I'm here.

"Are you okay?" I ask as we drive.

"Uh huh," she replies, but she's shaking.

I reach out and grab her hand. "It's going to be okay." She looks at me and nods but doesn't release my hand the entire drive to the farm.

Peter has forewarned my mother about our visit, and she's waiting on the porch for us. She's at Olivia's door the minute we pull into the driveway, enfolding her in her arms. "Oh, honey," she says, tears streaking down her face. "I'm so sorry."

Olivia shakes her head. "It's fine," she murmurs. "I'm fine." She's still shaking. I'm not even sure she realizes it.

"I think she should lie down," I say, directing Olivia toward my room with a hand on her back. I bundle her in the quilt that lies at the foot of the bed, but there's panic in her eyes when I stand to go. "Do you want me to stay?" I ask.

She nods, so I sit in my old desk chair beside the bed, frustrated by my inability to do anything for her. She stares blankly somewhere over my shoulder, still shivering.

"Scoot over," I finally tell her, and when she does I climb in beside her, sliding my arm under her neck and her back to my chest. We've laid like this before, more than once, but she has no idea. I'd feel a lot less guilty about it if there wasn't a part of me that *wants* to do this.

When she falls asleep, I carefully extract myself and leave the room.

"How is she?" my mother asks.

I take a seat on the couch. If I'm still feeling shell-shocked by what we found out this morning, I can't imagine how she's feeling. "Asleep," I sigh. "Aside from that, I have no clue."

My mother blinks back tears. "That poor, poor girl. Do you think that's what the nightmares are about?"

I've wondered it myself since I heard the news, except the timing doesn't quite work out. Her brother ran away—or whatever *actually* happened—when she was five. She didn't start having the nightmares until after she moved in with her grandmother, which would have been a year later. "I don't know."

My mother grabs my hand. "I'm glad she has you on her side."

I nod. Being on her side is about all I can do for her. And it's not nearly enough.

I GO BACK to campus to run the afternoon practice and call Jessica on the way.

"One of the students had a death in the family," I explain. "She's staying with my mom so I'm not going to be able to come by tonight."

"Okay, I can just meet you there," she says brightly. "I'll bring the two of us dinner."

I flinch at the suggestion, a little astonished that she's trying to turn Olivia's tragedy into a romantic moment for the two of us alone. I gently dissuade her, and there's a distinctly displeased note in her voice as she finally agrees, which surprises me. She's been so understanding about my mom all this time, but apparently that understanding does not extend to students.

After practice is over, I head to Olivia's apartment to pick up a few things. I assume she'll need her laptop. Clothes too, I imagine, though I'll have to tread lightly there. I have enough Olivia-based issues without looking through her underwear drawer.

I grab the key she keeps hidden under the planter—a terrible hiding spot—and let myself in, but come to a dead stop just inside the door.

The room is empty.

No couch, no table, no pictures, not so much as a cup on the counter. If I hadn't seen her enter and exit this apartment on multiple occasions, I'd assume I was in the wrong place entirely. I knew she was hiding something, or someone, that time I came here to talk to her, but I never dreamed she was hiding *this*.

In the bedroom, I find evidence of her, but that's only more unsettling. Her clothes still sit in a suitcase that's open on the floor. She has a laptop but no books, no desk, no lamp and no bed, just a sleeping bag on the floor.

I lean against the wall and close my eyes, realizing for the first time how bad things are and how alone she truly is. And that everything she has in the world right now, little that it is, depends on a scholarship...which depends on me.

～

SHE'S awake when I get back, sitting on my mother's couch still wrapped in the quilt, and her eyes harden when she sees her suitcase.

"Why didn't you tell me you were living like that?" I ask her. "I would have helped you."

She opens her mouth and closes it again. "I'm not a charity case," she mumbles. "I have what I need."

My mother comes out of the kitchen, where she's been baking —her go-to in times of stress. She sets a plate of cookies down and looks between the two of us. "You should go climbing. Will's an amazing teacher," she tells Olivia, "and climbing always helps him when things aren't going well."

The last thing I need is Olivia in a harness with her ass in my face for several hours. "I'm sure she doesn't feel like climbing," I mutter.

Olivia glances up at me. Perhaps she hears the unwillingness in my voice and that's what spurs her on, but she stands and casts off the quilt. "Actually, that sounds okay."

I consider that part of my life over, and it's a bad idea for the two of us anyway. But I don't seem able to refuse Olivia anything under the best of circumstances, so I'm certainly not going to today.

36

Olivia

We're standing at the base of a massive rock.

It looks close to impossible to climb. It's not smooth like glass, but it's not exactly laid out like a climbing wall either.

"I can't climb that," I tell him definitively.

"Yeah, you can," he says. "You'll be wearing a harness. I'm not going to let you get hurt." It seems like the kind of thing he can't promise, but I believe him anyway.

He leaps onto the rock and scrambles up and across it effortlessly, with no rope whatsoever, his body twisting and shifting as if this is a dance he's practiced a thousand times. It's the hottest thing I've ever seen in my life. Every muscle in his body is straining and delineated, his attention focused entirely on the movement.

"You just have to shift your weight," he calls. "And if you twist into it like I am, it won't require as much upper body strength."

I suspect he's making it look a lot easier than it is, but when he hops down I let him help me into a harness. He carefully knots ropes, checking and rechecking both mine and his own, before he climbs up again, affixing something into the rock, and pushing the rope through it. When he's finally satisfied, he slides back down with amazing agility.

"Ready?" His face is bright, and I don't think I've ever seen him quite like this. He's happy, but it's more than that. It's as if he is a hundred percent here, invested.

Every bone in my body screams that this a bad idea, but I nod anyway. I like seeing him like this.

I jump up on the rock just like he did, setting my feet in the most obvious place and desperately seeking something to grab hold of before jumping back to the ground. "You were fine until you panicked about your hands," he says. The next time, I climb back on the same footholds and he places a hand against my lower back to keep me there. "Do you feel that?" he asks. "If you balance on your feet and lean in, you don't even need your hands."

What I actually feel is his hand. Its heat and its breadth spanning my lower back, making it hard to breathe, much less find some elusive foothold or balance. I fumble with my hands until I find something to cling to, and then he releases me, though I wish he hadn't.

He has me practice moving across the rock. I'm a graceless, slow-motion version of his earlier display. "You made this look a thousand times easier than it is!" I shout.

He laughs. "You don't have to shout. You're still only a foot off the ground."

"Asshole," I mutter.

"I heard that," he replies, "proving you don't have to shout."

I go back and forth, time and again, and once I'm doing reasonably well he tells me I can start climbing up. I see now why he used to do this to get away from his problems: it requires such absolute concentration that I can't think of anything else.

Mostly. I'm about twenty feet off the ground when my mind

drifts to the feel of his hand on my back. I lose my balance and find myself suspended in midair, with him beneath me, laughing.

"You're doing great," he says. "You need a break?"

"No, dammit," I say, clipping into the bolt beside me. "I'm getting to the top. I don't care if it takes all night."

"That's my girl," he says proudly, and for a moment I sway in the air, stunned by how happy that statement makes me though I've got no idea why.

It takes an hour, and by the time I get to the top I've fallen repeatedly. My arms and legs are undoubtedly bruised and my muscles are shaking. I slide back down on the rope and collapse at his feet.

"What did you think?" he asks.

I let my body splay out over the ground. "I think you need to carry me to the car."

"But you loved it," he says. And then adds something quietly, wistfully, almost to himself: "I knew you would."

~

I GO to Will's room that night, but I'm unable to fall asleep. No, I'm too *scared* to fall asleep. I close my eyes anyway, but I see Matthew's face and I know exactly what his terror looks like. I've seen it a thousand times in that dream I have of us, sitting in the back of the speeding car. I see it now and my eyes fly open.

I can't scramble out of bed, get out of this room, fast enough.

I arrive in the living room gasping still, chagrined to find that it is empty. I turn on a lamp and the TV, letting some ridiculous reality television fight—grown women throwing drinks on each other—help clear my head. My pulse finally starts to slow. Matthew's face begins to recede.

"I'm not watching *Real Housewives*," says Will behind me. "That's where I draw the line."

I turn. He's freshly showered...and shirtless. I swallow,

unaware of what he just said or what I was doing a moment before, because he is tan and slightly damp and nothing but muscle, so pretty that for a moment I'm scared I might have made some audible noise of longing.

My eyes catch on his tattoo—high on his arm, nearly to his shoulder—and my hand reaches toward it. He's unnaturally still as my fingertips trace the pattern. He seems to be holding his breath. "Denali?"

"I got it done the first time I climbed it. I was going to do all seven summits and get a tat for each."

"Why isn't K2 on there then?" I ask, mainly to have some reason to keep my hand on his arm.

"Because that was the climb where I realized I wouldn't be climbing the other five." His voice is stilted, wary. He moves away from me and reaches into his duffel bag for a T-shirt.

Dammit.

He pulls the shirt over his head and I use the opportunity to ogle the shit out of his stomach when he does it. "Just before I climbed it, I called home. I thought my dad might actually be proud, but instead, he told me it was time I grew up. I hung up on him like an entitled little dick and went climbing, and when I got back to base camp, I learned he'd had a stroke. He was dead before I got home."

My stomach drops. "I'm so sorry. So you came home then for good?"

He shrugs as if the aftermath didn't really matter. "He wanted me to grow up. It was the last fucking thing he ever said to me, so it seemed like the least I could do."

What I hear in his voice is blame, and I don't want it to be there. Most people don't seem to take enough responsibility for themselves and their fuck-ups, but Will takes on more than his fair share. "You had a job, Will, and by the sound of it, a job you were good at. That's a hell of a lot more grown up than a whole lot of people."

"I had a duty to my family," he counters. "I should have been pulling my weight around here, and instead, I let my dad take it all on by himself."

He reaches for the pile of blankets on a chair and I stand and take them from him. "You sleep in the bedroom," I tell him. "I'm gonna stay up."

"All *night*? Olivia, you know I'll catch you if you have a nightmare," he says. "You haven't made it out of the house once since the first time you stayed here."

I shake my head. "It's not that." I hesitate. I don't even want to put words to it. "I don't want to dream about him," I finally admit.

"Your brother?" he asks, taking one of the blankets from me and spreading it on the couch. "I didn't know he was in those dreams."

"Sometimes," I say. "So—"

He turns off the lamp and lies down, patting the space in front of him. "Come here," he says with a sigh. Will feels guilty about so many things and I've become one of them.

"It's okay," I swallow.

"I'm tired, Olivia, and you're tired," he says, stretching out his arm. "So stop arguing and go the fuck to sleep."

"What a sweet talker." I laugh, but I lie down. He takes the quilt and tucks it around me. It's the last thing I remember.

37

Will

As tired as I am, I don't fall asleep. Once again, there are so many things wrong here, not least of which is the fact that I'm ostensibly doing this to comfort Olivia but happen to be hard as a rock while she lies a centimeter away sleeping peacefully. I took the precaution of shoving half the quilt between us after she fell asleep. *Not helping.* So, in essence, I'm perving on a student and cheating on my girlfriend, at least in spirit, and I don't know of another goddamn way to deal with any of it.

But the things that make sleep impossible and my shorts profoundly uncomfortable also make me happy that I'm here: the feel of her, the smell of her shampoo, the way her shoulders rise and fall, how at this moment all of her intensity and twitchiness are gone and she's so completely at peace. Today had to have been one of the worst days of her life, and yet it turned out to be one of the best I've had in years.

It wasn't just climbing. It was sharing it with her. I should have known she would love it, that it would strip her of every thought and emotion and let her be free of it all for a while. There are times, like today, when it strikes me that we are far more alike than different. And God knows I wish that wasn't the case.

38

Olivia

The next morning, Will is already up and dressed when I wake.

"I can be ready in five minutes," I tell him.

"You don't have to run today. Why don't you just take it easy? I can come back and pick you up in time for class."

I shake my head. Allowing people to baby you makes you soft, and I'm in no position to turn soft right now. "I think I need to get back to it."

"Fine," he sighs, "but you're staying here tonight."

"So bossy," I mumble, but it's seriously hard to pretend I'm unhappy about it.

~

AFTER PRACTICE IN THE AFTERNOON, he picks me up in the side parking lot so no one will see. We aren't doing anything wrong, but I worry anyway. It sure as hell would *look* bad if anyone saw us.

He turns to me just after he slides into the driver's seat. "Want to climb?" His whole face brightens as he asks, and even if I didn't want to go, I'd say yes.

"Don't you have to work on the farm?"

He grins at me. "Yeah."

"Am I finally seeing the naughty side of Will Langstrom?"

He arches a brow. "This doesn't even come close to the naughty side, Olivia."

Gulp.

I didn't think it was possible, but Will just got ten times hotter.

We head to the same rock we climbed yesterday, and he teaches me to lead climb, which involves clipping into bolts that are already in the mountain as I go up instead of relying on a rope anchored at the top. He also teaches me to belay, which allows him to climb with me on the ground, scared shitless that I'm going to accidentally feed him too much slack from the rope and kill him.

Watching him climb is an amazing thing, the strength and the agility and the gracefulness of it all.

"You look like Spiderman!" I shout.

His laugh echoes down through the rocks. "Hold the rope just in case!" he shouts back.

He's lighter, happier than usual on the way home—his laughter and smiles come easily—but that all ends when we pull up to the farm. There's a burgundy BMW convertible in his mother's driveway, and by the way he's stiffened at the sight of it, I assume that's a bad thing.

"Is it Peter?" I ask.

"No," he says, his shoulders sagging. "It's Jessica. My, uh, girlfriend."

My chest tightens. I know nothing about his girlfriend, but I know I don't want her here. "I'll deal with the horses and give you some time to hang out."

He nods, his mouth set in a hard line, and heads inside like he's facing a firing squad.

I go to the stables and take my time getting the horses groomed and fed. When I finally head back to the house, I hope she's gone, but even from a distance I can see her, posed like a pageant queen on the front porch with her long, perfect red hair swinging over her shoulder and her legs crossed.

And I loathe her. Even from a distance. It's not mere dislike. It's the kind of hatred that makes me wish I could strike out like a snake, fangs bared.

She rises and walks down the stairs with her arm extended. "You must be Olivia," she says with a wide smile that holds not a hint of friendliness. "I'm Jessica, Will's girlfriend."

I look her over head to foot. At the perfect hair, the perfect makeup, the expensive clothes. She's no one I'd ever have picked for Will. "Hi," I say flatly.

"So what brings you out here tonight?" Her voice is too bright, too clipped. She says it as if she's caught me trespassing and is diplomatically sending me on my way, which is my first clue that it bothers her I'm here.

So I plan to let it keep bothering her. "Excuse me?" I ask.

Irritation flickers in her eyes. "Why were you in the barn?"

"I was cleaning the stables," I reply. "You know what a disaster they've been since Jackson quit." Her smile falters. She didn't know Jackson quit, obviously.

Will walks out the front door, freshly showered, followed by Dorothy. The identical tension in their shoulders is really the first resemblance besides eye color I've ever noticed between them.

"I see you two have met," says Dorothy with a forced smile.

"Yes," replies Jessica. "Olivia was just telling me she was helping with the horses. If you needed help, you should have asked me, Dorothy."

What utter bullshit. I don't know how this girl affords a BMW or those designer heels she has on working for the university, but there's not a chance that *she's* cleaning stables.

"Olivia grew up working with horses," Dorothy explains.

Jessica walks around Dorothy and goes to Will's other side, grabbing his hand. "You should teach me what to do, so next time I can be the one to help. I'll need to learn eventually anyway, right?"

Whoa. What in the actual *fuck* did that mean? Is he *marrying* this girl?

Will swallows, looking between the two of us. "You ready to head out?" he asks her.

I still. I thought he'd be staying here tonight. I didn't realize just how much I was counting on it until now.

"Head out?" she asks. "But your mom made dinner. We don't spend enough time out here anyway. You know I love the farm."

"I thought we were eating out," Will argues, sounding a bit like a surly adolescent.

"We can eat out anytime!" she exclaims. "But how often can we eat with your mom and your star athlete?"

A lot more often than you think, Jessica.

It's uncomfortable, having her at dinner, especially when I don't know my role or what Will has told her. Dorothy asks me how our climb was over dinner, though, so that's one cat out of the bag. I tell her Will taught me to belay and she turns to him, smiling wide. "So you climbed?"

"Yeah," he says, his mouth twitching. "It was a pleasant change to have it be Olivia standing on the sidelines looking worried for once instead of me."

"I wasn't worried about you," I reply. "I was just trying to figure out how I'd get how home if you fell."

Will and I both laugh and Jessica looks between us with a

strained smile on her face. "*We* should go climbing sometime," she says to him.

He blinks as if she's speaking in some foreign language he needs to translate. Or maybe he just forgot she was there, though that's hard to imagine given the way she's clinging to him.

Jessica turns the topic to things that don't interest me—property values, restaurants, skiing. *Rich people shit*, I think dismissively, although to be fair Will and Dorothy aren't rich and I'm the only one here who seems bored.

It's only as the meal concludes that she turns to me, with that bland smile of hers. I don't even know what she's going to ask and I already don't want to answer. It's not her house. Why is *she* leading the conversation? "So, Olivia," she says, placing her napkin on her plate, "what are your plans for Thanksgiving?"

I rise and begin gathering dishes, wondering why she's asking because I'm certain she doesn't care. "I don't know yet."

"You have to come here," says Dorothy, "if you're not going home, that is."

"Oh, I disagree," says Jessica firmly. "She should go home. It's important to keep those ties strong when you go away to school."

I smile tightly, heading for the kitchen. "I'll figure it out."

Jessica follows me a moment later with a stack of dishes. "Isn't Will's family great?" she asks, setting her dishes down and moving mine away for no discernible reason. "I'm surprised Dorothy doesn't have a houseful of pets. She just can't resist a stray, you know?"

And with that, she gives me that sunny pageant smile and walks back into the family room.

∽

WILL LEAVES WITH JESSICA, and although I wish he were staying, it's a relief to escape his girlfriend's noxious presence. I sit on the couch with Dorothy.

"So that was Jessica, huh?" I say. "What a *lovely* girl."

"I think she was a little unsettled to find you here," replies Dorothy. "She's not normally quite so...tense."

"Will could do a lot better than that," I grumble. "I don't know what he sees in her." Okay, that's a lie. Anyone with two eyes knows what he sees in her. I guess I just expected more of him.

"Jessica is a nice girl," Dorothy sighs. "I sometimes wonder if it has more to do with pleasing his dad than himself but anyway, even if she's not who I'd have chosen for my son, it's not my choice to make. And she may be my daughter-in-law someday, so I need to make the best of it."

"You think he's going to *marry* her?" I ask incredulously. "*Her*? She's not good enough for him in a million years!"

Dorothy's face falls a little. "I think Jessica wants to get married," she replies carefully. "And she's pretty good at getting her way."

39

Will

The moment I saw Jessica's car in my mother's driveway, my stomach sank. I told her I couldn't meet tonight, but apparently she'd decided to take matters into her own hands. I prefer to keep the various parts of my life—the farm, coaching, Jessica—separate. Her presence felt like an intrusion, but what could I possibly say? Jessica is a separate part of my life, but somehow Olivia is not. Olivia *belongs* at the farm. But since it's something I can't even explain to myself, how could I possibly defend it to Jess?

My mother met me at the door, looking weary. "Jessica's in back on a work call," she said. "But you put me in a bad spot. How much does she know?"

I'd felt like a million bucks on the drive home. Suddenly, then, I just wanted to sleep. "She knows Olivia has slept here before some of the meets."

"And does she know *you* stay here too?"

"It was implied."

My mother clicked her tongue in disapproval. "In other

words, you never specifically addressed it and hoped she'd *assume* you were at your apartment. And she's about to see Olivia, who even the most secure woman would be jealous of, and discover you've been sleeping with her here."

"I haven't been sleeping *with* her," I snapped. "Jessica has nothing to worry about. You're making a big deal out of nothing."

She shook her head and walked back inside. "For all the girls you've run through in your short life, Will, you still don't know much about women."

I'd blown her off at the time but now, as I step into Jessica's apartment, it becomes clear my mother was right.

"Are you okay?" I ask. I want her to smile and move on, but I know she won't, which means we remain in this ugly sort of limbo until we've *talked*. And talks with Jessica don't necessarily go well. The only way you seem to achieve resolution is by promising something more than you are really willing to promise.

She sighs. "That's the girl who's been sleeping at your mom's house?"

"Yeah, I told you about her."

She sucks in her cheeks and her jaw shifts beneath them. "She's pretty."

Her words are a trap. If I agree, I open a whole Pandora's box of bullshit. But denying it is pointless. You'd have to be blind not to notice Olivia. Increasingly, of late, it seems I'm incapable of noticing anything else.

"I guess."

"So you were hanging out with her last night?"

"Jess," I groan. "Don't make this weird. She's just one of my athletes."

"*She* doesn't seem to know that."

"Believe me, Olivia is well aware of the fact that she's one of my athletes. I've never been fought so hard by someone in my life."

"That's not what I mean, Will. She acts like—" she trails off, her frustration mounting.

"Like what?"

"Never mind. I just don't see why she has to stay with your mom."

"She just found out her brother was *murdered*, Jessica," I say, hearing an edge slip into my voice. "Do you really want to begrudge her having people around while she deals with it?"

"No, but the people don't have to be you and your mom. It needs to stop."

I feel my temper inching up, and I do my best to keep my tone stable. "And why is that?"

"Because it looks bad. I work in public relations, and I'm telling you right now that *no one* is going to believe you're hanging out with a girl who looks like *that* out of the kindness of your heart."

"I don't give a shit what anyone believes," I snap. "She has the ability to be a world-class runner, and she's leading our women's team to its first winning season in a decade. If staying with my mom makes the difference, she's staying with my mom."

"As long as that's all she is to you."

I agree because it should be true. Because it needs to be true. There's no other option.

I GET BACK to my mother's around eleven. Jessica was clearly unhappy that I wasn't staying, but her lack of sympathy for Olivia left me not really giving a shit.

I'm just dozing off when I hear a noise from Olivia's room. She's flailing in the sheets, saying something over and over. I approach quietly as she grows more agitated.

"Stop crying," she pleads in a whisper.

I sit on the bed. "Olivia," I tell her, running my hand over her back as if she were a child, "it's okay. You're okay."

She grabs my arm and her eyes fly open. "Stop crying," she begs. "You've got to stop."

"Olivia, you're dreaming. It's okay."

"Please stop crying," she says and then she begins to weep, a small, childlike noise that is hard to listen to.

I pull her to my chest. "It's okay, Olivia. I promise. It's okay."

"Don't cry," she says, over and over. "Don't cry."

When she finally falls back asleep and I emerge from her room, my mother is waiting with her head in her hands.

"You heard that?" I ask, and she nods.

"What on earth happened to that girl and her brother?" she asks.

I wish I knew. And I'm equally scared that someday soon, I'm going to find out.

40

Olivia

I return to my own place on Wednesday.

Both Dorothy and Will encouraged me to stay, insisted really, but I said no. It can't be good for Will—he needs to be working on the farm instead of entertaining me, and he's risking his job at the school every time he does it. I guess it's also causing problems with Jessica, though I don't care as much about that.

Will drives me back before that morning's practice, swinging my suitcase out of his trunk. There's a hint of a smile on his face. "Enjoy the apartment."

He waits until my key is in the lock before he drives off, and then I walk in, and my jaw hangs open.

I blink once. Twice. I take two stumbling steps inside and shut the door behind me. This room was empty when I left on Monday morning. Now there's a couch, a coffee table, a dining table with two chairs, and a TV.

When did he do all this? And how?

I keep walking. In my bedroom there's now a bed, a night-stand, and a small dresser.

I call Will's cell, something I've never done before. "I've been vandalized," I say when he picks up. "Someone broke into my apartment and furnished it."

"That's an outrage," he replies. "There are some sick people in the world."

I laugh, and then grow quiet. There's nothing in the world harder for me than what comes next. "Thank you," I tell him awkwardly. "I don't know what to say."

"It wasn't a big deal," he replies. "Almost everyone I know has something extra they don't need. You were also offered a pie safe, whatever the hell that is, and a grandfather clock, in case you're interested."

When we hang up I hold the phone to my chest, trying to understand this tangled thing inside me. I feel full and happy and sad all at once. It's the first time since I moved out of the dorm my freshman year that I've had furniture, and I'm thrilled, but there's a part of me that wishes he hadn't done it. I suppose because it leaves me feeling the same way I do after spending time with Will.

Like I suddenly have something to lose.

⁓

THE FOLLOWING FRIDAY, Will picks me up to go to Dorothy's, and for once, it's not an act of charity. Dorothy's asked me to stay over and help with the horses because Will has to assist with school events for Parents' Visiting Day. I'd say yes anyway, but since I'm eager to be far away from campus this weekend, it's a win-win.

When we arrive at the farm, Brendan's car is parked outside. "I didn't know your brother was coming."

"Neither did I," he says between clenched teeth.

Dorothy and Brendan walk out together. "Olivia!" shouts

Brendan as if we're old friends, grabbing my suitcase and swinging an arm around my shoulder. "I'll take this in for you. Who's sleeping where?"

"Oh, Will's not staying—"

"She's in my room and I'm on the couch," Will cuts in firmly.

I suck in a breath. There is no meet this weekend for him to be concerned about, and he has his own place, which means he's sleeping here to protect his mom from *me*. I don't blame him, but I'm surprised by how much it hurts anyway.

"Worried I can't keep my fists of fury to myself?" I ask.

"Why would I be worried?" he asks with a smirk. "I've only witnessed you attempting to fight two people, excluding the time you took a swing at me."

"Come on," Dorothy says, tugging Brendan in. "Let's give them a minute."

Once they go inside I round on him. I suspect that if I were capable of crying, I'd be crying right now. "I would *never* hurt your mother."

His face softens. "I know that, Olivia. Maybe I just want to stay. Or maybe I can't stand the idea of you getting lost in the woods. Whatever it is, I'm staying."

I kick at the ground. "Fine, but I'll sleep on the couch. It's one thing before meets, but there's no reason you shouldn't have your own room tonight."

"Do you know how many miles of forest are out there?" he demands. "You think I'm gonna sleep for shit, worried that I'll wake up in the morning and discover you're gone? And if nothing else, I don't want my horndog little brother coming out to the living room every morning and watching you traipse around in your pajamas."

"I don't traipse around, first of all, and second of all, I wear *running clothes* to bed almost every night so it's not exactly sexy."

"You wear a tight little tank with no bra," he growls. "That's enough. Did you see the way he was looking at you just now? Multiply that times ten."

If I didn't know better, I'd think he sounded a little possessive. I like it. And I like that he seems so intensely aware of what I wear to bed. "Okay."

His eyes widen. "You're giving in, just like that?"

I shrug. "Sure. If it means that much to you, I'll do it."

"I guess that's why it's so much colder this afternoon," he says, opening the door. Brendan and Dorothy stand right on the other side, and I suspect they were listening. "Hell must've frozen over."

MY PLEASURE in being at Dorothy's is quickly muted by the arrival of Jessica, with her big fake smile and big fake laugh and big tits —sadly, those are probably real—and the way she's always pawing at Will.

She shows up once again in a suit that looks super expensive —what the hell does she do for the university anyway? I feel young and silly in my sweater and jeans. She hugs all of us, though her hug for me is decidedly stiff with dislike.

"You always do such a nice job with dinner, Mrs. Langstrom," she gushes as we sit down to eat. She glances pointedly at me. "If I'd known you had such a crowd, I'd have gotten here sooner to help."

"I've been cooking for a crowd on my own for as long as I can remember," says Dorothy.

"Well, you shouldn't have to," says Jessica, reaching beside her to clasp Will's hand. "And besides, I want to learn how to make all of Will's favorite things."

I wish there were a vomiting trough someplace close by. I catch Brendan's eye. It looks like he needs one too. "So where are we headed tonight?" Brendan asks, looking primarily at me.

"*We* aren't headed anywhere," counters Will. "I can't be seen drinking with my underage student."

I see his point, but it still irritates me. It's not like I'm ten—I'll be legal in two months. "You guys go," I tell them. "I have some TV to catch up on anyway." I see a wistful look cross Will's face and wonder if he might actually *like* our nights in.

"No," says Brendan. "Will and Jessica can go to one place, and you and I can go to another. Problem solved."

Will's jaw grinds. "That's not happening either." When we all look at him he sighs. "Fine, we'll all go out together but let's just make sure it's far from campus."

Brendan grins at me. "*And* somewhere that doesn't card. I know just the place."

"Why doesn't that surprise me?" asks Will.

BRENDAN'S PLACE is a country bar far to the outskirts of town. He seems to know just about everyone there, which is interesting given that he goes to school three hours away. He drapes an arm around my shoulders and introduces me to the staff as the next Mrs. Langstrom, and by the time we've ordered a pitcher, I'm fairly certain I've just met every semi-toothless person in the state.

Brendan's gaze follows mine over to Will and Jessica, who sit waiting at a booth, looking tense. "It's so weird that he's your coach. I mean, isn't that weird for you?"

I glance at him. "Weird how?"

"You're almost the same age, for one thing. And the two of you just have that vibe. You know, a couple vibe. When you guys argue, the air is just rife with sexual tension the whole time."

There's a small, quiet thrill at the suggestion. And I can't deny that I've felt some sexual tension over the past few weeks, but I'm not planning to admit it either. Especially not to Will's brother. "You're watching too much porn."

He smirks. "That's entirely possible but irrelevant. *Something* is going on."

Will's eyes meet mine over the crowd. He looks miserable. "Shouldn't we go sit with them?" I ask as Brendan pours me a beer.

"Nah," says Brendan. "My brother needs to realize how bored he is by Jessica on his own. And besides, it's so fun making him jealous."

I roll my eyes. "He's here with his girlfriend. The one thing he's not is *jealous*."

"Wanna bet?" he asks. "Watch." He puts his hand on the small of my back and then slowly lowers it until it's resting on my ass.

"Get your hand off my ass or I'll snap your wrist."

He grins at me. "Wait for it...three...two...one."

Will pushes between us. "What's taking so long?" he snaps, grabbing the pitcher.

Brendan leans toward my ear as we follow him to the table. "Told you."

Once the four of us are in the booth—me and Brendan across from Jessica and Will—awkwardness descends. I could talk to Will all day long, and I could talk to Brendan too, but Jessica... what does she have in common with anyone here?

Brendan tolerates the strained conversation for all of two minutes before he turns to me. "You know how to two-step?" he asks.

"I just moved here from Texas. I could teach a course on two-stepping."

He pulls me from the booth and leads me to the dance floor, where he promptly spins me and then dips me so low my head hits the ground.

He laughs. "You're so into me right now, aren't you?"

"Yes, there's nothing hotter than a guy who gives you a concussion while you're dancing."

"You're such a hard-ass," he sighs. "No wonder my brother's so into it."

"Oh my God. Shut up about that already," I groan. "You're making it weird." I give him my best stink-eye, but he's as impervious to it as his brother.

"Believe me, babe," he grins, "it was already weird."

Will and Jessica come out too, though Will looks like he'd rather be anywhere else. Brendan glances over at them. "If my brother hadn't been such an asshole lately, I'd do him a solid right now."

"Unless you know a place where he could go climbing at ten at night, I don't see what you could do anyway."

Brendan gives me a half-smile. "I do."

He steers me toward them, and then, without warning, releases me. "Switch," he says, grabbing Jessica's arm. He's the only one of the four of us who looks happy as he and Jessica dance away.

Which leaves me standing here with Will. We exchange one awkward glance and I turn back toward the table, but he stops me with a hand on my waist. "Fuck it," he sighs, grabbing my other hand. "This goes no further than this room."

I roll my eyes. "Did you really think I was going to *brag* about dancing with you?"

His mouth tips up for the first time all night. "They don't call me the Two-Stepping King of Colorado for nothing."

I just witnessed his lackluster dancing with Jessica, so I'm finding this hard to believe. "*Who* calls you that?"

"You will," he says with a cocky grin that could get him anything he wants from me, and I mean *anything*, "by the time we're done." He spins me one direction and the next, so fast that all I can do is follow his lead.

I pictured Will doing a lot of things, but never this. "Holy shit," I cry. "Where'd you learn to do that?"

"My mom. She taught us all these stupid dances under the impression that they were important skills to have."

I smile a little, imagining Dorothy forcing a teenage Will to learn to dance. I wonder if she has video. "And did they ever come in handy?"

"They've gotten me laid more than once," he replies, spinning me, and I'm so shocked that I nearly fly free of his hand, and he looks even more shocked than me. "I shouldn't have said that."

I spin close to him, so close that my chest is pressed to his and our mouths are millimeters apart. "Will," I say quietly, "I already knew this could get you laid."

His eyes meet mine and there's something fierce there, an intensity I've never seen in him. "Don't do that," he says, flinching. He pulls away and walks straight to the bathroom.

I go to the table, wishing I could bang my head on it. What the hell made me think I could say what I did? Will has Jessica, and even if he didn't, it's not as if he'd ever choose me.

It's after midnight and I'm just climbing into bed when there's tapping on my window. I pull up the shade and find Brendan standing there with that mischievous smile on his face, holding a six-pack aloft.

He winks. "Got to be some benefit to growing up in a tiny one-story house. Get dressed."

I grab a sweatshirt and climb out the window to join him. "So what are we doing?" I ask.

"Let's go to the stables," he says. "I need a little Jessica-free time."

Me too. Even though Brendan and I spent the rest of the night playing darts and avoiding them, just being in the same room with her ruined the evening. "You don't think he'll marry her, do you?"

He laughs. "Nah, even he won't take this guilty bullshit about my father that far."

"What do you mean?"

"You'd never guess it now, but Will was pretty bad in high school—he got arrested a few times and he and my dad fought like crazy about pretty much everything. My dad just had this idea that if Will could just straighten his shit out, he could land a girl like Jessica. That's what he'd say. 'You might even land a girl like Jessica.' And back then Will would make this face like he was being asked to eat a plate full of vomit. And now he's back home and fucking *serious* with her. It boggles the mind."

Dorothy said something similar, but it still feels like wishful thinking to me. As much as I don't want to admit it, there are plenty of reasons a guy would want to date Jessica. Even Will.

We get to the stables and he throws himself down in the hay and signals for me to join him. "So I have to ask," he says, popping open a beer. "Why do you sleep here before meets? No one will give me a straight answer."

Something in me softens as I realize that Dorothy and Will really aren't going to tell people. I guess, knowing them, it doesn't surprise me though. "You're going to think I'm a freak."

He shrugs. "Hey, I'm a registered sex offender. I'm no one to throw stones."

"*What?*"

"Little known fact: streaking during pledge week is actually considered a sex crime." He gives me a wide, absurdly cocky smile. "It was such a miscarriage of justice. I mean, look at me. Those girls were lucky to get an eyeful of this. Anyway, out with it. Tell me why my mom wants to adopt you and my brother is risking his job and sanity to have you here."

I hesitate. I've never *willingly* told someone my story. I was forced to tell Will, so that's different. But while it still humiliates me, having brought my secret out in the light to Will and Dorothy makes it seems slightly less dark than it did before. "I have these nightmares and I run in my sleep," I tell him. "Sort of like sleep-walking, but you know...really fucked up."

"Huh," he says, leaning back, completely unfazed. "So you get your entire workout out of the way and you don't even know you've done it? That's kind of awesome."

I laugh. His reaction is ridiculous, of course, but it's just such a relief that he's not looking at me like I'm possessed. "Awesome may be a stretch, but anyway, if I'm here, Will can make sure I don't run before meets."

He gives me a sly smile. "Can't he just sleep at your place and do that? It'd give you a lot more *privacy*."

I think of Will's rejection tonight and my heart sinks all over again. "He's not interested," I tell him. I swallow. "And neither am I."

"Not buying any of that," Brendan says with a grin, "but I've heard his brother is super hot. And available. If nothing else, it might help Will pull his head out of his ass."

I laugh. "Because things aren't tense enough between you two?"

Brendan's eyes seem to twinkle slightly less. "Would you believe," he says, finishing the beer, "that he used to be my best friend?"

41

Will

Everything that could go wrong tonight has, beginning with the moment Olivia pressed herself against me. Christ, you could probably see my hard-on from *space*.

And then there's Jessica, with whom everything is wrong. She's been tense as fuck all evening, but once she heard I was sleeping at my mom's it really went downhill. She doesn't speak on the way to her place, and when she finally does, I wish she had not.

"Olivia should find a family of her own," she says. *Jessica*, with her doting parents and her siblings and their annual ski trips and beach trips and traditions, telling me that the little we can offer Olivia is too much.

"Her only family member has Alzheimer's, so where exactly do you suggest she go find one? Because I'm sure she'd be all ears."

She exhales in exasperation. "You know what I'm saying, Will. You don't have to be the only person in her life. You've already gone above and beyond for this girl, but the charity has to end at some point."

I stare at her as if I've never seen her before, except the truth is that I have seen it. All through high school I saw it, but my father did not. He saw her as a *nice* girl. She was a cheerleader, the homecoming queen, while I was the kid routinely handcuffed in the back of a police car. He must have suggested a hundred times that if I cleaned up my act, I could wind up with someone like her. "Now that Jessica Harper," he'd say. "*That's* a girl you settle down with."

Have I been deferring to the opinion of someone who never really knew Jessica instead of listening to my gut? I think it's possible, but my head is such a mess at the moment I'm not sure I trust my own thought process. And the one person I'd like to discuss it with is the one who's got my head in knots. Olivia.

I PICK Jessica up on the way back from visiting day on Saturday. She shouts from the bedroom that she's almost ready, but then she peeks her head out. "Come sit in here," she says suggestively. "We have plenty of time until dinner."

I shake my head, avoiding her eye as I turn on the TV. "My mom asked me to hurry back." It's a lie, but right now the last thing in the world I want to do is sleep with Jessica.

She pouts. "Five minutes?"

"I'm gonna watch the game," I say, without looking back at her.

Olivia is out when we get to the farm. Brendan, naturally, is sitting on the couch watching football, not a care in the world. In moments like this, when I think about the two jobs I'm working to keep him fed and in school, I understand my father's anger toward me. He'd expected me to put the family first, begin to take on some of the weight, and like the selfish little prick I was, I looked at the farm and the trouble he had and couldn't run fast enough.

Jessica goes to look for my mom so I sit in the chair across from him, and attempt civility. "So how's school?"

He shrugs. "How's having two girlfriends?"

"I don't have two girlfriends," I exhale testily.

"Sure you don't, Saint Will," he says. "I've never seen a guy check out a girl's ass as often as you did Olivia's last night, but yeah, nothing going on *there* at all."

"I don't know what you're talking about."

"Cool. Because if you're not in those pants, I'd like to be, so I'm going to take my shot."

I feel like I can't breathe. The idea of him with Olivia is far too easy to imagine. They looked like a couple at the bar last night, and when he grabbed her ass, it was only Jessica's presence that kept me from violently detaching his hand.

"I told you this already. She's off limits."

"I know what you said," he laughs, "and I decided I don't give a shit. Tell Mom I got busted. Get her all upset just because you want to keep Olivia to yourself. You don't get to decide who she goes out with."

No, but I shouldn't have to watch it when it happens. "She can do what she wants," I reply. "But as long as I'm paying the bills, you can't."

"Congratulations, Will," he says bitterly, rising to his feet. "You've turned into Dad."

He's right and at the moment I don't fucking care. He's got everything else—free to do what he wants, no responsibility for the farm. He doesn't get Olivia too.

42

Olivia

I hate Jessica.

I *thought* I hated Betsy, but it turns out my feelings toward her are something more like mild irritation compared with what I feel toward Will's girlfriend. And the thing is, she isn't doing anything wrong tonight, not on the surface anyway. But I hate her for sitting on Will's lap before dinner. I hate the way she runs her thumb over his wrist and how he almost unconsciously wraps a hand around her waist. I hate that there's something triumphant on her face when she does it, something directed at me though she's not even looking my way.

Will goes into the kitchen with Dorothy and when we hear him laugh, Brendan rolls his eyes. "I guess he found his happy pills or something. He's been a moody fucker all weekend," he says.

Jessica winks at both of us. "He just had to work off a little steam earlier, if you know what I mean."

Bitch.

"Maybe I'll start visiting him during the day at work." She smiles at me. "You know, to take the edge off."

That's when I no longer merely hate her but decide I'd like to see her clinging to life. I want her just conscious long enough to know it's me pulling the plug.

I make it through the night with a great deal of jaw clenching and tight fists, and only begin to relax when they rise to leave. "Hey," she says, pulling me aside when Will leaves the room, "I'm so sorry about your brother."

She isn't sorry. We both know that. I nod, waiting for whatever it is she really wants to say. "So I hate to be the one telling you this," she continues, "but the Langstroms really aren't in a position to be helping anyone out right now. Things are tough for them and I'm just not sure they can handle the extra strain."

"I haven't been asking them for help."

"No, you know what I mean, emotional help, stability," she says. "They can't be your substitute family right now. They've got enough of their own stuff to deal with. Dorothy and Will would never tell you that, of course, but it's pretty obvious, isn't it?"

I hate every word out of her mouth, but I hate even more that she is probably right.

~

I LEAVE ON SUNDAY, determined that I'll only stay at Dorothy's when I absolutely have to from now on. But the pressure is getting to me. People expect me to win next week.

I have a nightmare on Monday night and my legs are dead when I get to the track Tuesday morning. Will's jaw clenches but he says nothing.

On Wednesday, when I arrive exhausted again and with small cuts on my forearms, he's had it. "You're staying with my mom tonight," he says. "You're stressing out and I can't afford for you to get injured or fatigued right before the meet."

I stare at my feet. "It's okay. I won't run."

"You know you can't make that promise," he replies. "And I thought you liked staying with my mom?"

I swallow hard. I do like staying with Dorothy. And I'm going to miss it. "I'm not a charity case. I appreciate what you and your mom have done but I don't need help."

"No one thinks you're a charity case," he sputters. "If you won't do it for yourself, then do it for the rest of the team. You've got us in line to win our first title. Think of what that would mean to everyone else."

I'm so tired I want to curl up in the bleachers and sleep. I can't win. I can't keep doing what I am without disappointing everyone. I can't prevent it without leaning on people who have burdens of their own. "Fine," I tell him. "I'll go."

"You should just stay out here until the meet," Dorothy says over dinner. "Get some rest and some good food?"

I can't get Jessica's words out of my head. *Dorothy can't resist a stray. They can't be your substitute family right now.*

"That's nice of you," I say tentatively, "but I've got plans."

"Oh?" she asks, head tipped, eager to hear.

My glance shoots quickly to Will and away again. It was stupid and impulsive, but it pissed me off so much when Jessica said that bullshit about working off steam last weekend that I finally told Evan I'd go out with him, something I know I'm going to regret. "I've sort of got a date."

Will's head shoots up. "A date?" he demands. "With who?"

I sigh. I didn't realize this dinner was going to be quite so invasive. "You don't know him," I reply. "His name is Evan. He's on the swim team."

Will's jaw locks. "Evan? You mean Evan Rainier? He's the captain of the team. Why the fuck wouldn't I know who he is?"

"Will," his mother scolds.

"Sorry," he mutters, but his jaw remains tight. "What exactly do you mean when you say that it's 'sort of' a date?"

I roll my eyes. "I'm just not interested in dating anyone. I told him that, but he asked me just to give it a shot."

"Awww," gushes Dorothy. "He sounds like a really nice guy, Olivia."

"Too nice?" Will asks, his shoulders rigid. He's recalling our previous conversation, wondering if I'm going to sleep with Evan, and I'll be damned if he's going to guilt me into saying I won't.

I raise my chin and look him dead in the eye. "No, he's definitely not *too* nice."

His fork hits his plate a little harder than it should and he pushes away from the table. "So you don't even like this guy and you're going to sleep with him?"

I explode then. I'll take criticism from him on a lot of fronts but this one? No fucking way. "Why the hell shouldn't I, Will? You sleep with Jessica and you don't like her! Why shouldn't I do the same?"

He looks like he's been slapped. "Jessica is my girlfriend. Of course I like her."

I laugh. "Bullshit! Every time you see her car here, your face falls. Every time she speaks, you wince. Not only do you not *like* her, I think a part of you actively *dis*likes her. I actually enjoy Evan's company. He's fun to hang out with, he's fun to talk to. Can you honestly say either of those things about Jessica? And before you answer, you should take a look at how much time you spend avoiding her and ask yourself why."

The kitchen is uncomfortably silent when my speech is over, and then Will stands and walks out of the house. Dorothy looks stunned more than angry, but I'm not sure. I just drove her son out of the house, after all.

"I'm sorry."

She looks at me, her face drawn. For the first time since I've known her, she actually looks her age. "Don't be," she says, "I think he needed to hear it."

But if that's actually true, I'm not sure why she looks so unhappy about it.

⁓

WILL STILL ISN'T HOME when I go to bed, which makes me think I've really taken things too far. He's always been so worried about me running in the woods and now he's not? Have I pushed him so far that he's given up?

It takes me a long time to fall asleep, waiting for the sound of the front door to open. I know I'm going to run tonight, and for the first time in my life, it's not about a meet or my brother or something that happened a long time ago.

It's about a boy.

43

Will

I'm driving away from the farm as fast as I can go, as if I can somehow separate myself from what she just said. I can't, because she was right. Every damn word out of her mouth was right.

It's not simply that I don't like Jessica. The truth is that I *dread* Jessica. I dread seeing her in my office, in my apartment or hers, or at the farm. There's nothing wrong with her. There's also nothing that makes me crave her, miss her, think about her when she's not with me. All these nights I've spent sleeping on my mother's couch were spent thinking about a girl, but that girl wasn't Jessica.

I'm mad at Olivia for pointing it out, and I'm mad at myself for not seeing it sooner. I turn the car around and go home, to sit on my mother's front porch with my head in my hands, realizing exactly how pathetic the truth is. I was never interested in Jessica. She was just another futile effort to please my father, an effort I made far too late.

I took over the farm like he wanted. I dated the girl he chose for me. I've spent two years paying penance as if these actions will let him know that I'm so fucking sorry for shit I said to him, and for letting him carry so much on his shoulders without ever once offering to help. But paying penance feels like it's sucking the life out of me, and it's never going to bring him back.

I've only just stood up when the door flies open. I leap forward, cursing myself for not going inside sooner, and barely grab Olivia before she gets down the steps. She screams and flails and finally gives in to me, collapsing against my chest with a weak, final cry.

I carry her to her room. It's funny that I grew up here, but in a short period of time it's become Olivia's room. It will always be her room, even when she's no longer here.

I lay her down on the bed, but she's still restless, so I lie down beside her. God knows I shouldn't though, perhaps most of all because I want to so badly. I think about falling asleep next to her almost as often as I think about seeing her naked, which happens more than I want to admit.

Once she's settled, I start to pull away, but she rolls toward me. And then, with her eyes still closed and fast asleep, she raises her head and kisses me.

For a moment, I'm drowning in sensation without thought, wanting this and wanting more. I only know soft lips, warmth, smooth skin, the feel of her body arching against mine, and I am desperate, greedy for more.

I come to my senses within seconds, but clearly not fast enough, given that my hands are on her waist and I'm nearly on top of her. She's still sound asleep and I'm on the verge of ... I don't know what. I scramble away and go sit on the couch, feeling sick with guilt, but not so guilty that I don't want to go right back in there and do it all again.

I've dreamed about what just happened. You're supposed to be grateful when you get the things you dream about, but I'm not. Because now that I've had a small taste of how it would be with her, I'm going to go through my entire life aware of what I don't have.

~

"IT FEELS like something is missing without her here," my mother says the next afternoon as she cleans the table. "The house feels empty."

I don't need to ask who she means, but I'm still not going to agree with her. Even if it's true. I grab a stack of bills and take them to the couch. "If you say so."

"Will," my mother says gently, "sometimes it's best to admit things to yourself, instead of pretending they aren't there."

I rub a hand over my eyes. Is it that fucking obvious how I feel about her? Apparently it is. "You want me to admit I like her? Fine, I admit it. Do I like her in a way I shouldn't? Yes, I think I have since the day I met her. There. It's all out in the open and it doesn't fix anything."

My mother sets the cloth down and turns to me. "If you like her so much," she asks, "then why are you still with Jessica?"

I exhale heavily. "I figured I should wait until after Thanksgiving since she told her family she wasn't coming home. But it's going to make things a lot harder—" Sometimes I think the only thing that's kept me from messing up more than I already have is the fact that I have a girlfriend. I'm with Olivia way too much and keep finding myself in situations where it would be so easy to make a mistake, like I did last night. But these are things I can't tell my mother. "I'm around Olivia a lot," I conclude, hoping she won't make me spell it out.

"Then maybe you shouldn't be sleeping here before meets," she says. She crosses the room and takes the chair across from me. "Obviously I'm not going to be able to stop her, but Brendan could."

My fists clench, a reflex. "No."

"Why not?" she asks. "He's as big as you, and nearly as fast. I'm sure he'd be willing."

Yeah, I'm sure he'd jump at the chance. "His *willingness* is exactly why he's not doing it," I sneer.

Her hands rest in her lap. She looks at them rather than me. "If you can't be with her, maybe you should move aside for someone who can," she says quietly.

I like that idea even less. I'm not stopping Olivia from doing anything. Hell, she's going out with someone tonight. The thought makes me flinch.

Brendan. Evan. The entire fucking world is full of guys who can take her away from me, and one day one of them will.

44

Olivia

EVAN PICKS ME UP AND, being a gentleman, he only makes a few references to how unbelievably shitty my neighborhood is. "It's not all bad," he says. "I bet you don't have to walk far to find meth."

He drives us out of the city and toward the mountains, and we wind up at a tiny shack that serves the best barbeque I've ever eaten in my life. There's a porch in back and a small stream weaves its way right through it. I didn't want to come tonight, and I'm still not sure I want to date him, but it's okay.

"So is this better than eating ramen noodles alone?" he asks.

"I don't know," I reply. "Are we talking shrimp flavor or the spicy chicken?"

His foot taps mine. "Admit it, you're having fun."

I smile reluctantly. "Fine. I'm having fun."

"Awesome," he says, leaning toward me. "Then I lied before, when I first asked you out. I am gonna try to kiss you."

It's a good kiss, just like it's been a good date. But it doesn't hold a candle to last night's kiss with Will.

The kiss.

I've spent the entire day stunned that it happened, pressing my fingers to my lips to recapture the feeling of it. At first it was my doing—I woke in the darkness as he was pulling away. I wanted him to stay, and I wanted a lot more from him so, half asleep, I took it.

His mouth was as soft and pliant as I'd imagined. And then came the shock to end all shocks: *he* deepened it. *He* sought it out. Groaning low in his throat and pulling me tight against him, he kissed me hard, like it was something he'd wanted for a long, long time. It was a perfect kiss—a life-altering kiss. Too bad he froze, as quick as it began, and jumped away.

Even now my fingers keep going to my lips, trying to recapture it.

He barely spoke to me this morning. Wouldn't even look at me. And it doesn't matter because now I know, whether or not he'll admit it, that some part of him wants this too.

45

The girls give me shit about my date the next morning. I mostly ignore it. I have no idea why I told them anything in the first place, but I'm back to focusing on the meet and they should be too.

Our shot at regionals is riding on this. Betsy's the fastest girl on the team aside from me and I've never seen her come in better than sixth, which means I have to be first to get us a high enough weighted score, and if I fuck up in any way, our season is over.

I go to Dorothy's on Saturday night. She's made a nice dinner, but I can barely choke anything down. She and Will talk while I sit here creating an endless mental list of all the things that can go wrong tomorrow.

As the meal concludes, Will takes a look at my full plate and sighs. "Let's go for a ride."

~

WE RIDE to the lake his father built for him and Brendan. I look at it while the horses graze, beginning to understand why Will is so conflicted about his dad. How can you love someone who treated you the way his father did? But how can you hate someone who also wanted to give you the world, who built you a lake just hoping to make you happy?

He sits beside me on the grass. "So you're nervous."

I give a tiny shrug. "You don't have to give me a pep talk. I already know. Just do my best and don't worry about the nerves and what happens, happens."

"Actually," he says with a grin, "I was gonna say, 'please don't lose'."

I choke on a surprised laugh. "Asshole."

"And also, just do your best. What happens, happens."

I tear at a piece grass beside my knee. "The whole team will hate me if I don't place tomorrow."

He shakes his head. "How could they possibly hate you for failing to do something *they've* also failed to do?"

"Because I'm the only one on the team capable of winning it." I know that sounds arrogant but it's the truth. The girls on the team work their asses off, but there's only so much hard work can do and the rest is genetics. "And if I hadn't fainted during the first meet, we'd probably already have a spot at regionals, but now we don't."

"Or you could consider that if you hadn't come to ECU we wouldn't have placed once all semester. *You* did that for us."

He may be right. It doesn't change the fact that we will all be disappointed if I mess up tomorrow. Anyway, there are other things I'd rather talk about. Like the way he kissed me the other night. I'd like to know if he enjoyed it. If he wished he could do it again. There are a thousand bad things in my head, things I push away all day long. But that kiss is a good thing and it's the only thing I'm not allowed to discuss with him.

"This conversation is making my stomach hurt. Can we talk about something else?"

"That detective left me a message," he finally says. "Apparently, you aren't returning his calls."

"I don't want to talk about that either."

"Liv," he says gently, "you're going to have to talk about it eventually."

"No, I won't."

"But why? You said yourself you'd never planned to try to find your brother as an adult. I know this whole thing has been a shock, but does it really change anything?"

He waits, and I know him well enough to know that he will ask, and ask, and ask until he's finally gotten the truth.

"It's not the possibility that he's dead. An adult version of Matthew would be a stranger to me. It's that if they are right ..." My voice catches, and still he waits. "If they are right then he would have been so little, and so scared." The sentence ends on a rasp, and I feel this odd grief come over me, pulsing against my eyelids, my jaw, trying to wrench itself free of my skin. My heart begins beating too hard, a race it can't win.

He scoots so that his body is tight next to mine, a welcome line of warmth, and puts his arm around me. I bury my head into his chest, relishing the feel of his fleece beneath my skin, the firmness of him under it, his smell and the sound of his heart so close to my ear.

"I would do anything to fix this for you," he says quietly, "and it kills me that I can't. Tell me what to do."

It takes me a minute to reply. "You already make everything better," I tell him. "And you're the only one who ever has."

He stills at the words. His breath, his pulse—it all seems to stop entirely. I look up at him and his eyes meet mine. I don't know what this is to him, but to me, it's something far beyond running or lust or even friendship. When did he become so important? I know all too well that it's not safe to care about anything this much.

I see panic, quiet and fleeting, pass over his face before he looks away. "Good," he says quietly, "I'm glad I've been able to help."

We ride back to the stables in silence. I'm equal parts embarrassed and angry. I don't know why I told him what I did. What did I think it would accomplish? I hang Trixie's tack up and brush her, quickly, eager to get away from him.

"So are you going out with Evan again?" he asks.

"I don't know," I say, without interest, walking out of the stables. "I'm not into relationships."

"You keep saying that," he says, following me out, inexplicably angry, "and you're full of shit. You wouldn't rather be alone. Even the lamest possible night you can imagine—eating at home, sitting around watching TV—is something you'd prefer to do with someone else."

I'm angry, and sad, and it's all welling up in my throat and my chest and my head, making me feel like it can't be held in.

"Yes," I hiss, coming to a halt. "You're saying that because I like to do those things with *you*. So if I told you I want *exactly* that —the two of us together doing every single lame thing we do— what would you say?"

I want to beg him to admit it. To tell me that all these things— watching TV and our time in the stables and the rides to his mother's house—are the highlight of his day, his month, his year, his *everything*, the way they are for me. *Please admit it, Will. Please.*

"I'm sorry," he says hoarsely. He draws his fingers toward his palms in tight fists. "I shouldn't have brought this up."

He turns to walk away.

I swallow hard, angry and desperate at once. He does not get to pretend this is meaningless. He doesn't get to pretend he feels absolutely nothing for me when I know he does.

"Did you like sleeping with me?" I ask. His body jerks to a halt. "I know you've stayed with me. Before the last meet. And the time we were in the hotel. You stayed when you didn't have to. Did you like it?"

He hangs his head. "Olivia, I'm not *allowed* to like it. I'm your coach. And that's all I'm ever going to be."

The words hit me like a fist. I want to stagger backward, throw my arms up to defend myself. He's already walking away, and I'm left behind, feeling like he's just stripped me of every reason I wanted to exist.

DOROTHY TRIES to get me to eat in the morning and it comes back up almost immediately. I wouldn't be surprised if I pass out again today. I don't want that for the team but at the same time it feels as if nothing matters anymore.

I never did fall asleep last night. Instead I spent the entire night trying to ignore the hole in my chest, and kicking myself for my stupidity. Did I *really* think he was going to abandon his job and his hot girlfriend for me? I've got no family, no money, a criminal record, and there's a strong possibility that I'll lose my scholarship before I graduate. I start fights, can't account for what happens when I'm asleep, and I'm incapable of any emotion but anger most of the time. Why would anyone give up anything for *that*?

"We'll see you Tuesday, right?" Dorothy asks, giving me a hug goodbye. "For Thanksgiving weekend?"

My stomach tightens. I can't. I can't spend another weekend around him after what happened last night, watching Jessica take all the things I want and can't have. It's time to finally cut the cord.

"Oh," I say. "I totally forgot to tell you, but I'm going home with Erin. Sorry about that."

Dorothy's face falls, and guilt spins in my stomach alongside every other bad thing brewing in there right now. But in the long run, I'm not going to be a part of this family, so it's probably time to stop pretending I am.

46

Will

I fucked up.

I know that I fucked up.

I just don't know what else I could have done.

I wanted to tell her that I want all the same things, and want them only with her. I want a thousand boring nights in, sitting on a ratty sofa listening to her malign newscasters and make fun of their guests. That I want to spend my entire life keeping her safe, even if it means sleeping on the couch outside her room to do it. That I've never wanted anything in my entire life the way I want her, and the idea of giving her up makes giving up climbing pale by contrast.

What good would it have done, though? I'm not going to wait a year and a half just to watch her move on to bigger things. And I'm sure as shit not going to try and convince her to destroy her future and stay here with me, in a small town where none of the things she wants can happen.

But I still fucked up, and with every minute that passes this morning, I can feel her growing more remote.

We arrive at the meet and she starts pacing, the way she always does, but today she wants nothing from me. She's the Olivia I first met, closely guarding her secrets, struggling beneath an unbearable weight, and certain that no one can help her carry it.

The gun goes off. She goes out at a dead sprint—as if it's the end of the race, not the beginning. As if she's running a 400 meter, not a solid three miles.

"What the hell is she doing?" groans Peter.

I flinch, already well aware of how this will unfold: when she starts to burn out and the top runners catch up with her, she'll panic and begin the mental self-flagellation she's so prone to. And then she will give up.

By the third mile, it all begins to unfold as I predicted and I watch, absolutely helpless to stop it. "Damn it," says Peter. "She just lost us regionals."

My temper flares. He's my boss and I should keep my mouth shut, but no one gets to blame *her*, not even him. "The team lost it," I snap. "She's the only one who got us close to it in the first place."

She comes in fourth, still the first from the team but several places too low to do us any good. When she comes through, I clap a hand on her shoulder. "It's okay, Olivia. You did your best."

She nods but there is defeat etched into the curve of her mouth and shoulders as she walks away. Nicole and Erin both throw their arms around her, but she doesn't react. It's not as if she's sad...it's as if she's absent. She never wanted to care about the team, and I think right now she wishes that were still true.

I say goodbye to all the girls once we reach campus. There's no practice tomorrow and school gets out Tuesday for break, so it'll be a week before I see them again.

A week before I see Olivia again.

She walks away and I watch until she fades from view, wishing there was anything I could have said to make her stay.

THE FARM IS A PRETTY DEPRESSING place to be for the next few days. It reminds me of the time after my father died, how we'd sit down for dinner and the sight of his empty chair seemed to diminish us all a little. My mother doesn't say it, but I suspect she blames me. I see it in her eyes, in the way her mouth tightens a little every time I say Olivia's name. The only person alive who appears happy about the whole thing is Jessica.

"No offense," she says as we drive to dinner on Tuesday night, "but it'll be nice to have a little family time without her there."

Family time? God, there are so many responses that come to mind. I just barely keep them to myself.

"And it's time she found a family of her own," she continues. "She can't be leaning on you guys as her only source of support."

"How exactly is she supposed to find a family, Jess?" I ask, my voice precise and angry. "Post an ad on Craigslist?"

"Will," she says, "don't get snippy with me. You know what I mean."

"No, actually I have no fucking idea what you mean."

"You always defend her," she accuses. "Ever since she got here, you've done nothing but make excuses for her, and she's totally taking advantage."

Jessica has a big family, and parents who dote on her. Her car and the fancy apartment she couldn't possibly afford on her salary are all benefits of having parents who can't deny her anything. It makes every word out of her mouth that much more appalling. "Taking advantage of *what* exactly, Jessica? My family's yacht and mansion?"

"Will," she says with a tremulous note in her voice, "this is a really hard week for me, okay? Please stop making it worse."

"Hard in what way?" I growl, irritated before I even know what she's going to say.

"This is the week we lost my grandfather," she says, pressing her index finger to the corner of her eye as if to stem the tears. "I miss my family and I'm thinking about my grandfather and now you're mad at me and it's hard, okay?"

We are almost into town and I should let this go, just make it through the evening, but I can't.

"When?"

"When what?" she sniffles.

"When did your grandfather die?"

"A few years ago."

"How many, Jess?"

"I don't know. High school. You're missing the point. I'm just saying—"

I turn the car around. I was going to wait until after the holiday was over but I just can't. She's sitting here expecting me to feel sorry for her over the death of a grandparent that occurred at least seven years ago, but can't muster an ounce of sympathy for someone whose entire family is dead or has abandoned her.

"What are you doing? We don't need to go home." She smiles, wiping away another invisible tear and then putting most of her faux-sadness aside. "I'm okay, just a little sad about not seeing my family. Let's go out. I'll be fine."

I take a deep breath, aiming for neutrality rather than scorn. "I'm sorry, Jess, but this isn't going to work out."

"Will, it's fine. I just needed a little cry—"

"No, I'm not talking about tonight. I'm talking about us. *We* are not going to work out."

Even with my eyes on the road, I can feel the way she recoils.

"You're breaking up with me?" she gasps.

"This just isn't working anymore, Jessica. I'm sure if you think about it, you'll see that too."

"But we aren't even having problems!"

"We've been having plenty of problems," I reply. "We just haven't discussed them."

"Is this about sex? Because *you're* the one who keeps turning me down. I tried talking to you about it—"

"It's not about sex."

"Then what? You can't just break up with me and not even have a reason!" she cries, almost unintelligible at this point. "Everyone thought you were about to propose and you want to take a break instead?"

"I was never planning to propose. I must have told you a thousand times I didn't want to settle down. And I don't want to take a break," I correct her. "I want to break up."

I pull up in front of her apartment complex. "Then why?" she demands. "I'm not getting out of this car until you've given me a reason."

"We have nothing in common, Jessica," I say gently. "If you think about it, you'll know I'm right. You don't run, you don't climb, you don't even like sports. And I don't do the things you do." In truth, I'm not sure what exactly she does away from me aside from work and shop.

"Right," she hisses. "I don't like those things, but your precious *Olivia* does, doesn't she?"

"She has nothing to do with it."

"She has everything to do with it!" Jessica screams. "Everything! We were fine until she showed up and it's been a steady downhill ever since! I *knew* you were cheating when you stopped sleeping with me."

"I've never slept with Olivia and I think you know that."

"Bullshit, Will! You think I'm stupid? You think I really believe you and that girl are spending all this time together and sleeping under the same roof, but you've never hooked up with her?"

"Yes, I expect you to believe it because it's the truth."

"You're going to get caught!" she cries. "You're going to get caught and lose your job and then your mom will lose the farm. Is that what you want?"

"I'm not sleeping with her!" I shout. "For the last time, there is nothing going on. Now please get out of my car."

"Fine," she says, climbing out, "but just for the record, you don't need to have slept with her. It's enough that you've been staying together at your mom's."

And then she leans her head back in and *smiles*. "When word gets about that, you're royally fucked."

～

"YOU'RE HOME EARLY," says my mother.

"Yeah," I sigh, flopping down on the couch and closing my eyes. "Jess and I broke up."

"Oh, I'm sorry," she says, striving to sound sincere, and failing.

I laugh. "No, you're not. You never liked her. You can admit it."

"Jessica had her good qualities," she counters, but even she laughs a little. "So what led to this?"

I turn on the TV, wishing she hadn't asked. "She started in on Olivia again and I kind of lost it."

We sit in silence for a moment while I flip through channels. "Olivia said she was going to Erin's?" my mother asks. "Where's Erin's family from?"

Even the mention of Olivia's name makes my stomach twist. She's the last thing I want to discuss.

"Why?" I ask, a little sourly. "You planning a rescue mission?"

"No," my mother snaps. "I'm just curious."

I try to remember where Erin calls home. Most of the girls are from Colorado, but for some reason, it seems like she was not. Her parents flew in for that meet they attended. And they'd had a layover in Chicago.

New Jersey.

Shit.

There's no way Olivia could have afforded to fly, and it was too far to drive.

I guess there's gonna be a rescue mission after all.

47

Olivia

I *lost.*

It's been over forty-eight hours since the meet and that's pretty much the only phrase I've uttered the entire time. I let them all down, but Will most of all. For him to have gotten us into regionals during only his second year of coaching—*that* would have meant something, and I took it away from him. I took it away from Nicole, who's graduating this year. And what's worse is I allowed it to happen. There was no excuse for it. I was fresh, ready, and if I'd given it any thought whatsoever, I'd have known I was going out too fast. But I was anxious and angry and bitter and a little too eager to leave those feelings behind me.

I did this.

A lot of the girls have called or texted to make sure I'm okay, which just makes me feel worse. I don't know how they can stand to be nice to me when I just screwed every one of them over the way I did.

Who haven't I screwed over, exactly? I hurt the girls on the team, I hurt Will, and worst of all I hurt Dorothy by canceling.

My entire life is one long series of fuck-ups, of people I've hurt, and I don't seem to be breaking the pattern.

My great-aunt once told me I was poisonous. And nearly six years later, I still can't say she's wrong.

~

ON TUESDAY NIGHT, someone bangs on the door. I've gotten so used to my isolation that I nearly jump out of my skin at the sound. But before I've even flipped the lock, I know who it is.

"You lied," Will says, storming in without waiting to be asked. "You fucking lied. You're not going home with Erin."

For a millisecond I feel something uneasy in my chest, but I fight it off as hard as I can. He doesn't want me, his family doesn't need me around, and it's time we all stopped the charade. "Fine, I lied, you caught me," I reply. "So what?"

"So why did you do it?" He walks an angry path through my apartment, back and forth, building up steam. "You lied to my mother's face."

My arms fold across my chest. "I'm not a charity case, Will. Your family doesn't have to take me in for every holiday. Consider yourselves off the hook."

"What the hell are you talking about?" he demands. "We *wanted* you to come."

There's a part of me that wants to believe him, which is fucking pathetic after what he said to me Saturday night. "Bullshit. You *personally* couldn't have made it clearer that you want to be away from me. And I'm guessing that losing the meet on Sunday only makes that more true. So yeah, I lied. Sue me."

His jaw opens and shuts. For a moment just he stares at me. "God, I want to shake you sometimes." He grabs my backpack off the floor and shoves it at me. "Pack your stuff."

"No. The Olivia Finnegan Charity Project you want to open has come to an end."

He raises his hands in the air, helpless with frustration, and slams his palms down hard on the counter. "Pull your head out of your ass, Olivia! For some inexplicable reason, my mother adores you. She's at home right now, heartbroken that you're not there, and it turns out you're lying to her in order to avoid it!"

I feel a small wobble in my anger, in my certainty, but I dismiss it. I wish I'd never gotten involved with his family in the first place. "You should've known not to count on me."

"Is that what this is about? Because you *lost*?"

I swallow. "No." My throat feels like it's closing in. "But I'm not a part of your family and that was pretty much the end of the cross country season, so I guess our work together is done." Just saying the words aloud makes me feel adrift in my own grief. I won't be seeing Dorothy again, or the farm or the horses. It's over.

He steps closer. "Well, my mother seems to think you're the daughter she never had. So like it or not, you *are* part of a family. Believe me, I'd have chosen someone a little more even-tempered and less quick to lie or throw a punch, but sometimes you don't get a choice." His eyes drop to the ground and his voice gets quieter, less willing. "We *all* want you there. You filled a hole we didn't even know we had and now you're gone and it's all any of us can see."

I want to scream, or lash out, but something inexplicable occurs instead. I feel like I'm about to cry. I hate that he's mad, I hate that Dorothy is upset, I hate that I lied and that I've been here alone wanting to be with them. I hate that I missed them all. My eyes are filling and my lip is trembling. It's humiliating, and it enrages me that he and his mother have made this happen. That thing inside my chest twists, too hard this time.

Suddenly he looks like he's been hit. "Are you *crying*?" he asks.

"No," I rasp, even as I feel tears rolling down my face. I turn away from him and head toward the bathroom. "Go home."

He grabs my arm and swings me back, into him, looking

astonished and saddened and hopeful all at the same time. "You *are* crying." His arms go around me, tucking me into him, my head just under his chin. "Liv, I'm so sorry."

I try to push him off and he holds on tighter. "It's okay to cry once in a while." My shoulders shake and I say nothing, but I no longer fight. The small explosion has triggered an earthquake, and it scares me. It seems as if there is no end to it, no bottom.

So I cry. I cry so ridiculously long and hard that it seems unbelievable to me and still the tears don't stop. He maneuvers me to the couch and wraps his arms around me, pulling me into his chest.

I cry for so long that it becomes silly, even to me.

"I can't stop," I whisper with a laugh that turns into another sob.

His hand runs over my hair. "I know," he says. "It's okay."

I cry until I'm exhausted, until the weight of fatigue steals over me. I cry until there's nothing left, and then I fall asleep.

WHEN I WAKE, the room is light. My back is to his front and I can feel something insistent pressing against my ass even through my jeans and his.

I laugh. "I guess you're awake, perv."

He groans. "That doesn't make me a perv. Every time I tried to move, you pushed your ass against me again."

I wiggle and I *feel* him groan as I much as I hear it. I love, a little too much, having that kind of power over him. "Don't notice you trying to move now."

"If you'd get off of me I would," he snaps. "You're a very hard person to be nice to sometimes."

I reluctantly sit up, and so does he, bending over to rest his elbows on his knees.

"From the feel of it, your girlfriend's a very lucky woman," I offer. Which is both the truth and as close as I want to come to an apology.

He remains bent over, mostly ignoring me. "We broke up."

My stupid, stupid heart begins beating fast. I know it wasn't because of me, and I know it won't change things. "Why?"

He's still staring at the floor. I'm not sure if it's because he's pissed at me or just trying to get his erection to go away. "I was with her for the wrong reasons and we didn't want the same thing. But back to the main subject—"

"Your dick size?"

He groans and laughs at once. "No, Olivia. My mother."

"Oh."

He glances over at me. "You know it'd break her heart if she found out you lied?"

The idea of it tears me up. Dorothy's been really good to me, and there haven't been a lot of people in my life I could say that about. "You're not going to tell her, are you?"

"No," he says. "Because you're going to come home with me and tell her your plans changed. So, as I said about eight hours ago, go pack your shit."

48

Olivia

"I brought you an early Christmas present, Mom," Will says when we walk in the door.

Dorothy's head pokes out of the kitchen and a smile breaks across her face that is too wide and too sudden to be fake. "Olivia?" she gasps. "What happened to your trip?"

I swallow. She really did want me here. It makes me feel like I might cry all over again. "My plans changed," I tell her, looking from her to Will. "Is that okay?"

She crosses the room and pulls me into a big hug. "*Okay*? It's so much better than okay. I'm thrilled."

Brendan walks out in a T-shirt and flannel pajama bottoms, running a hand through his riotous hair. "Holy crap, you people are loud." He blinks when he sees me and a sly grin spreads over his face, which prompts Will to step in front of me as if I'm naked.

"Hey, Houdini," Brendan laughs, "you realize that didn't make her invisible, right?"

OVER BREAKFAST, Dorothy suggests that Will take me climbing, but he shakes his head and says something about looking at a broken engine. I have no idea if it's true or if he's just making some excuse not to be alone with me. He was pretty fucking clear last weekend about what he wants from me, which is nothing. I suppose, in spite of this morning, that hasn't changed.

"I'll take her," Brendan says,

"Not a chance," Will replies. "I don't need my lead runner out for the rest of the season because you didn't secure something right."

I sigh. "The season is over. Thanks to me."

"Thanks to the *team* we're not going to regionals," he corrects. "And have you forgotten you've got the Cooper Invitational in two weeks? It's going to get national media attention. That's way more important for you than anything regionals could have done."

"So she doesn't even have a race for two weeks and you're crying about how she might get injured?" Brendan says. "Fuck that. I probably climb more than you do anyway, and there's no reason Olivia should have to sit around here just because you want to play with an engine."

Will gives him a look that might make anyone else cower. And Brendan just grins, with his middle finger extended.

～

"I DON'T WANT TO CLIMB," Brendan announces as soon as we get in his car. "It's too damn cold anyway."

I laugh. I sort of figured as much. "Stop involving me in your plans to piss off Will, please. And what are we supposed to do for the next few hours instead?"

He grins. "Something a hell of a lot more fun than climbing."

He takes me to a small one-street town about twenty minutes away, where we proceed to drink for the next five hours and then spend another two hours walking around while we try to sober up. It's dinner time when we get home, and when Dorothy asks us how climbing was, we both start to laugh.

"Am I missing something?" asks Will, that muscle in his jaw popping.

"Yeah," says Brendan, grinning at me. "You're missing a whole lot of something."

～

THE NEXT MORNING I'm up at six to help Dorothy. I don't have a hard time rising early, since I do it every day, but I do have a hard time rising early in order to *cook*.

Dorothy hands me a bag of potatoes as I stagger into the kitchen and I look at them blankly. "Um ... what do I do with these?"

"Make the mashed potatoes."

I look from the bag in my hand to her. "Uh, okay. Do I bake them first or something?" Like I said, my cooking skills are unbelievably limited. Aside from eggs, everything I know how to make involves ground beef and spaghetti sauce.

She laughs. "Is that a serious question?"

"Well, they need to be soft, right?" I scowl. "I've only made mashed potatoes from a box."

"You've never seen *anyone* make them?"

I shrug. "My grandmother stopped cooking when I was pretty young, and this is the only other kitchen I've been in."

She turns to me, her eyes sad. "Peel them, quarter them, boil them. We'll start with that."

"Seems like a lot of potatoes for four people."

"Peter's coming too," she says, as if that explains why she's got me working with about forty pounds of potatoes. I'm tempted to tease her about the fact that she blushed as soon as she said Peter's name, but I decide against it.

Will wanders in a little later, looking adorably sleepy and

unshaven, *and hot*. Who the hell looks totally doable just out of bed?

"Out," says his mother.

"Coffee," he replies, scrubbing a hand over his face. "You're not getting me out of here without coffee." He glances at me and grins. "My mom trusted you with a knife, did she?"

I narrow my eyes at him. "That was before she knew *you'd* be in the kitchen. Hope that coffee's fast. I'm feeling stabby all of a sudden."

He hops on the counter and watches me peel potatoes. "So is there anything I can eat *now*?"

Brendan's head leans in. "Me too."

"Have some cereal," Dorothy says.

Brendan groans. "*Cereal*? We're growing boys."

Dorothy shoos them away. "If the two of you grow any more, you won't fit in the house. Out."

"Mom," Will whines, sounding so young it makes me laugh, "we're *starving*." When that fails, he turns to me. "How about sneaking your favorite coach a few of those rolls?"

I feign surprise. "I didn't know Peter was already here." He laughs and gives me the finger at the same time, which is decidedly un-coach-like.

～

WHEN THE POTATOES are done we start working on the pies. "I guess you probably haven't done this before either," Dorothy says.

My mouth opens to agree, when I suddenly remember something. Standing on a stepstool next to my mother while she let me help her make pumpkin pie. A shudder passes through me. I remember her smiling when I poured in too much nutmeg by accident, and explaining later that a pumpkin is considered a fruit because it has seeds.

And the memory...doesn't fit. That's not the kind of person who just abandons her child, and I prefer the monster I've created in my mind—it makes it at least *possible* that some of the fault rests with her.

By 1 p.m., everything is done, or nearly so. "I guess it's time for us to get ready," Dorothy says, removing her apron. She leans out of the kitchen and yells at the guys to go get dressed. They both make similar sounds of protest, which she ignores. "We all kind of dress up, by the way. The boys hate it and every year they complain, but a rule's a rule."

"Oh," I say, biting my lip. "I don't know if I brought—"

"I bought you something," she says with a grin. "I hope you don't mind. I just saw it in the store and thought, 'Olivia would look gorgeous in that.'"

"You shouldn't have." They're nearly as strapped for cash as I am.

She shrugs. "I always wanted a little girl to dress up."

"You could probably still have a girl," I reply. Maybe it's just good genes, but Dorothy looks young. Too young to have grown sons, actually.

She smiles at me. "Shop's closed. And besides, I have you now, don't I?"

My eyes sting. I'm glad she's already turned away so she can't see it.

I follow her, touched but also feeling a bit of dread. Whatever she's bought I'm going to have to wear, which means sitting through dinner with Will and Brendan making fun of me the whole time. I'm already annoyed at both of them for it and it hasn't even happened yet.

While she goes to her closet, I pick up a picture of Will that sits on her dresser. He's a gangly little towhead, standing shirtless by a lake with a big crooked smile and a few missing teeth. I'm still smiling at it when she emerges.

"Wasn't he sweet?" she asks.

"Yeah," I sigh. He was adorable. There's something so free and unencumbered about him in the photo that it kind of breaks my heart. I've seen glimpses of it when we're climbing, but almost never outside of that.

She's holding up two different dresses. "I got you one for today and one for the fall athletic banquet."

Both the dresses are beautiful, but I don't wear dresses ever, so the idea of wearing either of them makes me feel squirmy and self-conscious. I laugh uneasily. "I guess the one that looks like lingerie is for today?"

"It's a slip dress," she scolds, "and no, that's for the banquet."

She has me take the dress that *doesn't* look like lingerie and try it on. It's a fitted cream sheath in matte jersey, pouring over my body like it was made for me. Dorothy sighs happily when I emerge. "I knew it would be perfect on you. Do you like it?"

For her sake I nod. "I'm just not used to wearing dresses I guess."

She smiles. "Maybe that's for the best. You're dangerous enough in running clothes. Now go put on a little makeup and I'll see you in the kitchen."

I go to my room and put on mascara and lip gloss, hating myself for how much I care. For how badly I want Will to like it, for blindly hoping it will somehow change things for us when he's made it so clear that nothing's going to happen. It's a course of action destined to fail but here I stand, undertaking it anyway.

I brought heels, thinking we might go out with Brendan one night, so I slip them on and look in the mirror one last time. My stomach sinks. I look good, and it won't be enough. He made that clear last weekend, didn't he?

I walk into the main area. Will's at the dining room table carving the turkey, wearing khakis and a button-down shirt, which is as dressed up as I've ever seen him. And he's gorgeous in it, of course. Even in that shirt you can see the raw strength of him, the breadth of his shoulders, the taut forearms. He looks hot and grown up and just ... I can't put my finger on it but it's something that makes my breath come a little short.

"Hey, Mom!" he shouts. "Do you want—"

His voice trails off as I come into his line of sight. He doesn't smile. He doesn't move. He just *stares*.

"You're looking at me like I walked in here carrying a decapitated head," I tell him.

"That'd be less surprising than you in a dress," he mutters, turning back to the turkey.

49

Will

Holy shit.

Olivia's in a dress.

A dress that flows over every curve. Curves even *I* didn't realize she had, and I've done more than my fair share of looking. I am temporarily struck mute. I want to tell her that she is gorgeous, breathtaking, astonishing. That the second I saw her my stomach dropped with something that goes so far beyond lust that I can't even name it. I can't tell her any of this though, so I do what I've always done.

I try to pretend she's no longer there.

❧

PETER ARRIVES and we all go to the table. He doesn't take my father's seat at the end. Instead, he sits next to my mom and leaves the seat for me. I guess he's just trying to be respectful, but I wish he hadn't. I'd kind of banked on talking to him about sports and ignoring Olivia entirely, but now he's talking to my mom and Olivia's straight across from me, so pretty that my eyes trip over her, stutter, stall, every time I look up.

It was hard seeing her with my mom in the kitchen, seeing the way she seemed to cure a certain loneliness in my mom that me and Brendan and my dad never did. It was hard seeing how much she belongs here, and knowing it's never going to happen. It was hard looking at my brother's smug smile. I don't know where they went yesterday, but I know they didn't climb for eight hours.

And now it's hard sitting across from her, desperately trying to keep my boss from seeing how I feel about her. I don't know why the fuck my mom had to invite Peter, but if it comes up that Olivia is staying here, I know for a fact he'll make sure I'm not staying here too. And with the way she looks right now, that might be the safest course of action.

"How's school, Brendan?" Peter asks. "You gonna graduate on time?"

Brendan shrugs as if it doesn't matter when most of my salary is what's paying his goddamn tuition. "I don't know. Don't see myself using that degree anyway."

"Oh?" asks Peter. "Why's that?"

"I got a buddy who's trying to line us up jobs with a bike tour company next summer."

I feel my blood begin to boil. "Bike tours?" I ask. "If you're going to piss away your time, why don't you piss it away by helping around here?" *Jesus, I sound exactly like my father,* bitter and demanding and unfair. I hate it and yet I'm still angry.

Brendan laughs. *Laughs.* "Right, because working on a farm is just as rewarding as biking through Europe."

Even before Olivia, I'd have been angered by his response. But now I'm enraged, and it has far less to do with the farm than it does the fact that he has choices. If he wanted to, he could take Olivia out tonight. He could sit across from her in a restaurant and feast on the sight of her in that dress and wonder how the hell he got so lucky. He could be the one who takes that dress off of her when they get home. And most importantly, he could be the one to follow her when she leaves here next year.

I want those things. I want them so badly that when I imagine them, the way I am now, I feel a little unhinged. I lower my head, thinking about the climbs I'll never climb and the girl I'll never have, and worry I'm going to explode in a fit of rage, right here, at the unfairness of it all.

Brendan says something I don't catch and he and Olivia exchange a look. He looks at her like he knows things, as if he's privy to her secrets. If he ends up with her, I won't be able to fucking stand it. I won't.

I hear my text tone chime across the room just as we're finishing up and practically leap from the table. I just need to get away from all of them for two seconds, away from the idea of Brendan with Olivia, or *anyone* with Olivia, before I lose it.

I walk slowly to the other room with my phone, checking the text mostly for show. It's from Jessica, her tone breezy as if Tuesday night never happened. She wrote several times yesterday, asking if we could talk, which I ignored. I assumed she'd gone to Denver, but nope. Her text now says she's on her way here. *I have a little gift for your mom*, she says, *and then maybe the two of us can have a chat.*

And here I thought my evening couldn't get any worse.

50

Olivia

Will's been weird all through dinner. He seems angry, though at whom I'm not sure. And I'm a little angry at him too. Or actually, I'm just hurt. I knew getting dressed up would change nothing, but I thought maybe ... I don't know what I thought. Will is as blind to me in a dress as he is to me in anything else, and it shouldn't come as a surprise.

"Jessica's coming over," he sighs as he comes back to the table. "Apparently she got you a gift, Mom."

The whole time he says it he's looking at me, as if I'm a live grenade.

"What's the matter?" I ask.

He runs a hand through his hair. "When we broke up, she made some accusations involving you."

Every head in the room turns to me. It's not their intention, but it makes me feel like I'm at fault, and I wish I hadn't come. I rise. "I'll just go home."

"No," says Dorothy hastily, "absolutely not. You're not running off just because Jessica got the wrong idea."

"There's not time anyway," Will says. "She'll be here any minute now."

"I'll go to the stables," I say, heading for the door. "I can groom the horses a bit."

"You're in a dress," Will objects, but I'm already out the door, and I want to be, because I shouldn't have come in the first place and I don't know why it's taken so long for me to get that. I wanted to be here, yes, and I wanted to make Dorothy happy. But more than anything I wanted time with Will, one more chance for him to change his mind. And of course he's not going to, but now, because of me, Peter will be aware something is amiss. And God only knows what Jessica will say when she gets here. She isn't a stupid girl—she'll look in Will's room and see my stuff. She'll notice my plate on the table or see my facewash in the bathroom and then she'll make trouble for no reason.

Brendan catches up with me as I near the stables. It's nice of him but I'm really just coming here to lick my wounds, and I prefer to do that in private. "You don't need to come," I tell him. "You were still eating."

"It was worth it to watch my brother's head explode when I left," he replies. "Besides, you need to tell me what the hell is up with Peter and my mom."

I find myself fighting a smile. "It's pretty obvious what's up, isn't it?"

"Yeah, but how long has it been going on?" Brendan asks, aghast. "And what does Will say about it? I mean, Peter's his boss. That's got to be weird."

As unhappy as I am, I laugh. "I think Will doesn't have a clue, shockingly enough."

Brendan shakes his head. "That's not shocking at all. His head is totally up his ass about his own feelings, so why wouldn't they be about Mom's?"

I thought I wanted to be alone but I realize, as Brendan talks, that this is exactly what I needed: to not feel like an outcast or a charity case. And maybe I'm still both those things, but at least I've got company.

I grab the brush and begin to groom Trixie while Brendan lies there comfortably, watching. "You could help, lazy ass."

"I could," he replies, "but that would take work away from you, and I know how you love it. Besides, what endearing nickname would you give me if Lazy Ass no longer fit?"

"I can think of plenty," I reply. "Believe me."

"I'll have you know I'm extremely dedicated to things I care about."

I raise a brow. "Oh, is that right? Like school?"

He grins. "Let's not get carried away."

Voices approach. Jessica's high voice, her dumb fake giggle. Will's low rumble. Brendan and I glance at each other.

"This is bad," I whisper.

For once Brendan's not smiling. He might even look as worried as I do.

Jessica walks into the stables and her eyes narrow on me with a degree of malice even *I* am not accustomed to.

Will walks in behind her with his jaw rigid. "Jessica insisted on coming out to say hi to Brendan."

"I knew *you'd* be here," Jessica says to me.

Brendan steps forward and pulls me against him, his arm wrapped around my waist. "Do you have a problem with my girl-friend, Jessica?"

"Your *girlfriend*?" she asks. "Since when?"

He glances at me. "How long has it been, baby? It was that first night I made you sneak out the window? Four weeks? Five weeks?" His story rings true because, I suppose, it is true. Not a word about it is a lie, but then he failed to mention that absolutely nothing happened.

"Yeah, about five," I agree.

"Bullshit," says Jessica.

"You don't believe me?" Brendan asks, and then he turns me

toward him at the waist and presses his mouth to mine. He holds me there tight, not letting me pull away, opening my mouth with his tongue, grabbing my ass as he does it. It goes on way longer than it needs to, and I stagger a little when he finally lets me go. He gives me that sidelong grin of his and slaps my ass for good measure.

Jessica turns on her heel and storms out. Will stands there a second longer and there's something in his face now aside from anger. He looks hurt. So hurt that I want to run after him as he turns to follow her out, which is insane, given how many damn times *he's* rejected *me*.

I lean back against the pillar that stands between the stalls. It feels as if something has shifted, has been made unstable. "You shouldn't have done that."

Brendan shrugs. "I may have just saved his job. It'd be worth it even if I didn't. Did you see his face?"

I raise a brow. "Why do you enjoy torturing him so much?"

"That's just what brothers do. And besides, he needs someone to light a fire under his ass."

"I think maybe you ought to find a better way to do what brothers do," I sigh, picking up the grooming brush I dropped when he attacked me. "Like coming back to help for a while after you graduate."

"Help?" he says. "Why? Will's got it under control."

I look at him in disbelief. "Do you really think that, Brendan? He's working two jobs to keep you in school. Your dad left so much debt they can't even afford full-time help anymore. Will doesn't want you to know, but this place is a sinking ship and you're swimming away as fast as you can while he bails water."

He looks stricken. "Great. So he's doing all that and he thinks I'm trying to steal his girl on top of it."

"I'm not his girl," I counter.

I hear noise outside and my head raises just in time to see Will coming at us, looking only at Brendan.

"Oh fuck," mutters Brendan and seconds later Will's fist is airborne, connecting with Brendan's jaw. Brendan takes the hit, stumbling backward.

I still haven't emerged from my shock when Will grabs my wrist and pulls me outside the stables. "What the fuck was that?" he demands. "Are you dating him?"

My jaw drops. "I can't believe you just punched him. And of *course* we're not dating."

"No? Then why the fuck did you let him kiss you?"

"What choice did I have?" I cry back. "He lied to save your ass and I went along with it. You should be grateful."

He presses me to the wall, pinning me there with his hands at my shoulders, his face an inch from mine and angrier than I've ever seen him. "Well, I'm not," he snaps. "So don't do it again."

He is solid muscle as he presses against me, and the anger inside me is morphing to something else, something hot and liquid and weak. I can feel his breath against my mouth, his angry eyes registering the difference in me just as I register it in him. And then his mouth descends, crushing mine beneath his, pulling me into him with his hands tight on my waist.

There is no uncertainty, no hesitation. There's something urgent, almost desperate in it, and I am senseless to everything except for him. His mouth, his tongue, the rasp of his breath, his hands beneath my dress, sliding along my thighs.

I've never wanted anything so much in my life and it's too much to take in, to memorize. His soft mouth and the rasp of unshaven skin and his smell and his warmth. It's too much, too good, and yet not close to being enough.

He pushes away from me suddenly, wide-eyed. "Oh God," he breathes. "I'm so sorry. I can't ... This should never have happened. I'm sorry."

My stomach bottoms out as he walks away. I want to chase him down and refuse to let him leave like this again. I want to slide to the ground and weep. I'm so angry and sad and turned on, all at the same time, that I have no idea how to react.

But most of all, I'm stunned.

Will kissed me.

Will kissed me like it was something he couldn't live without. As if he was suffocating and I was oxygen.

He kissed me as if I wasn't optional.

I'm still leaning there when Brendan walks out a moment later, rubbing his jaw. He looks at me, in my very obvious state of dishevelment, and grins. "I knew it would work."

51

Will

I return to the house and sit at the table, not even trying to disguise what I feel. It's pointless anyway.

"I guess things didn't go well with Jessica," my mother says, looking at my face.

"No, not really," I sigh.

I may have avoided getting into trouble with Peter, but Jesus, what a fucking disaster this day's turned out to be. And as much as I want to blame everyone around me—Brendan, Olivia, Jessica, even Peter—the problem is me.

My mother pours coffee and chats with Peter while I take inventory of the situation. I just kissed the girl I *coach* while my boss was waiting inside the house. I didn't care that it was wrong in a thousand ways and couldn't go anywhere or mean anything, that it would only create more problems to be solved and more memories to be forgotten. I just didn't care. I wanted her and for a second, before I finally came to my senses, I planned to have her, right there against the back wall of the stables with my brother a few feet away.

And I still want all of those things, just as much as I did.

My mother asks if Brendan and Olivia are on their way back. My eyes shift to hers for only a moment, trying to hide my thoughts. For all I know, Olivia's not even going to come back to the house. "I'm not sure."

My mother hesitates for only a moment, reading something in my answer and then turning back to Peter. The two of them seem to have an endless stream of things to talk about, things I didn't even know they had in common. He's in her book club, which I'd always thought was some female thing, and their mutual friend Tina, apparently, drinks too much wine and thinks her husband is having an affair. I guess I should have realized my mom had a life outside of us and the farm, but it's weird to realize that her outside life overlaps to the extent it does with my boss's. I don't especially like it, but it's coming in handy right now, when I'm on the verge of losing my shit.

Brendan and Olivia walk in a few minutes later. I should be worried about what they'll say, or about how mad my mom's going to be when she hears I punched Brendan, but honestly all I can do is look at Olivia. With her hair messed up and her lips kiss-swollen she only looks more beautiful to me. I can't believe that I did what I did. And I also can't believe I stopped.

"My God, Brendan!" my mother cries. "What happened to your face?"

He shrugs, taking a quick look at me. "Got hit by a falling rake. It's cool. I should probably be more careful with shit that's not mine."

Olivia doesn't meet my eye once, and I wonder what that means. Maybe she's mad at me for walking off the way I did. Or maybe she's mad at me for kissing her in the first place, though I find that difficult to believe. When I remember the way her whole body arched into mine, her sharp inhale as my mouth moved to her neck, I know it was mutual.

∾

PIE IS SERVED. Surprisingly, we manage to get through dessert without me assaulting anyone or violating NCAA regulations.

"I'm going to head home," I announce once we've finished cleaning up, giving my mom and Olivia a quick glance to silence any objections.

Peter and I walk out to our cars at the same time. "Will—" he begins, and then he trails off. Finally, he shakes his head and settles a hand on my shoulder. "You've grown into a fine man. I know I can trust you."

And here I thought I couldn't feel any worse.

∾

I GET BACK to the farm late, when I know they'll all be asleep, and I'm back out the door the minute the sun's up. Yes, I'm avoiding her. It doesn't feel like I have a choice. Right now some gate I've had shut tight, on lockdown, is swinging wide open just waiting for her to walk through.

The mechanic arrives to fix the combine. The whole ride out to the field he's telling me some story about a seed separator, and I'm hearing that small hum in Olivia's throat as she responded, remembering how it felt to run my hands up her thighs.

I'm avoiding Olivia because I'm weak. Because the worst part of me wants her to be the one to pursue it, to not take no for an answer, and somehow absolve me of guilt. Except unless she tied me down—a possibility I'm *definitely* going to imagine later—it's entirely on me. And I can't do that to her, or to Peter.

My mom takes the golf cart out later and brings me lunch. "Looked like you were never planning to come back in," she says.

I shrug. "Lots out here to get done."

"There's almost nothing to be done out here that can't wait," she replies. "So why don't you tell me why you punched your brother and are spending the day out here hiding?"

I should have known she'd never fall for Brendan's 'I got hit by a rake' story. I run a hand through my hair and release a heavy sigh. "He kissed Olivia," I tell her. "He said he was just trying to cover for me with Jessica, but he didn't have to take it that goddamn far."

She looks at me and shakes her head. "Will," she says, "you're so in love with that girl you can't see straight. Something has to change or this is going to turn ugly fast."

My temper flares. *Something has to change.* I'm so sick of hearing that. "What can I possibly change, Mom? I can't quit. We can't afford it. I could probably get her a scholarship with another school. Now that she's winning, I could probably get her in a D1 school, but I'm not uprooting her like that when she only has three semesters left. Plus, I can't even imagine what it would be like knowing she's off in some new city and there's no one to stop her—"

"What if Peter tried to find you a position somewhere else at the school?"

"I still wouldn't be allowed to date her. It's all pointless anyway. She's leaving here after graduation and I'm not."

She cocks her head to the side and sucks in a cheek. "I wouldn't give up on everything just yet," she says softly. "These things have a way of working out when they need to."

She, of all people, should see there's no room for optimism in our situation. "Nothing's worked out for me in a long time, Mom. And I don't see a lot of point in hoping that's going to magically change."

"Well, we'll worry about that later. In the meantime, come back and take that girl climbing. She's working herself to the bone trying to keep busy and the last thing she needs is more work."

"I figured she was busy being entertained by *Brendan*," I say snidely.

"Your brother loves you," she replies. "I know he's got a strange way of showing it, but I think he's trying to help."

Olivia is pissed. She doesn't even look at me as I approach, and I can tell by the rigidity of her stance that it's intentional. She has her guard up again, the way she did when she first arrived, as if she expects to be hurt. I hate that, but I can't exactly fix it either.

"Let's go climbing," I say. She wants to stay mad, but she wants to climb more. I can see it in her face as she reluctantly agrees.

We don't say much on the drive. Maybe she's waiting for me to begin, to explain. Or maybe the truth is so obvious that neither of us feels the need to address it.

As we turn left on the highway, she looks toward me. "This isn't the direction we normally go."

"Yeah, I figure you're ready for a bigger climb."

She almost smiles, and it's the first glimpse of happiness I've seen on her face today. "Are you *actually* admitting I've done something well?"

I give her a half smile. "Nah, just admitting you're not quite as terrible at it as you were."

"Terrible?" she scoffs. "You're gonna eat your words, asshole."

When we arrive, the doubts sink in. I've chosen a really difficult, technical climb and for all the wrong reasons. I was looking for something hard enough to silence the awkwardness between us, put it on the back burner, but now I'm worried I may get her killed in the process.

"I was kidding before," I tell her. "You've done really well so far, but now that I'm looking at it I don't know if this is a good idea."

"Feel free to wuss out," she says over her shoulder. "I'm climbing it."

Fuck.

Someone has already established the route, but I don't necessarily trust it, so I go up first, checking the bolts to about the halfway point, which is as far as I'm letting her climb. I hang my weight off each one to assure myself they can hold hers. When I'm satisfied, I climb back down and grab the ropes.

"Your goal today isn't to hit the top," I tell her. "It's just to get some practice dealing with these kind of angles. There are a couple moments when you're going to feel like you're leaning backward. Just know that I've got you, okay? If you don't have the grip strength yet, you can just slide back down."

She rolls her eyes, as cocky as ever. "I've got the grip strength," she says. It should irritate me, but instead, I feel a shot of lust so strong that my fist tightens around the rope in response.

It doesn't go away as I watch her begin to scale the cliff face. She goes at it like she's on the attack, and something about her intensity makes me long for a whole lot of things I can't have.

She scrambles to the mid-point far faster than I imagined she could.

"That's good!" I shout up to her. "Come on back down."

She looks down, arching a single eyebrow. "Right. After you said I was terrible, you think I'm giving up halfway?"

Shit. I didn't bank on her not listening to me and why the hell *wouldn't* I bank on it? When has she *ever* listened to me? "I didn't say you were terrible," I shout up to her, "but seriously, Liv, the climb gets harder and you've got to be tiring out. I haven't checked the bolts above where you are right now either. Don't be stupid."

"The next time you don't want me to act stupid," she calls back, "don't make the grave error of telling me I'm terrible at something."

She resumes her climbing, going past the midpoint, and all I can do is watch. She's still safe at the moment, not far above the last bolt I checked, but not for long. I have no idea who established this route and how long ago it was. For all I know, a good breeze could knock them loose. I wish to God someone were here so I could hand off the rope and scramble up after her, but I'm stuck watching her, angrier than I've ever been.

"Olivia, stop!" I demand as she clips onto the new bolt, but she ignores me. Exhaustion has set in too. There's a strain I can see in her hands and shoulders that wasn't there before, and I'm not sure if she's doing this to punish me, but it's fucking working. I struggle to think of some way to make her stop while at the same time I marvel at her. Sometimes her grace and agility seem unnatural, and I wish … Fuck. I wish a whole lot of things and not a single one of them will ever happen.

"Come down now!" I finally bellow. "I'm serious, Olivia. Now! You're too tired and you're going to get hurt."

She ignores me.

"I'm never taking you climbing again if you keep going!" I threaten in desperation.

"I'm never climbing with you again anyway, asshole!" she shouts back, and I hear that wounded thing behind her anger. "Who the fuck do you think you are anyway? You kissed me and then you just ran off like I was going to stalk you or something."

"Olivia, that's not why I ran. Please, come down and we'll discuss it."

That's when it happens, when her hand slips above her and she starts to fall. I watch her progress through my worst nightmare, falling, screaming, the first bolt ripping out of the mountain under her weight and sending her hurtling downward. I'm frozen, so terrified that all I can do is watch, knowing if the second bolt doesn't hold, she'll die. It will be too great a fall and her weight will pull out the bolts beneath or she'll swing into the cliff face like a wrecking ball.

It can't take more than two seconds, but it is the longest,

slowest two seconds of my life waiting to see if the bolt holds, the bolt I didn't secure for her.

The rope goes taut as it pulls against the bolt, and it holds, but the momentum sends her swinging against the face of the cliff anyway. For a moment, I'm speechless. I can't find the words to ask if she's injured. It's been a long time since I've prayed but, in that millisecond, I pray as fervently as anyone ever prayed for anything.

"I'm okay!" she shouts down to me as if she knows.

My heart is still in my throat. "Just hold still. I'm going to lower you down."

"I'm okay," she says again. "I can climb."

"No," I reply, my voice far too harsh. "Don't even think about it."

52

Olivia

I'm bruised and my heart is still beating fast enough that I can't believe it doesn't just explode as Will lowers me. He's going to yell at me for climbing after he told me not to and he was *right*, damn it.

As he lowers me to the ground, I brace for a lecture. Instead, his arms are around me before I've even hit the ground. His front is pressed so hard to my back that I can feel his heart racing, just as fast as mine.

He buries his face in my hair. "Jesus Christ. You scared the shit out of me."

"I'm sorry," I begin, turning toward him. "You were right and I—"

Something in his eyes makes my stomach clench the way a flower contracts before it bursts open. His mouth lowers and captures mine, silencing my gasp of surprise. It's a heedless kiss, one that holds nothing back and shuts down my brain entirely.

"I thought you were going to die, Olivia," he growls. "If you ever do that again, I'll kill you myself."

His hands cup my ass to pull me tight against him. Desire for him coils in my belly, makes me strain to be closer to him as his hands slide into my shirt, spanning my back, pressing his fingertips to my overheated skin. His hand runs from my waist to my breast, cradling the weight in his hand and his exhale shudders against my lips, making me arch against him in a silent demand for more. More pressure, more contact, more skin.

"We've got to stop," he groans, but his mouth is still on my neck, his hands sliding up, beneath my bra.

I reach between us, snaking my hand into his waistband. He inhales sharply as my hand slides down to wrap around him, and not that I'd expected any differently, but there's a lot to grasp. "Olivia," he hisses. "I ..."

I run my hand over his length, loving the way his whole body jolts when I do it, his eyes squeezing shut.

"Oh fuck," he says. "Stop. We have to stop."

I ignore him, running my thumb over the tip of him, slick and swollen and ready.

The air catches in his throat even as he grabs my wrist to stop me. "Please," he begs, resting his forehead against mine, his voice a harsh whisper. "I'm not sure I've got enough self-control to stop if this goes any further."

If he's under the impression that will discourage me, he doesn't know me very well. "Good."

His lips press to my hair and he pulls back. "Jesus, I don't know what I'm doing anymore," he says. "If things were different ... but they're not. Nothing's changing. Nothing's going to make this okay. We both know that. I've tried so hard to do the right thing and then this shit happens, like you falling and Brendan kissing you, and I just lose my fucking mind. I don't even know what to say. I'm sorry. I'm so sorry. Based on what's happened, I should be driving straight to Peter and handing in my resignation, and I can't even do that."

I want to be angry at him right now but I can't. He looks so torn, so guilty. Will wants to help all of us. He wants to save me, he wants to see Brendan get through school, he wants to save the farm and give Peter a winning season and do the right thing by everyone, and I'm the one making it impossible, making him put it all at risk.

I tell him I understand. I ignore, for the time being, the part of me that doesn't. Because if he really cared enough, he'd just ask me to wait.

THAT NIGHT I climb into bed knowing that it's my last night in this house for a long time, possibly forever. It has to be that way, if only for my own sanity. Dorothy, Brendan, the farm—none of these things are in my future. Nor is Will, and that's the part that kills me. He cares—just not enough. And somehow that's almost worse. Because I'd have waited a decade for him if he'd just asked.

My chest aches, my throat goes tight. "Don't you dare cry," I hiss. I push it back down, that sadness. I'm not going to cry over Will.

I'm not going to cry about anything.

My mom calls me her early bird. "Please go back to sleep, baby," she'll murmur when I climb in her bed in the morning. So it's weird to find Matthew up before me, standing in the doorway.

"Dad's home," he says quietly.

"Oh." My stomach drops.

My father was gone for a while this time, long enough that I started to feel like I could take a deep breath again. Long enough I almost forgot what's it like to be scared when we wake, wondering how things will go when we get downstairs.

We walk into the kitchen together, sitting at our places in silence while my mother finishes putting breakfast out. I know immediately when I sit that this is not one of the good days. He has that look, that awful stillness. Today, the solid ground we use to edge around him will be a tightrope.

We begin to eat, silent and tense. My mother's face is drawn, but he ignores her, ignores all of us. He doesn't eat, but instead, opens bills, one after the other, growing angrier and angrier. I feel a tightness in my arms and chest as if I'm being squeezed in from all sides.

And then he holds one bill longer than the others. The air in the room seems to compress around him while we wait. "What is this?" he asks my mother, holding the bill in front of her face. His quiet voice is bad, far more dangerous than his loud one.

I can smell the fear coming off of her as she answers. "Daisy was having seizures," she says, her voice too faint, showing weakness. She shouldn't show weakness—even I know that. My father can smell it, can smell fear, the way a predator can smell blood.

And he reacts the same way.

"I didn't ask you what the fuck was wrong with the dog. I asked you what the bill's for."

"The medicine," she whispers. "The vet said she needed it or they'd get worse."

I'm only five but I know she needs to stop talking, stop explaining, stop acting like she's done something wrong.

He says nothing. He holds still for a moment, and we wait for his hand to fly out, to send her sideways from her chair with a startled cry. But instead, he turns toward Daisy, curled in the corner of the room.

"Let me show you what we do with a sick dog," he says.

Daisy doesn't sense danger. She nuzzles into him as he reaches for her. Sometimes, just when I think a terrible thing is going to happen, it doesn't. And then I feel stupid for fearing it, as if I must have been crazy to expect things to go poorly. He cradles her in his arms and she relaxes. We all relax.

And then my father grabs Daisy's neck and twists.

She's still in his arms, her eyes open, unmoving. There is utter silence. I can hear my own pulse, nothing else. And then we begin to cry, a symphony of tears and pain and disbelief. My mother gasping, choking on her tears.

"Oh my God," is all she can say. "Oh my God oh my God oh my God."

"You killed her!" my brother weeps.

"Stop crying," my father says to Matthew. "And go dig a hole."

But Matthew ignores him, his face flat to the table, his whole body loose and boneless with grief. My father pulls his collar so his face comes off the table.

"I said stop your goddamn crying and go dig a hole!" he yells.

I stop crying so fast that I choke a little. I stop as if it will make up for the fact that Matthew cannot. Matthew's always been soft in ways I'm not, and it's the only thing about me that's ever made my father happy.

Stop crying, Matthew. You've got to stop. Look at me, *I plead silently.* You can stop just like I do. Look at me.

Even my mother has come to her senses. She grabs Matthew's hand and through her own tears urges him to calm down, to go on outside like my dad said. But he doesn't. He can't. His tears are a form of insanity, suicide, and he just can't stop.

I jump up so fast my chair falls behind me. "I'll do it!" I cry. "I'll do it!" My voice is hysterical with enthusiasm. "I can dig the hole!"

My father nods. "That's my girl. Glad someone in this family takes after me."

My brother looks at me. I see blame in his face, hatred. I did it for him, but suddenly I'm a monster now, just like my dad.

53

Will

Her screams wake everyone in the house.

I'm there first and seconds behind me my mother and Brendan arrive, huddled at the door, staring at us in shock.

"I dug the hole," she says, scraping at her throat as if she can't breathe. She gasps for air once and then again. "I dug the hole."

She's curled up in a ball, knees squeezed tight to her chest. I try to pull her toward me but her whole body has gone so stiff that nothing moves. "It's okay, Liv. You're just having a bad dream. It's okay."

"No," she says, choking again, grabbing her own throat. "It wasn't a dream. It was me. *I* did it. I dug the hole."

"Dug what hole?" I ask, trying to pry her arms apart.

"Where he buried Matthew," she says. "I dug the hole."

Her story is hard to listen to.

She tells it in bits and pieces, with her hands covering her face the entire time. How her father drove her down the road to dig the hole for their dog and found a spot in the woods. All day long she dug. There was a tree above her, raining down acorns at unpredictable intervals, and by the time he came to get her it was dark and she had small pinpoint bruises covering her arms. The next morning, Matthew was gone. Her father said he'd run away. When she finishes talking, she's crying so hard that she's gagging, and I wonder if she'd be better off if she could forget.

I stay beside her all night. She sleeps sporadically, always waking with a gasp as if she's just remembered all over again. It's just before dawn when she wakes again, staring at me with her glassy, unseeing eyes on the pillow we share.

"We need to talk to the police, Liv," I tell her.

It's the first time I've ever seen her look terrified. Even when she fell yesterday, it wasn't like this. "No." She shakes her head. "I can't."

"Olivia, your father killed him. You know he did. If he's still alive, he needs to be stopped."

"I *can't*," she says. "I just can't."

~

I leave her asleep in the morning and go back to the office. I find the detective's card tucked carefully into the right side of my desk calendar. Somehow I think I knew that it would be me, not Olivia, eventually making this call.

I report what occurred last night, and he tells me he'll need to interview her right away. "She's not going to talk to you," I sigh. "She's as scared of talking to you as she is almost anything."

"I still need to try," he says. "Secondhand information from you doesn't get us anywhere."

I blow out a breath, leaning back in my chair and staring at the ceiling. "Look, can't you just interview the other adults involved? At least try to confirm the story through her mother if you can find her?"

"Her mother's been dead almost fifteen years," the detective says, "so I don't think she's going to be much help at this point."

My chair hits the ground. "*Dead*?" I whisper. "Jesus. Olivia doesn't even know. She thinks her mother just abandoned her."

The detective gives an unhappy laugh. "Look, buddy. I don't know what stories this girl's been feeding you, or feeding herself, but she knows her mother is dead. She watched it happen."

I rest my forehead in my hands, feeling...blank. My brain is slow to catch up, but it's pretty easy to figure out how her mom must have died. "So ... was it her father? Is he in jail?"

"Not my case, but it looks like there was nothing to pin it to him. Olivia was the only witness and she claimed to have seen nothing. It's probably what saved her life, because if she'd talked, you can bet your ass he'd have come after her."

I feel something icy crawl along my back. "So if her father's still on the loose," I ask, "is Olivia even safe?"

"I think it's fair to say that as long as this guy isn't in jail, Olivia will never be entirely safe. Especially," he adds, "if she starts remembering."

~

I OPEN MY LAPTOP SLOWLY, unwillingly. A part of me, like a part of Olivia, doesn't want to know. Wants to continue believing the version of events she's created in her head.

It isn't hard to find articles about it once you know what you're looking for. Had I even once typed in her mother's name months ago it would have been the first thing I'd found. Is it really possible that Olivia hasn't? Yes. Something has warned her away from looking too carefully at anything for a long time, has assured her that she can't handle what she'll find out.

There's a photo in the first article, and it hurts to look at it.

Olivia, tiny and smiling beside her mother, who looked very much like Olivia does now. The article says she was stabbed forty-two times. Olivia ran nearly four miles in the dark and was found unconscious the next day, still bleeding from the wound on her back.

The night running. The scar on her back. The way she seems to black out when she's attacked. If I'd even tried to guess at the source, I'd never have come up with something quite this awful.

I CALL the nursing home once more. This time, I don't ask for Olivia's grandmother—I ask for her next-of-kin, kicking myself for not thinking of it before. Olivia was only sixteen when her grandmother was admitted. There's no way she'd have had the wherewithal or the funds to fly her grandmother to Florida and get her into a home.

They refer me to Olivia's great-aunt. A woman who doesn't appear to have lifted a fucking finger for Olivia, as far as I can tell. I'm pissed off before she's even picked up the phone, so it's a struggle not to blame her as I introduce myself. I explain what Olivia's remembered and the woman makes a noise of disgust.

"Well, it might have been nice if that girl could have told the police back then, wouldn't it?" she says.

I press the bridge of my nose between thumb and forefinger, trying to rein myself in. "She didn't remember anything until just now," I say between clenched teeth. "She's still under the impression that her parents abandoned her."

She clucks her tongue again. "That stupid story. Anya let her keep believing it, but let me tell you, I'd have put a stop to it right away. She knew good and well what happened. She nearly bled to death. You don't just forget something like that."

I swallow. "What story?"

"Oh. Olivia'd get so hysterical when people spoke about it

that everyone finally gave up. So Anya started saying 'when your mother went away' and they left it at that."

I'm so out of my depth at this point it feels like I'll never surface. "Is there anyone else I can speak to? Who did Olivia live with after her grandmother got sick?"

There is defensiveness in her silence. "You understand I couldn't take her in," she finally says. "I'm too old to be raising someone, especially someone troubled like that."

I brace myself for an answer I clearly won't like. "So who did she live with?"

"She just stayed in the house by herself. She was fine. Anya had been sick for a long time and Olivia was used to taking care of both of them. She was better off on her own anyway."

She's still sputtering, making excuses, when I hang up the phone. And then I stare out the window, seeing nothing.

It's so much worse than anything I could have imagined. I wanted to protect her, I wanted to help her open some doors and let light into the places she closed off. Instead, I may have opened a door that should have stayed closed.

It's time to come clean before I do more damage.

TELLING PETER ABOUT OLIVIA'S nightmares, what the police said, and how I've been stopping her from running at night all leads to the somewhat obvious fact that Olivia and I have been sleeping under the same roof.

"Will," he groans, rubbing his eyes. "I'm gonna pretend you didn't just say that, okay? Because if you tell me you're sleeping under the same roof, I have to tell you to stop, and we both know you're not gonna. So I'm going to pretend you never said it."

I give him a small nod to mask my surprise. Peter's not the kind of guy who's comfortable with ethical violations. I can't believe he's letting this slide. "So what do we do?" I ask.

"I'll see if I can find a specialist, because this obviously isn't the kind of thing one of us should be pushing her to remember," he says. "In the meantime, don't tell her anything. She's got the Cooper Invitational next weekend. Let's just get her through that, maybe even finals, before we open another can of worms."

I sigh, agreeing with him even if it doesn't feel right. Olivia's had nothing but bad breaks all her life. Telling her the truth right now could destroy her chances next week, and she's not asking for the truth. She's asking for a shot.

So I'm going to do whatever it takes to give it to her.

54

Olivia

When I wake, Will is gone.

I sit up, pressing my knees to my chest, resting my head against them.

I helped bury my brother. How did I not put it together for so long? How did I convince myself he was alive? And if I managed to forget about my father killing Daisy, about digging the hole... what else have I forgotten? My head feels like the creepy basement of a haunted house—best left unexplored, evil lurking in every dark corner. I'm scared of what else might be in there, waiting.

And I wonder if Will is scared of it too.

When he returns to the house, something has changed. He's kind, but he's also guarded in a way he wasn't before. I suppose if I'm wondering what else I've done and who else I've hurt, it's unfair to be mad at him for wondering it too. But it's clear that if I ever had a chance of convincing him to care enough about me to make something work, it's gone now.

∼

OVER THE NEXT WEEK, the whole team still practices together, but only three of us even have a reason to train until after winter break is over and it's obvious. Most of the team is phoning it in and just barely. Will doesn't look at me once without guilt on his face, and I don't look at him once without seeing what I will never have. That same ambivalence I felt the morning of the last meet, as if nothing matters and nothing ever will, still weighs me down. Running was once everything because I'd never had anything better. And I still don't have anything better, regardless of what I might have hoped, so I really need to pull it together by Sunday. After the final practice of the week, Erin hands me a bag of cookies.

"Here," she says. "They're good luck."

"What makes them good luck?"

She shrugs. "Nothing, but it was either that or my good luck underwear, and I figured you didn't want that."

I grin. "Yeah, I'm pretty sure that good luck underwear is non-transferable."

She gives me a hug. She's a hugger. I guess I've gotten used to it. "We love you whether you win or not, Finn," she says. "And if you haven't figured that out yet, you're an idiot."

∼

THERE ARE nine of us flying to Oregon for the Cooper. Peter with Dan Brofton, and two others from the men's team, plus Will, me, Nicole, Betsy, and Dorothy. A regulation requires a female chaperone anyway, so all of her costs are covered by the program.

We arrive in Portland late Saturday afternoon and are given our room assignments. I'm with Dorothy, of course.

"Still need a chaperone I see," mocks Betsy. "Right up until the last minute."

"It seems to work for her, though," says Dorothy pointedly, "since she came in first the last time I roomed with her. Maybe I should chaperone *everyone*."

Damn, I laugh to myself. *Dorothy has claws. No wonder we get along so well.*

We all eat together. Peter and Dorothy sit at one end of the table. They talk easily, eat off each other's plates without asking. They seem like they've been together forever.

"Who out of this handsome bunch are your kids?" the waitress asks them.

Peter grins. "All of 'em."

A question, confusion, crosses Will's face then. A moment of insight he blinks away. For someone who's normally pretty perceptive, he's shockingly slow to pick up on this. That or he just refuses to.

After Dorothy lies down, I go to the other bed in his room and stretch out. He's getting stuff ready for the morning and doing his level best to pretend I'm not here. It pisses me off.

"It's the last meet," I say, rolling to face him. "You gonna miss me?" My tone is playful, but my meaning is not.

He glances at me, his eyes darting to my stomach before they return to my face. "Your shirt is riding up," he says hoarsely.

I glance down and shrug. "I'm sure two inches of skin won't kill you. Answer the question." I run my finger over my lip and his eyes focus there. He looks like he wants to take a bite of something.

He returns to his packing. "It's not like I won't still see you," he says. "You'll stay with us over break, right?"

I sigh and sit up, swinging my legs over the edge of the bed. Here I go again, trying to make this more than it is. "Why?"

He sets the First Aid kit down and turns to me, his brow furrowed. "Because..." His jaw sets. "Because we want you there. Because you're important to my family."

I rise, crossing the room until we stand two feet apart. "And that's all?"

"Liv," he groans. "It's all you're allowed to be."

That ache in my chest, the one that never quite leaves, blooms again like a fresh bruise. I'm not sure how many times I'll have to get the same answer before I stop asking. "That," I reply, walking past him to my own room, "is why I'm not staying with you over break."

55

Olivia

Peter's got us all gathered in a group the next morning, offering the same speech he always offers. I like him, and his words might even do me some good, but today I'm too nervous to hear a word.

I felt okay when I woke up—nervous, as always, and unable to eat, as always, but okay. It was only when we got to the field that it started to fall apart. The air is cold, but it can't account for the chill that seems to climb under my skin.

"Something's wrong," I tell Will. "Something's off."

"Nothing's off," he soothes. He reaches out to touch me and stops himself, letting his hand fall. "It's just nerves."

"No, this is different. I feel sick," I tell him. "I think I'm going to throw up."

"You're not sick," he says firmly. "Don't do this to yourself. Or go ahead and do it to yourself. But you know once you're running it'll pass."

I nod, but this time, I'm not convinced. Maybe it's just my failure at the last meet, but I don't think it is.

The women are called to the line. I taste metal in my mouth as we wait, and then it's in my stomach, climbing through me. There's some issue with the timing equipment, and the lot of us twitch and jerk nervously, knocking into one another. I'm worried if I get elbowed one more time, I'm going to take a swing.

At last the problem is fixed. The gun sounds and I take off too fast, trying to escape the chill that's climbing up my spine, the certainty that I will fail. I think of Will on the sidelines right now, how he's watching me and how his stomach is sinking because I'm doing just what I did at the last meet.

I force myself to pull back and let the other girls set the pace. I'm so agitated that it feels painfully slow, but as the distance increases I feel better, stronger, more certain. I even out, going head-to-head with some girl from Stanford. Everyone expects her to win, but I can hear the violence of her exhale, the rasp in her inhale. We aren't even two miles in and she's struggling, whereas I feel like I could run this pace all day long.

I break ahead. It's early, for me. A risk. Maybe I don't have another two fast miles in me, but today I want this. I want it for Will and Peter and Dorothy as much as I do myself, and I think it's possible I have it.

I hear the crowd at the finish long before I can see them, and I begin to sprint. The finish line comes into view, and the noise of the crowd rings so loud I can't hear my own breath. Their roar grows deafening as I break through the tape.

My heart is pounding in my ears. A cameraman from ESPN is running alongside me as I push forward, gasping for air, looking for only one face.

And then I find it.

Will breaks through the crowd and throws his arms around me.

"You did it, Liv," he whispers, his breath warm against my ear, his body wrapped around me. Winning a race like this was something I dreamed of my entire life. But this moment with him—it's the best part. It's the part I'll always remember.

He slowly lets go when Peter and Dorothy jog up. "19:22!" yells Peter. Meaningless to most people, but all of us get it. I was only five seconds off the 6K world record. Closer to it than anyone I've ever known.

I'm pulled through the crowd, congratulated and hugged by complete strangers.

Even Betsy is almost nice when she gets in. "19:22," she says, shaking her head. "I still don't like you, but holy shit that's fast."

"How does it feel to come within seconds of breaking the world record?" a reporter asks.

I give the answer I'm supposed to, tell her I'm shocked and thrilled, and that it's the best day of my life. And the whole time I watch Will, knowing I'd give it all up for him—my wins, the team, my future—if he only wanted me enough to take it.

WHEN THE AWARDS ceremony is over, we head back to the hotel. Dorothy's already packed and waiting in the lobby by the time I get out of the shower. I dress fast and am zipping up my suitcase when Will walks in, head down, hands in his pockets.

"Please reconsider about staying with us over break," he says quietly. "I swear on my life nothing will happen."

I laugh. The sound is sharp and unhappy. "You think I don't *want* anything to happen?"

He digs a hand through his hair. "I'm just saying that we can get past this."

I set my suitcase down and perch on the edge of the bed. "That's just the problem, Will. You *can* get past it. I can't. If you wanted me enough, you could have had me. Or you could have asked me to wait until I graduated. But you didn't, and you won't, and do you know how hard it is to have to look at you?" My voice grows raspy and I pause because I refuse to cry over him again. "To look at you and know that you made your choice and you didn't choose me?"

He flinches. "Olivia, it's not a matter of choosing." His voice is rough. "I don't have a choice."

"You do," I whisper. "It'd just be a little over a year. You could ask me to wait. You could ask me right now and I'd do it. Gladly. But you're not going to, are you?"

He closes his eyes and that muscle pops in his jaw. He says nothing.

I grab my suitcase and walk to the door. "That's exactly what I thought."

56

Will

"I went to see Olivia yesterday," my mom tells me.

It's been a long three days. I haven't seen or heard from Olivia once.

Three long days during which the same phrase plays on repeat in my head: *I lost her.*

It's not that I ever thought she'd be mine. I'd just refused to consider that there'd come a day when she wouldn't be. I thought I could steal all these moments from her: at my mother's house, on the track, climbing. Store them up as if they'd do me a damn bit of good once she's gone.

"How was she?" I ask.

"Just like you," she says, setting a laundry basket down on the couch. "Doing her level best to pretend she's okay when she's clearly not."

There's a *flatness* to her voice I dislike. "You sound like you're blaming me."

"I *am* blaming you, Will. You're in love with her. Have you even told her that?"

I push away from the table. After everything I've done wrong, I can't believe I'm finally doing the right thing and she's mad.

"It wouldn't do any good," I say through gritted teeth. "I can't be with her anyway."

She clenches a T-shirt tight in her hands. "Will, for God's sake. She's a junior. It's not that long until the student thing isn't even an issue."

My temple throbs. I've never thought of my mother as naïve or unrealistic but both words sit on the tip of my tongue. "Right. And then what? She comes and lives on some shitty farm, with no coach and no group to train with? Where she can't get endorsements and doesn't have the money to fly to big races? She gives up her future for *this*?"

"You can't know how things will play out," she argues. "That's over a year away."

"Mom," I say, rising to conclude this conversation, one I've had with myself many times. "I know the only two things I need to know: that I can't leave and she can't stay."

By SATURDAY NIGHT, the night of the banquet, I think I'd cut off a limb just to lay eyes on her again. I crave her like a drug. It won't solve anything and I don't care. I just want to see her.

I've spent the entire week arguing with myself, and each day I grow a little more desperate, my arguments growing wilder and less probable by the minute. *Maybe I could* is how every single thought begins, each one borne of desperation. *Maybe I could get a third job so I could fly out to see her. Maybe once Brendan's out of school I'll be able to afford it. Maybe she'll decide on her own that she doesn't want to run after college.*

It's weakness on my part and I just need to get through this banquet without giving into it. Thank God there's a bar.

My mother is already here, sitting with Peter. I have no idea how *that* happened. I could have taken her if she wanted to go so badly. I trust Peter, but I hope he's not getting the wrong idea about this.

I head to the bar. I'm going to need something, possibly a whole lot of something to make this experience palatable. I grab a beer and drink half of it before I even head to the section of the room reserved for the team.

I'm halfway there when my eyes meet Jessica's. I suppose she's here in some public relations capacity, although it's definitely the kind of thing she could have punted to someone junior to her. She's been leaving me tearful, angry voice mails every day since Thanksgiving. In roughly half the calls she tells me she misses me and wants to talk. In the other half, she tells me I'm going to be sorry I treated her the way I did.

She smiles wide and comes straight to me, throwing her arms around my neck and kissing my cheek. "Will!" she squeals. "It's so good to see you."

"Is it?" I ask, standing stiff, waiting for her to disengage herself.

She laughs, linking her arm through mine. "Just because we've broken up doesn't mean we can't be friends, silly."

I raise a brow. "I don't know, Jess. You said in that last message that my mother should have aborted me. I don't say that to most of my friends."

She waves it away. I wish she'd let go of my arm. "I was hurt, Will. You hurt me. But I'm okay now, really."

Uh huh. "Good. Well, I better go sit."

"Come with me," she says, pulling at my elbow. "I saved you a seat."

At that very moment, Olivia walks in. She's in a green silk dress that matches her eyes, pours over her curves, and reveals only a hint of cleavage while allowing you to imagine what you *can't* see too fucking easily. Her hair is straight tonight, falling over her shoulders and down her back, highlighting her long neck and the angles of her face.

As always, I seem to settle on her mouth. I don't know that I've ever seen her wear lipstick before and, for some reason, this opens an entire Pandora's box of fantasies. I want to see it smeared. To kiss her so hard that neither of us can breathe. To pull back and find that mouth ajar, panting, the lipstick a pink blur around the edges.

My God, I want it so badly I'm not sure how I'll get through the goddamn night without having it. That and all the things that follow it. My hands sliding that silk dress over her head, learning every inch of her the way I've dreamed about for months.

Except right now her eyes are focused on the point where Jessica's arm is linked with mine, and her expression—raw and wounded—is like a knife to the chest. I step away from Jessica, grabbing my drink and draining it.

"I'm sitting with my mom," I tell her firmly.

She looks from me to Olivia. Her eyes glitter. "I see what's going on."

"There's nothing going on," I reply, walking away. "With her or with you."

"Doesn't Olivia look gorgeous?" my mom asks.

My eyes dart across the room again. Her green dress shimmers, catches the light, catches on her curves. "She looks like she needs more clothes," I grumble.

"*I* bought her that dress," my mother says with a brow arched. "It fits her like a glove."

"Yeah, exactly," I retort. "That's sort of the problem."

My gaze is still on her, though. Moving up from her hips to her waist to her chest, back up to that mouth of hers. I picture it again, the lipstick smeared, her breathless under me.

And then a single hand cups her hip bone, visible through the thin silk, and I'm ejected from my fantasy at high speed.

My lust morphs into rage over the course of a single breath.

Evan. She came here with *Evan*. *Why the fuck is she with him? She said she wasn't interested. She said he wanted something serious. She said ...*

She said she wanted me, and I turned her away.

She's moving on, doing whatever she needs to get by. *The same thing I'm doing*, I think, as I rise to head back to the bar.

WHEN EVERYONE finally takes their seats, I discover that she and Evan are at the table on the other side of mine, giving me a painfully direct view of the two of them. He is physically incapable of keeping his hands to himself, and I'd love to relieve him of that problem. Whenever she stands, his eyes are on her, devouring her. He paws at her when she returns, jumping to pull out her chair but managing to get his fucking hands over approximately seventy percent of her body when he does it. And if he tries to look down her dress one more time, I'm definitely taking him out.

I go to the bar again and move from beer to whiskey. I don't normally drink much, but tonight's a special case. It's either this or I completely lose my shit in front of hundreds of witnesses.

Food is served which I can't taste. Awards are given out that I don't notice. She is more real to me than anything in this room or out of it, the only thing I can see.

No one knows her fears like I do. No one knows how fragile she really is, how sweet. They don't know that she cries in her sleep and that she curls her whole body up against me as if she'd like to crawl inside. But *I* know these things. And for all the fighting we've done, there aren't two people in this room as made for each other as the two of us. My world is constructed entirely of artificial rules about what I owe people—my father, my family, the school. But somehow it excludes the only thing that matters to me.

Her.

If it weren't for the goddamn farm and the school, she'd be here with *me* tonight.

I watch her say something to Evan and he nods, wrapping a hand around her waist and pulling her toward him as she begins to rise from her chair. He kisses her. It's just a small peck, nothing like what my asshole brother did, but that's when I'm fucking done.

"Enough," I say quietly as I stand.

I don't know what possesses me to follow her. I know, with every bone in my body, that it's the wrong thing to do. That I have no claim on her. But I saw that kiss, saw the look in his eye, the one that says he intends to leave with her soon, and I found myself on my feet.

She's halfway down the hall by the time I reach her. She looks over her shoulder warily when she hears me, but she is too late. I'm already there. I grab her elbow before she has time to react and pull her into a classroom.

She stiffens and pulls back, ready as always to fight. Squaring off, eyes flashing and hands on her hips. Seething before I've even said a word.

"You have no right to—"

That's when I cup her jaw and capture that mouth I've longed for the whole goddamn night.

57

Olivia

His mouth comes down on mine, obliterating my pathetic attempt to object. He seizes it thoroughly, with such certainty, as if he's spent his entire life practicing for this precise moment. His hands raking back through my hair, his tongue finding mine as he presses against me. His mouth moves over my neck, and he groans, a noise of both despair and satisfaction.

"You didn't want me a week ago but now you do?" I start to push back, but he holds me tight against him.

"I just don't want you stuck in a shitty small town when you graduate. It was never about not wanting you."

I know there are things I'm supposed to remember, other reasons why I'm supposed to object, but they escape me. I am only this—my body ripe and raw and overexposed, pain and pleasure at once. I've wanted this too long, his hands on my skin, my body pressed against his and his mouth creating a trail of kisses down my neck.

It's right.

I've known nothing in my life with such certainty as the fact that what's happening right now is all I'm capable of wanting, that nothing in the world matters more to me.

His hands move from my hips to my breasts, and then he pulls one strap of my dress down, trailing slow, open-mouthed kisses over my shoulder and collarbone, almost reverently. Nipping with his teeth and soothing it with his tongue. He pulls the dress down to my waist, unclasps my bra with a single hand. He cups my breasts, bringing his mouth to them in the same way, sharp and sweet at once and creating a need in me so intense that it borders on pain. I gasp and arch toward him, submitting entirely as my head falls backward against the wall.

He pulls back just enough to see my face. His eyes are such a vivid blue as he searches mine, looking there for something he desperately needs. Permission. He wants permission. As if I'd ever tell him no.

"Yes," I whisper. "Please."

"You're sure?" His voice is hoarse with desire.

And when I nod he pushes the dress over my hips and allows it to slide to the floor. His hands follow, skating over my hips, down my thighs, and I stand before him now in nothing but panties and heels.

"That fucking dress nearly did me in," he says, smoothing my skin as he kisses me again. He pushes against me, his suit against my bare skin, his erection pressed hard to my stomach, a quick pulse there as if he is desperate for friction.

He slides his index finger under the elastic of my panties. The moment he touches me, my whole body jolts. "Fuck," he hisses, squeezing his eyes tightly shut. "You're already soaked."

His finger slips back and forth, lightly, in torturous circles before it pushes inside me.

"Oh God," I whisper, my body bowing toward him. He adds a second finger and this time his groan is louder than mine.

"Jesus, Olivia," he growls. "You're going to be the end of me."

I unclasp his belt and unzip his pants reaching down to pull him from the confines of his boxers. He is thick and heavy in my hands, hissing as my fingers wrap around him, tugging gently. "Stop," he exhales after a minute. "I'm not gonna last if you do that and there are so many things I want to do first."

He pushes my panties down and lifts me up almost simultaneously, turning to deposit me on the table beside us. He kisses me once, hard. "Lie back," he commands.

He drops to his knees, spreading my legs so I'm displayed before him, the slide of his fingers making me arch off the table. Suddenly, his fingers are joined by quick swipes of his tongue.

"Oh my God," I gasp. "Will ... just—"

His mouth and tongue lick and brush and pull, creating tiny flames that begin there and spread all the way to my toes. I try to scoot backward, but his free hand clamps down on my thigh, holding me in place.

"I've dreamed about doing this every goddamn night for months, Olivia. So let me."

I can't even nod in agreement because suddenly everything inside me is swirling together, muddied, building so quickly that I can't tell where I am or where I'm going.

"Oh," I gasp. It's so insufficient, that word. This is completely uncharted territory for me, to cede control the way I am, to hand everything over and be so exposed to someone. It's so much pleasure it borders on pain, tearing sounds from my throat involuntarily. And then his fingers push inside me and I explode with a cry of ecstasy and surprise, arching against his mouth.

He doesn't pull back, but instead slides his hands beneath my legs and tugs me closer, buries his face to create wave after wave of something I never thought would happen in the first place.

When it finally begins to recede, when the small of my back rests on the table once more and I'm capable of speech, he finally stands, his face contorted with longing and triumphant at the same time.

"Holy shit," I breathe. I'd like to be more eloquent right now, but I've got nothing.

He leans over to kiss me and when he does I wrap my legs around his waist, bringing him against me so suddenly that he gasps in my mouth. "Olivia," he groans.

"Please," I whisper. It seems impossible for anyone to be more satisfied than I am right now, yet I still need the very thing he wants most, the thing he is so certain he shouldn't give.

He looks tortured and pulls back but I tighten around him, pressing him against me. "Don't even think about stopping right now."

He shifts his hips just enough that he is pressing right there, not inside me but mere seconds away from it. In a single pulse, he could be buried inside me. "Is this okay?" he asks, his voice tight. "Do we need ..."

"No," I beg. "Just do it."

He pushes in, barely. He's so thick that already I'm stretched to the point of pain.

He flinches, inhaling sharply. "Oh God, Liv," he whispers. "God, that's so good. Just give me a minute, or this is going to be over before it starts."

Finally, he moves once more, going slowly, a low noise deep in his chest as he finally shoves all the way in. "Are you okay?" he asks between clenched teeth.

I nod as I adjust to the size of him, pain still outweighing the pleasure. It's when he starts to withdraw that the margin shifts, that the pain recedes as a burst of pleasure crawls up my spine, sucking the air from my lungs. It feels *too* good, something so vast and all-consuming it can't possibly end well. I *never* finish this way but *oh my God...*

If it were ever going to happen, it would be now.

His next thrust is faster, more certain, but he stops entirely at my sharp inhale. "Did I hurt you?" he asks.

"No." I'd laugh if I were capable. He didn't hurt me. He

stunned me. His strokes come slow and rhythmic then, as he leans over, finding my mouth with the table bracing his weight, his arms taut.

"I've wanted this for so fucking long," he says, holding still inside me.

"Keep going," I beg. "Don't stop."

"Patience," he croons. "You have no idea how hard it is not to come right now."

I grab his ass and push upward, ignoring his warning, thrilling at the low grunt he makes as he bottoms out. "Liv," he growls, "goddammit." His hips jerk back and then forward, almost involuntarily. It's all I need.

I cry out, my neck craning back as it happens again, everything inside me bursting into color. He thrusts quick and hard, desperate now, and then stiffens with a single guttural noise as he pushes in one final time.

He falls against me, his mouth against my neck, his breath warm on my skin. It's closer than I've ever been to another person, and I would like to stay here, just like this, forever.

But after a moment he pulls away. I open my eyes, ready to beg him to come back, but the words die on my lips when I see the look on his face.

58

Will

I t's a little like waking from a dream. I imagine it's a little like when Olivia wakes from hers, a moment of wonder followed by a much more sickening moment of *what the fuck have I done?* She's still stretched out before me, and before I've even pulled out, I can feel that twinge, the growing impulse to do it all over again.

The best sex I've ever had and the biggest mistake I've ever made just occurred simultaneously. The guilt and astonishment twine around each other, leaving me unsure what I think or feel about anything. It was wrong. No matter what other considerations there are, I just slept with a student. I slept with someone who looked to me for guidance and protection, even if she'd never admit it was the case. She would argue that it was okay because she has feelings for me, but how can she possibly know? As fucked up as her life has been, and with all the ways she's needed to lean on someone this semester, how can she tell the difference between love and need, or between love and gratitude? She can't. Somewhere inside I knew that, and because I wanted her and I was jealous, I chose to ignore it.

She looks up at me and her smile fades. "What are you thinking?" she asks. There's dread in her voice. Her jaw hardens. "You regret it."

"Olivia," I sigh, pulling her to my chest. "It's not that. It was... amazing. I just need to figure this out."

"Figure what out?"

I bury my face in her hair. I don't want to be having this conversation with her. I wish there was a way I could just hold her and take her home and work this all out on my own later. But there's not. "What happens next. I mean, it shouldn't have happened. We both know that. I took advantage of—"

"No," she snaps, pulling away. "You did *not* take advantage of me. Are you really going to let the way it might look to everyone outside this room dictate whether or not it's okay?"

Except it's not *everyone outside this room*. It's me. I didn't do this after careful thought, after balancing my duty to her and the school with the things I want. No, I let my anger and my need obliterate every reasonable thought. I gave in to something I've exerted unholy restraint to avoid until now. And in doing so, I've let myself down and—far worse—I may have put her scholarship at risk.

I pull away, planning to reach for my boxers and my pants, which still hang mid-thigh, but grab her dress and bra off the floor first instead. The sight of her naked is getting me hard again already, and that's the last thing I need right now. "Please get dressed," I beg hoarsely. "I can't think straight when you're naked and we have to get back out there before someone notices we're gone."

She wrenches it from me. "So you want me to go back and continue my date with Evan like this didn't just happen?" she asks, clasping the bra and pulling the dress over her head.

No. *Fuck*. "Olivia, your scholarship and my job are both on the line here. I just … I've got to figure this out and do it before anyone else does. So what matters most is that we both get through the banquet like nothing happened."

"And then what?"

Her anger and her *fierceness* don't put me off in the least. They make me want to pin her down on the table and take her all over again. Jesus, I *need* to do it all over again. But not here. Back in my apartment, where we'll have time. And a bed. "Can we please just get through the next hour?" I ask, my voice harsher than I mean it to be. "Jessica is out there. My boss is out there. Hell, my *boss's* boss is out there. The most important thing either of us can do right now is act like nothing's wrong."

She slips her heels back on and moves to the door, her head high and her posture rigid. She's doing what I asked but I hate that she's leaving mad.

"Olivia, wait—"

"For *what*?" she demands. "You just fucked me on a table and now you're sending me on my way. What more could you possibly need to add to that?"

She walks off. By the time I'm dressed and back to the auditorium, she and Evan are gone, which is both a relief and a worry. My mother turns toward me when I sit. "Is everything okay?" she asks in a tone that clearly indicates she knows it's not.

I look at Olivia's empty chair. "I fucked up, Mom," I say quietly.

Her hand slides over mine just for a moment. "Then stop wasting time here and go figure it out."

How am I going to tell Peter what I did? How am I going to pay for Brendan's last semester with no income?

I could solve those issues by lying to everyone, but how will I live with myself if I do? How will I face Olivia every day knowing I sacrificed her for my mom and the farm and the school all over again?

There is no answer. I lie awake all night, alternately appalled at myself for my bad decision-making and reliving it in my head, wanting it again so badly that I find my hips pressing into the mattress.

It's nearly daylight when I give up on sleep and decide to do the one thing that has ever successfully cleared my head.

I go climbing.

In spite of my rustiness, I choose a difficult climb, knowing I need something so consuming that it will obliterate all other thought. The air is so cold that my hands are numb by the time I've got my gear on, but I scramble up anyway, hammering the first pin in, and moving higher. Twisting and straining, moving quickly until my shirt is sticking to my back and sweat begins to drip into my eyes. I clip into the next bolt and pull my fleece off, throwing it to the ground before I keep going.

I'm halfway up the mountain face when a single thought occurs to me.

I wish Olivia were here.

This was once my sweet spot, climbing alone, and now it's shifted and expanded to include her. It feels *empty* in her absence. The farm, my job, my *life* were once central but now are merely white noise that surrounds her.

I stall, clinging to a small handhold, only a single foot making contact with the rock, realizing that she isn't just a part of my life now. She is *all* of it. And even if I made a mistake, even if it means that I will gravely disappoint Peter and mess up things with the farm, I will find a way to follow her when she's done here.

Because of all the things in the world I love, that I have a duty toward, she is first.

And she is the one I won't give up.

59

Olivia

I told Evan I was sick.

It was easy enough to be convincing. I've never felt more ill in my life. I thought when Will came to me that things had changed. Sleeping with him was beyond anything I'd ever imagined. And then he opened his eyes and told me to return to my date. Said he needed to think. And that was the difference between us.

I did not need to think.

I *knew*.

And he should have too.

I don't sleep. I sit with my back pressed against the headboard. How can I possibly stay here now? I can't imagine three more seasons of wanting him, of seeing him daily and remembering that look on his face as I left.

There's a knock on the door. Despite everything, I throw it open assuming it's Will. Assuming he's made a different decision than the one he seemed to have made earlier tonight.

Jessica stands on my doorstep. Her mascara is smeared and

her dress has something spilled on it. She pushes right past me and in my shock I allow her to.

"I'd invite you in," I say, finding my voice, "but it looks like you already took care of that on your own."

"I *know*," she hisses, her eyes narrowed. "I know about you and Will."

Despite a lifetime of lies and bluffing, I'm not the one who stands to lose if this goes south, and that changes things. I try to look bored, but I have no idea if I'm succeeding. "There's nothing to know."

"I followed you!" she cries, her voice tremulous. "I saw him take off after you at the banquet and I followed him. And believe me, *neither* of you was quiet."

My heart begins to race. Already, though, I'm forming a defense. It's her word against ours. Her story is meaningless unless I back it up. "I have no idea what you're talking about," I reply. "I went to the bathroom. I don't know where he went."

"You lying little bitch," she says.

And then, taking both hands, she shoves me.

I feel that rage in the pit of my stomach, my father's legacy. For Will's sake, I push the darkness away. I can't be the thing to make this situation worse than it is. "I don't know how much you know about me," I say, digging my nails into my skin, "but I can guarantee that if you lay another finger on me, you'll regret it."

Her arms cross and she laughs angrily. "You'll be the one with all the regrets. Do you know how much dirt I have on him? I have photos of him dropping you off at your apartment at seven in the morning. You were drinking with him when you were underage. I witnessed that myself. I pulled the hotel bills—you had fucking adjoining rooms at your meets. Let's see how much he wants you when you're the reason he gets fired next week."

My stomach rolls. She has him cornered, and it's entirely my fault. All that's left is the truth and the weak possibility she can be reasoned with. "If you cared about him at all," I whisper, "you wouldn't think of threatening his job. You know they need that money."

She raises a brow. "And if you cared about him at all you'd leave him alone. Do you really think you're going to make him happy? Look at all the *problems* you have. Can you honestly say you're the kind of girl he should end up with? Raise kids with? Look at the way you've risked his career with all this bullshit. Is *that* love, Olivia?"

I want to lash out at her, but I can't deny the basic truth of what she's saying. Nothing about my arrival at this school has benefitted him. I can't possibly make him happy the way someone else can, someone pulled together and from a good family and, well, not crazy.

I feel like I'm standing at the cliff's edge and jumping is the only option left, so I exhale and prepare to jump. "What do you want?" I ask.

"Obviously," she replies, "I want you to leave."

60

Will

Peter is just pulling up when I get to his house.

Under normal circumstances, I'd find it odd that he was out and about so early, but right now I'm a little focused on my own shit.

He takes one look at my face. "Does this have anything to do with your long disappearance during the banquet?"

I raise a brow. "You seem to already know exactly why I'm here."

"Will, only an idiot could have looked at the two of you last night and not seen the truth." He unlocks his door and nods for me to come in. "I don't want you to tell me what happened. I imagine there's something, but if you tell me, then it changes the way I have to respond. You understand what I'm saying?"

I do. If I tell him we've slept together, then the university launches an investigation. My name will be everywhere. Her name will be everywhere. Her scholarship could get called into question.

I swallow all the admissions that sat on the tip of my tongue.

"I'm here to resign," I tell him. "I don't know how the hell I'm going to support my mom, but I'm no longer able to perform my duties as a coach."

He nods. "I accept your resignation. And speaking as your friend, not your boss, we will come up with another solution, okay? I can cover Brendan's spring tuition, and we'll find you something that pays nearly as well."

I shake my head. "We can't accept that. You've done too much for us as it is."

"We'll talk about that later. In the meantime, maybe you should go tell your mom the good news."

I scrub a hand over my face. "My mom? I'm hard-pressed to see how she'll think me losing my job is good news."

He gives me a half smile. "No, but you winding up with Olivia is. I get the feeling she's had her heart set on it for a while."

Yeah, I think. *She's not the only one.* I can't believe that after all these months of wanting Olivia and swearing to myself I can't have her it's all finally within reach. "I'll tell my mom later," I reply with a smile of my own, "but there's someone else I need to go see first."

~

I TEXT HER, but she doesn't reply.

I call, but she doesn't answer.

I knock on her door, but I get silence in response.

Now that the decision is made, now that I'm no longer her coach, waiting feels like an impossible burden. I want to begin. I want to tell her everything and promise I'll find a way to make it work. If she's even a fraction as willing as I am to make this happen, we'll succeed.

While I wait to hear from her, I go to my office and pack my stuff. Better to do it now, over the weekend, without witnesses. I'm not sure how my resignation is going to get played out, but everyone will be looking for the worst possible cause, and unfortunately, in this case, they'll be right.

I call her again, text her again, and get no answer. *Where the hell is she?* As the morning goes on without a word from her, my dread grows. I know she was upset last night but was she upset enough to give up on me entirely?

I go back to her apartment. When she doesn't answer, I grab the key under the pot and go in. When I do, it seems like all the air has left my body.

Because the furniture remains, but every last thing she owns is gone.

61

Olivia

The buses run pretty regularly to Denver. Before daylight, I was already past the perimeter of the city, moving away from the mountains I'd grown to love.

I'll give Jessica credit for being thorough. She made me leave right away and demanded I do so without explanation. She took my cell phone, just to be on the safe side.

She's assuming my absence is all she needs to win Will back, and who knows? Maybe it is.

In Denver, I call Erin from a pay phone. I gloss over the whole I-just-slept-with-our-coach part but tell her everything else—what Jessica has proof of and what she is threatening. I ask if her brother will let me stay with him in LA just long enough for me to find a job and save a little money. No, LA isn't where I want to end up, but right now I just need to get on my feet and I'd prefer not to do it in a women's shelter, where I'd get robbed or kicked out for fighting within a few days.

But the whole thing worries Erin. "What do I tell Will? I mean, you know he's going to ask."

He's not going to *ask*. He's going to *flip*. I can see it unfold and it makes me sick. The way he'll worry. The way he'll blame himself, and *call*, and go to my apartment to find me gone. "Tell him I got sick of living in a small town and that I thought my chances were better somewhere else."

"Why would he believe that?"

That one's easy. Because he said it himself.

~

THE BUS RIDE from Denver to LA is exactly twenty-two hours long.

I pretend I'm just going on a short trip because it's easier than thinking about the fact that I've left him behind for good. Does it matter anyway? Better to leave now than to spend the next fifteen months falling more deeply in love with someone I'm not going to end up with.

During one of the stops I call his work line, knowing it's late enough there's no chance he'll answer. My voice is breezy and careless as I tell him it was never going to work and that ECU is a waste of my time. I want to apologize, to ask him to tell his mother goodbye, but I don't because I'm about ninety percent sure I'll cry and ruin the whole charade.

And when I end the call, I *do* cry. I might never hear his voice again, and he and Dorothy will always remember me as an ingrate who took everything they offered and threw it in their faces without a backward glance.

On Monday morning, just as we're approaching LA, I get an email from a guy who says he represents Fumito—some fledgling Japanese shoe company—and wants to Fed Ex me a proposal. I write back and give him Erin's brother's address in LA. I just hope he lets me stay long enough to receive it.

I should be happier about the endorsement than I am. I mean, this is all I wanted, right? But the truth is that what I want even more is to be able to call Will right now and share the good news. Without that, it feels a little hollow.

62

Will

I t's my mother who holds it together while my life falls apart. One of us has to be sane here and it sure as shit isn't me.

It's my mother who sits beside me while I call Erin and Nicole and, finally, Evan. No one knows anything. Neither the school nor her landlord has heard a word.

And I have no clue who else I can even ask. All I can do is sit with my head buried in my hands, so fucking frustrated by my own stupidity, by the way everything in my life has seemed beyond my control and now Olivia, the most important part of it, is too.

And I did it to myself.

My mom sits beside me. "She's not the kind of girl who stays hidden for long," she says quietly, wrapping her arm around my shoulders. "You'll get your chance to fix it. This, right now, is the worst part."

A small part of me listens, and believes her.

Until the police call.

～

THE DETECTIVE who's handling Olivia's brother's case says the details of her story checked out. They found animal bones mixed in with her brother's, and there was an oak tree at the burial spot like she said.

"It's very important that we get ahold of her right away," he says. There's a whisper of anxiety in his clipped voice.

I close my eyes. "I have no idea where she's gone. But even if you find her, I'm not sure she's going to talk."

He hesitates. "I'm not worried about that right now," he says quietly. "After we got confirmation about the bones, we went to pick up her father for questioning. He was gone. It looks like someone tipped him off that she's talking."

The breath leaves my body. *She* wasn't talking. Everything they know, they know from me. "You don't have any idea where he went?"

"Our fear," he says, "is that he's gone after her. So it's pretty important that we find her first."

63

Olivia

S ean, Erin's brother, is high as a kite. I can see cocaine residue laying right there on the coffee table.

"Olivia!" he says. "Hey, hey, this is so awesome, so fucking awesome. It's gonna be fun, right?"

He tells me he's going to a party. "You like to party, right? That's cool?" I assume he doesn't mean with cake and gifts.

"I'm in training," I reply, "and I probably ought to just rest up so I can go find a job tomorrow."

He flops on the couch and grabs his phone. "A job?" he asks. "I got you covered."

~

WET-N-WILD IS a strip club where Sean is apparently best friends with everyone.

I'm not old enough to tend bar for another week, and I'm technically not supposed to serve drinks either, but the owner says he will overlook it. It's pretty clear he plans to *overlook it* by focusing on my ass instead, based on the length of the skirt he hands me, but so be it. I can't keep living with Chris Cocaine for long, obviously, so I need to make some damn money. Especially since nothing has arrived yet from the endorsement guy. I can't even find Fumito shoes online when I look, and now the whole thing feels a little shady.

I start at Wet-n-Wild the next afternoon. By 5 p.m., I'm sick of being indoors. I'm sick of bass. I'm sick of having sketchy businessmen graze my thighs as I bend over to set their drinks down.

What is Will doing right now? He's probably working at the farm, where it will be bright and crisp. And perhaps he's worried about me. I really hope he's not.

The crowd starts to pick up after nine, and I'm making okay tips, but it's begun to feel like I'm in a prison I will never leave. My feet are killing me in these heels they make me wear and I'm craving sunlight and fresh air more than I ever dreamed I would.

"You can make a lot more money up there," one of my customers tells me. "Or in back."

I'm not entirely sure what goes on in back, since lap dances occur out here, but I assume it's something I don't want to be a part of. I glance at the stage, where a girl is rolling around in more cash than I'll make in a week of waiting tables.

Even that moment of hesitation makes me feel like I'm in some bad TV movie. *A promising athlete fallen on hard times explores her dark side.*

I turn away. I'm only here for a few weeks, just until I get enough money to head to Seattle, and then I'll start training. This is *not* how I'm going to end up.

I miss Will. I'd like to tell him about this, though I doubt he'd be amused. I grit my teeth as I remember that it's not going to happen. That I'm never going to see him smile again or watch that muscle pop in his jaw when he's annoyed. That I'm never going to see him above me again like he was at the banquet, focused and desperate and trying not to come.

It'll be fine. I've been stabbed before, I've been assaulted. I was hit by a car and broke four bones. I came home one day and discovered my grandmother had no idea who I was. I survived all of that. I'll survive this too.

"Come here, sugar," calls a businessman with three other guys, all in suits. "We want a lap dance."

I shake my head. "Sorry, I just serve drinks."

"Even better. A lap dance virgin. I'll give you five hundred dollars to come dance for my friend."

I shake my head again. "Sorry."

Five hundred dollars. Five hundred dollars for three measly minutes of dancing? I must be insane to turn it down. I just worked *three hundred sixty* minutes for sixty-five freaking dollars. They wouldn't even be allowed to touch me, although this club seems to have a very *flexible* approach to the rules.

But it's a slippery slope. If I take five hundred for a lap dance tonight, then tomorrow I'll be wondering if I should take a few grand to do something far worse.

The next guy swats my ass, and the guy after him asks if I'd consider going to the back room. And I have to stand here being cheerful and cute about it so I get my tips at the end of the night. Sean assured me this place was "cool" but I'm thinking he was talking about the customer experience, not the employee one.

As time goes by, The Suits are drunker, rowdier. Their leader flags me down again. Asks me again about the lap dance. "Come on," he wheedles. "My buddy here's getting married."

I smile and put my hand on my hip, imitating the kind of girl I've always hated. "Now you know I can't do that," I say with an accent I don't actually have. "How 'bout I get y'all another round instead?"

I go back to the bar and wait for their drinks. All of them drinking whiskey on the rocks and chomping on cigars they aren't allowed to smoke, the biggest caricature of all time.

"I'll give you two grand," he says when I return. "Two grand to give my friend here the best lap dance of his life."

And I hesitate. Because I need to get out of here. Because I need to be in Seattle so I can maybe find a way to keep running and stop wishing I'd died when my brother did.

"Twenty-five hundred dollars!" he shouts. "That's my last offer."

I set the tray down. *Hello, slippery slope.*

64

Will

Erin folded the moment I told her Olivia was in danger, and within twenty minutes I was on my way to the airport. I still can't get my head around how far Jessica was willing to take things. But what I feel most is *wonder*: Even though Olivia and I had just argued, she was willing to give up everything for me.

Once I find her, I swear to God I will never, ever take her for granted again.

I arrive in LA around six-thirty and go straight to her brother's apartment. No one's there, so I wait. And wait. When Sean does finally arrive, it's almost comical how panicked he looks to find me on his steps.

"Hey man," he says warily. "I'm empty-handed if that's what you're here for. I'm gonna party at Avalon tonight."

"I have no idea what you're talking about," I tell him. "I'm here looking for Olivia."

"Oh," he says, backing away as if he thinks I'm going to throw a punch. I guess I probably do look slightly unhinged right now.

"My sister told me about you. I don't need any trouble. She's not even staying here."

I'd laugh at this too if I wasn't so worried. Erin must have warned Sean about Olivia's dad, but this guy's math could use some work. I haven't shaved in a few days, but I doubt I look old enough to have a grown daughter.

"I'm not her father, moron," I sigh. "I'm her coach."

He laughs nervously. "Oh, yeah, I guess that makes sense. She's probably at work."

"She already has a job?"

"Wet-n-Wild, this strip club on Fifth Street."

"*Strip* club?" I don't even recognize my own voice.

"It's not even a mile from here," he says, as if my actual concern was the distance.

I catch a cab, rubbing my hands over my face. She's in a strange city, broke and desperate, and it's entirely my fault. She clearly has no fucking clue how I feel about her. I quietly pray this is the end of it, and that things aren't about to get worse.

65

Olivia

ell done, Olivia. Only you could manage to lose a job on your first day of work.

So now it's barely ten p.m. on a Wednesday night. I've got seventy dollars in my pocket instead of the twenty-five hundred dollars I'd planned on after a full day's work. And if I call a cab, I'll be down another ten.

It sucks, but I can't bring myself to regret it. I can't believe that asshole thought he could put his hand *there* and get away with it. Maybe some of my rage was just at how arbitrary it all is. What kind of world do we live in where Will *can't* do that but a complete stranger *can*?

I start walking. It's just a mile, but it's a long fucking mile to walk dressed like a hooker.

It's eleven in Colorado right now. I wonder what Will and Dorothy are doing. I wonder if they're still angry or maybe they've just moved on to being relieved. Eventually, they will. How could they not? Poor Will's barely had a decent night's sleep since I joined the team.

But I miss them. My eyes burn and blur as I think of Will sitting there on Dorothy's couch alone, probably feeling guilty since that's how he is. I miss him. I miss everything I had and everything I never got with him and I'm pretty sure I always will.

By the time I get back to Sean's, I'm beat. Not from the walking or the long day, but from my own misery. I find the keys he left me under the mat and walk in, dropping my heels off to the side of the kitty litter box and flipping on the light.

"Hello, Olivia," says a voice.

A voice I'd forgotten I knew.

I freeze. Only my hands move, shaking so hard I can hear Sean's keys rattling against each other.

It's the voice I've heard in every nightmare I've ever had.

I want to scream but hear only the unholy rasp of my breath whistling through my throat in tiny, panicked bursts.

The nightmare was faceless, blank, something purely evil and inhuman. And now, in a single second, it's standing before me—and I remember *everything*. I remember what he did, after my mother told me to hide in the closet.

I remember the snap of her arm breaking as he twisted it and the sound of his knife, the one he used to gut fish, sinking into her skin. And when I ran to her, throwing myself between them and the knife went into my back...I remember that too.

She screamed at me to run and I did, panicked and scrambling off the floor, knowing he would chase me. I ran as hard as I could, I ran until the world seemed to close in on the edges and even the moonlight was squeezed out of my vision.

I woke in a field of corn, sticky with blood and alone. That's when I realized he'd never chased me at all, and that I'd left my mother behind to die.

And now he's come for me at last, the monster who chased me in all those dreams. He bridges the distance between us and wraps his hands around my throat. They are gentle, though, almost a caress. "You went to the police, didn't you?"

"No," I whisper. I'm not following the rules—*don't apologize, don't show fear*—but I can't help it.

His hands tighten, ever so slightly. "But you told someone something, didn't you?"

I grab my father's wrists and attempt to pry them off, but my grip strength is no match for his. "Let go," I hiss. Instead, they tighten further.

I think of him breaking Daisy's neck...

And Matthew's neck...

I pull harder at his hands, just enough to drag air through my throat, to push it back out. And to scream as loud as I possibly can.

66

Will

I arrive at the strip club, braced for the worst, and they tell me she was fired for punching a customer. It's the first time I've smiled since I found out she was gone.

That's my girl, I think, rushing back outside. My cab is gone, so I start jogging toward Sean's, still carrying the backpack I brought with me.

I've just turned the corner to her apartment when I hear a scream—her scream—and start sprinting. My heart hammers as I fly up the stairs and run down the hall.

I fling the door open to find her there—silent, limp, her arms swinging by her sides and her father's hands around her neck. He starts to turn just as my fist makes impact, crushing the side of his face.

The two of them fall together and then lie crumpled on the floor. Lifeless.

It feels as if my chest is caving in. The horror just seems to... empty me. I fall to my knees without realizing it's happened, pulling her to my chest. She is boneless and still in my arms.

"No," I say. "No. No. No." I want her back—not this shell, but *Olivia*, with her smart mouth, her bad attitude, her wary smile. I want everything back, everything I had and took for granted, all of the bad, all of the good, and I'm shouting at her, pleading, knowing it's too fucking late and that the moment I stop shouting I will have to accept it.

And then she gasps.

There has never been a sweeter sound than her gasping inhale.

I lower her just enough to see her face. She's confused for a moment, as if she's just coming out of a deep sleep, and her small smile, her pleasure when she sees me, breaks my heart a little. The fact that I'm capable of putting that look on her face amazes me. I'll never take it for granted again.

It's only when she looks at her father, still unconscious, that she seems to remember, and the smile fades.

I pull her to my chest and cling to her. "Fuck, Olivia. I thought ... fuck." I can't even say it. I just know I don't ever, for the rest of my life, want to feel that kind of terror again.

After a moment, I reluctantly let go of her to call 911 and bind her father's wrists, though I doubt he's going to be conscious anytime soon. And then I'm holding her again, running my hand over her hair, trying to reassure myself she's really okay.

"You could have died," I reply, choking on the words, realizing how close we came. "I'm sorry. I'm so fucking sorry."

"You didn't do anything wrong."

"I did everything wrong," I reply. "And I swear I'm going to fix all of it."

THE POLICE ARRIVE with guns drawn, though I told the dispatcher her father was unconscious. They point their guns at me instead, and it's not until Olivia screams at them that they realize I'm not the culprit. Her father is still unconscious when they take him away, but I'm relieved to see that he's already handcuffed.

Olivia is taken by ambulance to the hospital despite her protests, and not for a single moment of that time do I let go of her hand. She seems fine, but I don't think I'll ever get over seeing her the way she looked when I ran into Sean's apartment.

"I guess Erin told you," she finally sighs when we get a moment to ourselves. "I knew you'd feel guilted into coming after me if you found out what Jessica did."

I look at her in astonishment. "I'm not here because I feel *guilty*. And I don't know how the hell you thought I'd choose my job over you."

"You *did* choose your job over me," she replies. "You chose it when you sent me off the night of the banquet to pretend like everything was normal. I understood why you did it but ..."

"I quit, Olivia."

Her eyes widen. "You *what*? You can't do that! Jessica got what she wanted. I left. She's not going to tell."

"It had nothing to do with Jessica," I reply. "I quit hours after the banquet ended. I just had to do it in a way that wouldn't jeopardize your scholarship or get Peter in trouble."

"You *can't*," she insists. "What about the farm? What about Brendan?"

They're the same questions I was asking of myself a week ago, and now I can't believe I ever thought they could hold equal weight to her. "I made my choice when I followed you at the banquet. I put you first then. Everything else will have to work out somehow."

"You don't have to do that," she argues. "It was sex, not a promise ring. You never once suggested it was anything more than that, so stop trying to do the honorable thing and go get your job back."

I lean in, letting my lips graze her forehead. "I've been far from honorable for a long time," I tell her. "And I'm not being honorable now either. I'm here because I love you. Because I'm so in love with you, I can't see straight."

She turns away from me.

I pull back, feeling my first queasy flash of uncertainty. I don't know how I thought she'd react, but it wasn't like this.

"I don't see how that can possibly be true, Will," she says quietly. "We both know how fucked up I am. How could you want to be with me knowing what you know?"

I reach out, gently cupping her chin to face me. "I'd give anything to change your past, but at the same time it's made you who you are," I tell her. "The things you think are so terrible? I *love* those things. That fragile part of you, the way you freeze when someone tries to hug you or compliment you or acts like they care—I can't separate that from everything else now, so I love all of it. I should have told you that a long time ago."

She doesn't reply, just looks at me wide-eyed as if everything I've said to her is a surprise when it shouldn't be. Everyone but the two of us saw it months ago.

I run my hands through her hair and lean in. "In case you haven't done this before, this is the part where you tell me you love me too."

"Have *you* done this part before?" she asks.

I grin. "Yeah, about five seconds ago. And she didn't say it back."

She smiles. "I love you."

I brush her lips with mine, wishing there were a way to save the needy little noise she makes when I pull away.

"More," she whispers. The doctor's going to be in any minute but I give into her, relishing the softness of her mouth and the heat of her tongue and fuck...

"We've got to stop," I rasp, pulling back again.

"I'm not wearing *anything* under this hospital gown, Will," she says with a smile that goes straight to my dick. "Wanna see?"

I groan aloud.

This girl is going to be the end of me. But I guess I've known that since the day we met.

67

Olivia

I t's well past one in the morning when we are finally released and into a hotel room nearby. I was on my feet in the strip club for seven hours and then nearly died, so you'd think I'd be tired, but...there's something about the prospect of sharing a room with Will that has me all kinds of awake.

Will drops his backpack on the bed and our eyes meet. I want a whole lot of things from him right now, but not until I've rinsed off the hospital and the strip club and, yes, the attempted murder.

"I need a shower," I tell him, biting my lip.

He stills for a moment, something the tiniest bit feral in his gaze, and then he nods and sits on the bed. "Go ahead," he says, "do you need a..." His words trail away, catching on me as I peel off the skirt before he averts his eyes. "Do you need a T-shirt to sleep in?"

I raise a brow. "You're allowed to look now, you know."

"I think it's best if I don't," he says, swallowing. "Just go shower. You need some rest."

Rest? A small, slightly appalled laugh comes from the base of my chest. "So you're saying that you're no longer my coach and we're alone in a hotel room and you want me to get some *rest*?"

He sighs, pinching the bridge of his nose. "Olivia, in the last few hours you were assaulted and nearly died. You *just* got out of the hospital. So yeah, under those circumstances, I want you to rest. We have lots of time to do this the right way."

"Oh my God," I groan. "You're not going to do, like, candles and rose petals and shit, right? While you recite poetry, maybe play some slow jams on your guitar?"

"I'm pretty sure there's some middle ground between being sensitive ponytail guy and the guy who fucks a girl as she's exiting the hospital."

I stare at him in open-mouthed astonishment. He's really doing this. Or, I should say, he really *thinks* he's doing this.

I shrug, as if conceding the point. "You go first then. I'm going to call Erin before it's too late."

I watch him walk away, and even go sit next to the hotel room phone.

The water starts, and I hear the shower door slide open. That's when I strip off the rest of my clothes and walk into the bathroom, pausing for a moment to take him in—perfect arms, tight ass, water streaming off that delectable v where his waist meets his hips.

He is perfection. And *mine*.

"Olivia," he sighs, opening his eyes to find me ogling him. "What are you doing?"

I step into the shower. "Don't mind me." I lather the soap in my hands. "I'm just here to get clean." My hands slide over my skin, down to my thighs and between my legs.

"Liv," he groans, half-plea and half-warning. To my delight, I notice that he's already hard and I haven't laid a finger on him.

"Oh, how rude of me." I wrap my slippery hands around him. "I should clean you first."

"You just got out of the hospital," he says through gritted teeth. During the entire time I've known him, he's been in charge. Yes, I often defied him, but there was never any doubt about which one of us held the power.

Right now though, with my hands slipping over his rigid cock, it's definitely *me*.

"Maybe you'd feel better about it if I was sitting," I say as I drop to my knees, washing away the soap before I take him in my mouth.

"*Fuck*," he gasps, and in that single word I hear him cave. His fingers press to my scalp, running through my hair. When I glance up, I find him watching me, eyes at half-mast and feverish. I think I could come from his reaction alone: his low groan, the way he strains not to push hard into my mouth, his hips still jutting forward softly despite his best efforts.

"You've got to stop," he says gruffly. "I'm not going to be able to hold back much longer."

I like his loss of control. I'm on the cusp of resuming my task when I find myself lifted from the floor entirely, my back pressed to the shower wall.

He takes the soap and runs it between my legs, and then takes his fingers to push through the soapy trail he's left behind. "Will … oh God, that's amazing."

"I'm going to make you come in every way possible tonight," he growls against my ear, his fingers slipping and sliding until I think my knees are going to buckle. He is rigid in my palm, beginning to thrust up into it, as he seizes my mouth violently.

"I want you inside," I plead. "I want you to come like that." With a speed I didn't imagine possible, he lifts my legs around his waist and pushes inside me hard, just the way he thrust into my hand.

"That's so good," he groans, his mouth pressed to my damp neck. He pulls out and presses back in, faster and harder than before, as my back slides against the shower wall.

I'm far from virginal. I've always enjoyed sex. But this is something else entirely, a pleasure so sharp that it almost hurts, that it draws goose bumps and elicits cries from my throat I seem helpless to stop. For the first time, I'm not worried about whether I'll finish but about whether I can hold off a little longer.

"I'm close," I gasp. I meant it as a warning but the second he pushes in again something bursts open inside me like a bomb. He hammers into me, prolonging everything until suddenly he stiffens, groaning into my neck, sinking his teeth into my skin as he comes.

He buries his face there, his mouth moving, pressing tiny kisses anywhere he can reach while he catches his breath. "I think it's time we got really crazy and tried this thing called a bed next."

"I've heard of those," I reply. "They sound dangerous."

He turns, still holding me, still *inside* me, and starts walking to the room. "You have no idea."

68

Will

We arrive in Denver a little after four the next day. I walk through the airport marveling at the fact that we're here together, and that I'm holding her hand and that it's all really happening. I walk through also marveling at the fact that despite the hours we spent naked last night and this morning I want her all over again. We have an hour drive ahead of us and my mom and Peter are waiting at the farm, but I think we're going to have to work in a pit stop.

She goes off to use the bathroom while I wait for the bags. When my phone rings and I see Jessica's name, I start to shut it off but think better of it. She's been calling me incessantly for days, and I guess it's time to get this over with. Now that I know how much of what we just went through is her fault, I have a few things I'd like to say myself.

"Will!" she cries when I pick up. "Thank God. I've been calling and calling. I heard you quit!"

"I did quit," I tell her calmly.

"But *why*?" she gasps. "I know I implied it, but I never would have told anyone about Olivia sleeping at your mom's."

"I don't think you *implied* it. You used it to blackmail Olivia into leaving."

She's silent for a moment, recalibrating. "I don't know what she told you, but you know what a liar she is."

I draw in a breath, struggling to maintain my temper. "Jessica, I didn't even learn it from her, so don't try to bullshit me."

I see Olivia's suitcases coming and reach for them while Jessica continues trying to justify herself. I'd have ended the call if my hands were free. "Look I've got to go," I finally say, cutting her off, "but I just wanted to thank you."

She draws in a breath. "Thank me? For what?"

"Because I don't think I'd ever have known how much Olivia really meant to me if you hadn't run her off," I say. "And it made me realize a lot of things. Like you know how I was so sure I didn't want to get married soon?"

"Yes," she snaps.

Olivia is walking toward me now with a little sway to her hips and a knowing smile. I want to see that smile every day for the rest of my life. "I was wrong," I reply, and I hang up the phone.

Olivia reaches me and I pull her close, letting my lips brush over hers once and then a second time. "Maybe we should stop by my apartment first," I suggest. "Just to get cleaned up."

She laughs. "Is that what the kids are calling it these days?"

"Don't hear you saying no," I reply.

"Will," she says, moving toward me and placing her mouth next to my ear, "I never say no."

～

I LOVE MY MOM, but she is the ultimate cockblocker. She calls when we're driving home, demanding we come straight to the farm. She and Peter and Brendan are all waiting, and she is already standing by the door.

When we arrive, my mom runs from the house, already crying, and pounces on Olivia.

"Let's give them a minute," Peter says to me, watching them walk in. He looks as uncomfortable as I've ever seen him.

I brace myself. I already resigned. Is it possible Jessica made problems anyway? "What's up?" I ask him.

"A few things," he says with a frown. He shoves his hands in his back pockets, his eyes focused on the ground. "The first is about the farm. On your mother's behalf, I entered conversations with the school late last year about allowing the agriculture program to lease a fair bit of it, year-round."

This is, obviously, not where I thought he was going. It's a relief but still makes little sense. "Lease it? Why would they do that? They have their own land, right?"

He explains that demand for corn has decreased, and our land would provide a perfect test case to prove the benefit of switching crops. "They're willing to pay your mother far more to lease it than your father ever earned off crops in his best year," Peter says, "and she'll get twenty percent of the profits, once there are profits, to boot."

"And what happens when the lease ends?" I ask.

He shrugs. "They might want to renew. If not, I'm planning to retire in the next few years and was thinking I could try my hand at farming."

I cock my head. I've known Peter my entire life. I've never once heard him express an interest in the farm. "So *you* want to buy it?"

"Not exactly." He hesitates. "What I'd like to do is marry your mother."

I blink, wondering if I've misheard him, and then I laugh. "*What?*"

He scrubs his face with both hands. "Your mother said you weren't ready."

I know I didn't get much sleep last night, but this conversation wouldn't make a damn bit of sense even if I had. "*Ready for what? She knows you're thinking...*" I shake my head. "Don't you think you ought to *date* first?"

"Will," he laughs, "I've been seeing your mother for over a year now."

I glance up then. Olivia and my mom are both standing at the window watching us, and Olivia appears to be laughing. I don't understand what the fuck is happening. "But *how*? I mean, when did this all take place?" But even as I ask, I'm thinking about Thanksgiving—about all the people they knew in common. And how they attended the banquet together and how she'd heard about Olivia from Peter before she'd heard about her from me.

And then I think about the morning after the banquet, when he was just pulling up to his house as I arrived, and I flinch. "On second thought, I don't want to know."

We walk to the house together while I slowly—*very slowly*—come around to the idea. I guess it kind of makes sense. My mom has known Peter since before I was born, and I've thought many times about how much I hate that she's out here alone.

I almost feel capable of faking normalcy until we walk inside...and I find Brendan with his arms around my girlfriend. His smile fades when he sees me over her shoulder—possibly related to the fact that I am about to throw a punch.

With an exaggerated sigh he releases her. "Chill, dude. I was just saying hello."

I glare at him. "Just use words next time."

"But Olivia gives such good hugs," he counters, glancing at her chest. "She's got to be at least, what, a D cup?"

She laughs and crosses the room to me, wrapping her arms around my waist. "That was your last hug, asshole."

My mood is slightly less forgiving. It's going to be a while before the memory of their kiss stops pissing me off.

"It's the middle of the week," I say, struggling to sound civil. "Shouldn't you be taking finals?"

He shakes his head. "The school let me take them early. I thought you might need some help around here."

Brendan hasn't given a shit about the farm since the day he was born. When he was little he used to come home suggesting non-farm jobs to my father, as if possibly my dad just didn't *realize* he could be a pilot or fireman instead. "Help?" I ask, my voice rife with disbelief.

I wait for the punchline but it doesn't come.

"Yeah," he says. "It means 'providing assistance to.'"

"I know what it means, idiot. Are you saying *you* came back to help with the *farm*?"

He shrugs. "Unless you want me to help take care of your girlfriend, which I'm also open to."

I almost smile. Almost. "This will surprise you, but no, I'm not really open to that."

IT'S JUST BEGUN to snow as we leave. Snowflakes cling to her hair, to her lashes, making her seem other-worldly, lit up from within. She looks up at the sky and laughs, her delight almost childlike, and I'm flooded with warmth. I love her so much that it feels like there's not even room inside me for all of it.

"What's with the look?" she asks. "You don't want to date me now that I'm geeking out about the snow?"

I shake my head and step toward her, wrapping my hands around her hips, and taking it all in—her wide smile, her moonlit eyes, the snowflakes glowing in her hair. "Just the opposite," I say softly. "I'm looking at you and wondering if it's possible I've gotten this lucky."

Her smile changes then from delight to something else, something warm and surprised, quietly pleased. "We're both lucky," she says, rising on her toes to find my mouth.

By the time we get in the car, our hair is soaked and we're both shivering. I crank the heat and head down the long road from the farm, but when I reach the highway, I don't turn toward campus.

"Where are we going?" she asks.

It didn't even occur to me to take her home. I suppose I should have asked her, but fuck it, I'm not letting her set foot in that neighborhood again. "You didn't think I was actually going to sleep in your apartment, did you?" I tease. "I'm big but I'm not bulletproof, and we've already been involved with the police once this week."

"Okay, but you're not going to be weird about it, right?" she asks. "You were so weird that first time I slept in your apartment."

I roll my eyes. "Yeah, you mean the time my hot student sat up in bed and flashed me her tits? Nothing to be weird about there."

"I assumed you'd seen breasts before mine."

"Yeah, but yours are exceptional," I reply, pulling into the parking lot. Just thinking about that morning has me hard as a rock.

I grab her bags and head for the door. "There *is* one way tonight will be like the first time you stayed," I warn her, putting the key in the lock.

"Oh, what's that?"

I set the bags inside and pull her in behind me without bothering to turn on the lights. "You're not seeing anything but my bed until daylight."

69

Olivia

There's not a lot of time for us to revel in our good fortune. I've got school and finals to catch up on, and he has the farm and job interviews. As much as I enjoy watching him walk out of the apartment in the morning in a suit, I'm more excited by the job he finally accepts at the week's end— leading small group excursions for a tour company. It doesn't pay as well as the university did, but it means he'll be climbing again. There's a light in his eyes that was missing all fall as he describes it to me.

Naturally, word of our relationship spreads across campus fast. My response is "no comment" to all but a few people, and Evan is one of them. Even though we barely dated, I knew from Will that he'd been worried when I disappeared. It only seems fair that he know the truth. Not the part where I slept with Will during the banquet I attended with *him*, just the rest of it. And he isn't surprised.

"I kind of guessed it around the time you disappeared and Will went batshit crazy," he admits.

I also tell Erin and Nicole. Erin, because she already kind of knows, and Nicole because she's way too nosy not to figure it out on her own.

"I want *all* the dirt," Nicole says, slightly too eager.

"You're not actually saying you want me to talk about, like, physical stuff, right?" I ask.

She looks at me blankly. "Of course I am. You think I want to know what he eats for dinner? You've at least got to tell me how big his d—"

"I'm sure you can guess," I say, cutting her off. "And that's the very last detail you'll request, ever. Understand?"

She ignores me entirely, turning to Erin. "I told you he'd be huge, didn't I?" she crows.

～

THE DAY that I officially become an adult coincides with the day I officially stop living alone. On December twenty-first, we return the furniture Will borrowed from various people and take the last of my meager possessions to his apartment. Erin and Brendan both come to help, though Brendan's version of "help" involves a lot more lying around than you might imagine.

"I still can't believe you're doing this," Erin says in wonder as we enter Will's apartment together. Brendan is, at the moment, "helping" by watching TV. Erin glances at him for one long moment and then looks back to me. "I mean, it's weird, right? Isn't it weird?"

Nothing has felt less weird in my life. Here, with Will, I feel like I'm finally *home*. "No," I reply, kicking Brendan's feet off the coffee table.

"It's just so random," she says. "I mean, I knew you guys were tight but it's like finding out that Brofton is sleeping with Angelina Jolie. It's just, you know, he's *Will* ..."

"Yeah." I smile. "I know." Sometimes I look over at him, when he's in the kitchen or getting dressed or stretched out on the couch waiting for me to lie beside him, and I can't really believe it either.

She throws her arms around me before I can back away. "This is the first decent break you've ever gotten, Finn. Don't fuck it up, okay?"

I promise her I won't, and though I'm not much good at keeping promises, I feel pretty good about this one.

∾

PETER, Brendan and Erin all join us that night at the farm, where Dorothy has made every food she knows I like. I don't mention it to them, but it's the first time anyone's celebrated my birthday since I was ten, which makes even a small gathering feel a little overwhelming. I swallow hard and dig my nails into my hands to avoid tears when Dorothy comes out of the kitchen carrying a cake with my name on it, singing "Happy Birthday." Sure, maybe I can cry now, but it doesn't mean I'm going to start crying when I'm *happy*. Dorothy gives me more dresses, and Will gives me my favorite gift ever—new racing flats.

"How did you know?" I ask. I hate the shoes the school provides, but it's something I've never mentioned to him.

He laughs. "You scowled every time you put them on. It was hard to miss."

Much later, after we've come home and celebrated in other ways, he lies, sated and sleepy while I trace small circles on his back. His back fascinates me, still tan and all muscle. I've seen guys pose in a gym and look less cut than he does at rest.

"We just moved in together," he says out of nowhere, turning to face me, "and we've never actually been on a date."

I shrug. "We've eaten in a restaurant together."

"With my *mom*. Usually fighting."

"It doesn't bother me," I say, studying him. "Does it bother you?"

He rises up on his forearm, his lips brushing one temple, and then the other. "You remember that dress you wore on Thanksgiving?" he asks. "I spent the entire meal imagining you in that dress on a date with Brendan and it made me crazy that it couldn't be me. And now it can be."

I smile at him. "I'll put the dress on right now if it means that much to you, but I kind of thought you liked the fall banquet dress better."

He grins. "That one has a special place in my heart too. But it's not just the dress. It's also that you haven't ever really dated—"

"I've been on dates."

"With someone you *liked*?" he asks. "Someone you planned to keep seeing?"

I roll my eyes, an admission of defeat.

"Then you should probably try it while you have the chance, Olivia," he says softly, his mouth pressed to my ear, "because I'm going to be the first and the last."

I want to not smile at that but I can't help myself. "The *last*, huh? Pretty sure of yourself."

He rolls us over until I'm on my back and looms over me, clearly no longer *sleepy*. "Yes," he says. "I've never been more sure about anything."

～

I WAKE the next morning to find him walking out of the bathroom, half-dressed. "I'm gonna be at the farm all day. I'll pick you up at five thirty for our *date*."

"Won't you need to get ready?" I ask.

He sits on the edge of the bed. "I'll get ready at my mom's. If we try getting ready at the same time, we'll just wind up in bed."

"What's wrong with that?" I ask. "I like winding up in bed with you."

He smiles. A sweet, sheepish smile that makes my heart flip over in my chest. "Because I'm wooing you."

"I'm already wooed," I say. "Take off those jeans and I'll show you just how wooed I am."

For a single second he glances at me, his resolve faltering a bit, but then he grabs his T-shirt and pulls it over his head. "Five thirty."

Sighing, I climb out of bed. "Isn't that kind of early for a date?"

"Yeah," he says with a grin, pulling me between his legs, "but I don't think I can stay away longer than that. Wear the dress."

IN THE AFTERNOON, I put on makeup for the first time since the banquet. I feel excited in a small way, but mostly I feel ridiculous. He knows I don't look like this normally. He knows I couldn't care less about food, aside from Dorothy's pie. And we've now gone a full seven hours without sex, so I guarantee that when he walks in, I won't be thinking about dinner.

Overall, I just have a bad feeling about this, especially because I'm sure he and Jessica went out like this all the time. I picture them talking about grown-up things: Medicare reform, foreign films, ECU school policy, and none of that is me. I'm good at meaningless banter. Maybe I'm good at seduction, occasionally —at least I seem to be where Will is concerned. But I've never thought of myself as the kind of girl you *date*, and I suppose my fear is that, tonight, Will might start to agree.

There's a knock on the door just as I'm finishing up and I find him there, freshly showered, in suit pants and a button-down shirt without a tie. I should be used to this by now—I've seen him dressed up before, but God he wears his clothes well.

He steps in, his eyes lingering on my mouth. "You're wearing lipstick."

I swallow. "I can take it off." I step closer, sliding my hands up his arms, wanting very much to reach for that top button.

"Don't," he groans. "Believe me, I like it." He pulls me closer, his mouth ghosting over mine, making my skin prickle as it might if I were chilled, or scared, but in the best possible way. I want more, but he puts his hands on my hips and removes himself carefully, like one of us might break. "We should go."

"Will," I sigh, "you don't have to do this."

"I *don't* have to have a really good meal with my beautiful girl-friend?" he asks dryly. "Thanks for letting me off the hook. Why are you being so weird about this? It's just dinner."

"I don't know," I sigh. "It's just something I don't have much experience with and I guess I don't like feeling unsure about things."

He stares at me for a second, and then he starts to laugh. "So the same girl who threatened to feed Piersal his own balls and put another guy in the hospital is scared to go out to *eat*?"

I roll my eyes. "It sounds stupid when you put it like that."

"Do you trust me?" he asks. His face is earnest as he waits for my reply.

It's a question I don't even need to *contemplate*. I trust him more than anyone alive. More than I trust myself. "Yes."

"Then come on," he says, lacing his fingers through mine. "Let's go on a date."

~

WE DRIVE into town and he parks beside a restaurant I've seen before but never dreamed I'd one day enter. It looks expensive, and I want to dig my heels in and refuse, but I bite my lip and take his hand instead.

Warm air whips around us like a blanket as we walk inside.

It's all dark wood and white linen and candlelight, like something out of a movie. Will squeezes my hand, knowing instinctively that my anxiety just grew by a mile.

The hostess is a girl about my age, maybe a little older, pretty and showing way too much cleavage. Will gives her his name and she smiles at him—and *only* him—like he's a winning lottery ticket, grabbing menus while she licks her lips and tugs her low-cut dress even lower.

We follow her through the restaurant, her hips swaying so much you'd think she was in a Shakira video, and then she leans over as she seats us, letting her cleavage spill forward, to ask Will if the table is okay. He absent-mindedly tells her it's fine, with a polite smile, but I shoot her a nasty look as she walks away.

His eyes meet mine. "What's the matter?"

"Did you seriously not notice the way she was acting with you?" I demand. "She practically shoved her rack in your face."

He looks genuinely, adorably confused. "I didn't notice anything."

"I'm not sure how you failed to notice *that.*"

He laughs, but it sounds slightly disgruntled. "You're finally spending some time in my shoes."

He's got to be kidding. How many times did I have to watch Jessica pawing at him? "*Your* shoes? You're the one who had a girl-friend all fall!"

"I've put up with plenty, believe me," he says with a scowl, setting down the wine list. "Brendan? Evan? Brofton hitting on you on the bus? The football team with that fucking song they used to sing?"

"None of that meant anything," I sputter.

"Right," he says. "It meant so little you barely noticed it. Just like that girl doing whatever she theoretically did meant so little that I didn't even notice."

He's right. The football players, Brofton—they barely registered because I only had eyes for Will. Is it so inconceivable that he might feel the same way?

"Maybe," I say with a reluctant smile. "You know it's our first date and we're already arguing. That can't be good."

He laughs. "I bet arguing with me made you feel right at home though, didn't it?"

And the funny thing is that it *did*. Neither of us are different here, as I feared we might be. He's the same guy who often annoys me and always thrills me, the same guy who can get me to undress with simply a look, and right now he's watching me across a candlelit table with a smile I've never seen him give anyone else. "I'm probably never going to want to talk about Medicare reform," I warn.

He raises a brow. "And you're under the impression I *will*?"

I smile. "I guess not."

He reaches across the table and grabs my hand.

"Just so we're clear," he says, "this is still the best first date I've ever had."

"Me too," I reply. I rub my leg against his and his eyelids lower ever so slightly, his mouth the tiniest bit slack. I think about how many times I've seen that look on his face without realizing what it meant, that it was the look he has when he wants something and is doing his best to restrain himself. "You might even get lucky if you don't irritate me too much."

His tongue darts out to tap his lip. "Olivia," he says quietly, picking up the menu, "I assure you I'm getting lucky no matter how irritating you find me."

BY THE TIME we reach the apartment, foreplay is completely unnecessary and even unwanted. He pushes my back against the wall just inside the door, his mouth landing on mine as he slides up my dress, his hands skimming my thighs.

"Oh *God*," he groans when his fingers slip between my legs.

I reach for his belt and undo it as we move toward the table. I'm not sure which of us is leading the other. I only know that there will be time for something slow and measured later, but that's not what either of us wants right now. He turns me so that I'm face down, and I remain there, breathless as I listen to the sound of his zipper sliding, feel him push against me and then into me with a groan of relief. He holds my hips in place, bending over to kiss the curve of my neck, murmuring my name. My back is damp, soaking through the dress and I don't care as he moves faster, as his words grow incoherent. He pushes so hard that my hands cling to the far end of the table, as if it's all that separates me from a long, hard fall. One more push, the table sliding across the floor, and I come.

He lets go with a sharp cry, then flops over me, his front pressed against my back, his mouth buried in my neck. "I love you," he whispers. "God, I love you so much."

There is something desperate in his voice, something I feel too. He's as scared to lose me as I am to lose him. And gratitude blooms in my chest, because I'm not sure anyone ever felt like this about me until now.

For the first time in my life, I feel safe.

70

Olivia

Not all of my problems are solved in a day, or in a month. It takes more than just Will to fix me. Under duress, I start seeing a psychologist who specializes in PTSD, someone Peter found. I don't particularly enjoy it, but at least she doesn't suggest that a nice bubble bath can fix all my issues.

For a long time, I'm cagey when Will suggests marriage and kids. I still don't trust who and what I am enough to promise the best of myself to someone else. But slowly the nightmares abate. One day Erin points out that I'm the one who initiated a hug. Something has changed inside me, flowered, without me noticing.

And when Will turns to me, at Peter and Dorothy's wedding, and tells me he wishes it was us up there at the altar, I tell him I wish it were too.

~

A YEAR to the day after our first kiss, the one that took place while I pretended to be asleep, I collapse on the couch beside him after afternoon practice, freshly showered.

"How was work?" I ask.

"Good," he says, lifting my legs and placing my feet on his lap. It's something I'd never have allowed anyone to do a year ago, but my days of barefoot running are over. On the rare occasions when I have a nightmare, I'm not even out of the bed before Will's stopped me.

"I took a family climbing at Garden of the Gods. It was their kid's first climb and you wouldn't believe the smile on his face once he got about twenty feet up."

"You're not taking any future children of ours climbing. I hope you realize that."

"Of course I will," he says with that sideways grin of his. "You know you're incapable of telling me no."

"In *bed*, yes. Parenting, no. But since today's our anniversary I'll let you think you're right."

He shakes his head. "Our anniversary isn't until December."

"But the first time we kissed was a year ago today. I know you remember it. In your bed at the farm."

His eyes widen and his jaw drops just a bit. "You were *awake*? You did it on *purpose*?"

I laugh. "Of course I did."

"Jesus," he says, grinning at me. "You were even more evil than I realized."

"You loved it."

"I loved it *too* much. Thinking about that kiss tortured me for weeks," he says, lifting one foot gently and kissing the arch in a way that has me trying to stifle a moan and failing. "You like that?" he asks.

"Yes," I say, my voice the tiniest bit breathy.

"Your feet are soft now," he says, kissing the arch again. "Almost like girl feet."

"These girl feet can still kick your ass in a race."

His mouth moves to the top of my foot, to my ankle. "We both know that's not true," he says with a low laugh.

"You're just dying to race me, aren't you?"

"That wasn't entirely what I had in mind." He smiles lazily at me, a *suggestive* smile, and my heart thumps once—*hard*. "I'm just saying that all the barefoot running in the world won't make you as fast as me."

I swing my legs off his lap. "That sounds like a challenge." I stand and begin backing toward the door.

"I was just trying to get laid," he says, but he jumps to his feet with that gleam in his eye, a tiny hint of wildness about to be set free.

"I think you need to earn it," I reply, and with a whoop, I'm bolting out the door, past the parking lot and into the fields newly glazed by moonlight. I run hard but it's a *good* hard, and I feel the entire world in my bones—not a horrifying one from a time gone by, but this one with the wind and the dry grass crackling beneath my feet like tiny fireworks. Here are the things I love: I love the smell of winter coming in, I love the burn in my muscles as I sprint across the field and the icy air whipping through my lungs. And I love the boy behind me, the one who's closing in fast. I love him so much that I slow my pace, realizing that, for the first time in my life, I want to be caught.

EPILOGUE

After Olivia graduated, we left for Seattle, where she began to race long distance.

I went back to work for the same guide company I was with before, but it wasn't the same. A funny thing happened after I got everything I thought I wanted: I didn't want it quite so much. I still loved climbing, but I'd grown to love other things so much more. There came a point when I could no longer stand the look on Olivia's face when I left for an expedition, or the fact that no matter how hard I insisted I'd come back in one piece, we both knew it was never entirely in my control.

But mostly, I gave it up because I missed her. Two months in Peru, the trip I'd dreamed of, was the longest two months of my life. I missed her first marathon win during that trip. I timed the decision well, since it turns out that—much to our surprise—Olivia was pregnant.

So I moved on to other things, things that allow me to be where I am today, waiting at the seventy-mile point of the Western States Endurance Run, a hundred mile race she has a damn good chance of winning.

"How much longer, Daddy?"

Olivia's been running for eleven hours. Our son has asked this question several times an hour since she started.

"Any minute now," I tell him.

"That's what you said last time," he tells me reproachfully, reminding me a great deal of his mother.

"Should we go down to the bottom of the hill and run back up with her?"

He's off like a shot. *His mother's son to the end.* We jog to the bottom of the incline and wait, and despite her exhaustion, her face lights up when she sees us.

"Mommy!" shouts Matthew. "You're winning!"

She laughs, fatigue cutting the sound a little short. "There's still thirty miles to go, baby. No one's winning yet."

"Daddy already *told* me you're going to win," he informs her, sounding a little put out.

She smiles at him. "Well, he *is* the one with the fancy degree, so I guess he'd know."

I thought I would miss climbing when I went to medical school, but I like what I do. And it certainly comes in handy when you have a wife who tries to run a hundred miles at a time. I'm nearly done with my residency, but I have a feeling things will still be pretty busy even when it's over.

When we get into the rest station, my mother brings the baby over, and Olivia holds her with that kind of awestruck look she tends to get sometimes when she's watching the kids, as if she can't quite believe she's created them.

"How do you feel?" I ask, pulling off her shoes. Blisters, bad ones, are unavoidable in this race, and she has several.

But when she looks at me her smile is dreamy. She takes in the family around us, the family we made, and her eyes grow damp. "I feel complete," she sighs. "And it's all because of you. You saved me, you know that?"

She sets off for the last leg of the race, giving me, Matthew, and the baby each a quick kiss. We begin packing up our gear to head to the finish line, where Brendan and Erin wait. I still think that them dating is a recipe for disaster, but Olivia reminded me that people thought the same thing about us once upon a time, so I'm keeping my mouth shut.

"How's our girl holding up?" Peter asks.

"She's good." I smile. "I think fatigue is setting in. She almost got emotional." I shake my head. "After all this time, she's still under the impression that I saved her."

"You did save her, Will," my mother replies. "And she saved you."

I guess she's right. And one day I'll tell Olivia exactly that. But right now? It's time to go to the finish line and watch my girl win a race.

THE END

Want Brendan and Erin's story? Turn the page!

ALSO BY ELIZABETH O'ROARK

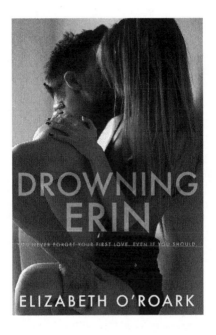

You never forget your first love...

But you should, if you're marrying his best friend.

ALSO BY ELIZABETH O'ROARK

What if you discovered you were living your life for the second time--
and you were still in love with someone from the first?

"Seriously one of my top, top reads--not of just 2019, but ever."- Amazon
Bestselling Author Maria Luis

Turn the page for a sneak peek!

PARALLEL

I had a nightmare as a child. A nightmare that visited me again and again. I've never forgotten it, not a single detail, although if my parents hadn't kept the psychologist's report, I'd probably assume the years had added and detracted from it in various ways. But they didn't. It's all in writing, exactly as it rests in my head.

Quinn, age four, was brought into our clinic due to recurrent nightmares. Parents report that patient wakes several times a week, crying for her "husband" ("Nick"), and claiming they've been separated by someone. Patient insists she "isn't supposed to be here" for hours and sometimes days afterward. There are no further signs of psychosis.

At first those nightmares—their weirdness, their specificity—made my mother scared for me. Over time though, she also became scared *of* me, and that taught me a lesson I'd continue to find true over the coming years: the things I knew, *real* things, were safest kept to myself.

QUINN
2018

Déjà vu.

It translates to *already seen*, but really it sort of means the opposite: that you *haven't* already seen the thing, but feel like you have. I once asked Jeff if he thought they actually call it *déjà vu* in France or perhaps keep a better, more accurate expression for themselves. He laughed and said, "you think about the weirdest shit sometimes."

Which is so much truer than he knows.

"Everything okay?" he asks now, as we follow my mother and his into the inn where we will marry in seven short weeks. I've been *off*, somehow, since the moment we pulled into town, and I guess it shows.

"Yeah. Sorry. I've got the start of a headache." It's not entirely true, but I don't know how to explain this thing in my head, this irritating low hum. It makes me feel as if I'm only half here.

We step into the lobby and my mother extends her arms like a game show hostess. "Isn't it cute?" she asks without waiting for an answer. "I know it's an hour from D.C., but at this late date it's the best we're going to do." In truth, the lobby reminds me of an upscale retirement community—baby blue walls, baby blue carpet, Chippendale chairs—but the actual wedding and reception will take place on the lawn. And as my mother pointed out, we can no longer afford to be picky.

Jeff's mother, Abby, steps beside me, running a hand over my head, the way she might a prize stallion. "You're being so calm about this. Any other bride would be in a panic."

It's posed as a compliment, but I'm not sure it is. Losing our venue two months before the wedding *should* have made me panic, but I try not to get too attached to things. Caring too much about anything makes perfectly reasonable people go insane—just ask the girl who burned down the reception hall her ex was about to get married in...which happened to be the reception hall *we* were getting married in too.

My mother claps her hands together. "Well, our appointment with the hotel's events coordinator isn't for another hour. Shall we get some lunch while we wait?"

Jeff and I exchange a quick look. On this point we are both of one mind. "We really need to get back to D.C. before rush hour." *Are my words coming out as slowly as they feel?* It's as if I'm on delay somehow, two steps behind. "Maybe you could just show us around?"

My mother's smile fades to something far less genuine. She wants giddy participation from me and has been consistently disappointed with my inability to provide it.

She and Abby lead the way, back to the porch where we entered. "We've already been discussing it a bit," Abby says to me over her shoulder. "We were thinking you could walk down the stairs and out to the porch, where your fa— *uncle*, I mean, will wait." She pauses for a moment, blushing at the error. It shouldn't be a big deal at this point—my dad's been gone almost eight years—but I feel that pinch deep in my chest anyway. That hint of sadness that never quite leaves. "And then we'll do a red carpet out to the tent."

Together we step outside. It's a gruelingly hot day, as are most summer days anywhere near D.C., and this thing in my head only gets worse. I vaguely notice my surroundings—blinding sun, a technicolor blue sky, the rose bushes my mother is commenting on, but all the while I feel displaced, like I'm following this from far away. *What the hell is going on?* I could call it déjà vu, but it's not really that. The conversation occurring right now, with this group of people, is wholly new. It's the place that feels familiar. *More* than familiar, actually. It feels important.

They're discussing the lake. I'm not sure what I've missed, but

Abby is worried about its proximity. "It would just take one boatful of drunks to create chaos," she says. "And we don't want a bunch of looky-loos either."

"Most boats can't reach this part of the lake," I reply without thinking. "There's too much brush under the water on the way here."

Abby's brow raises. "I didn't realize you'd been here before. And when did you ever sail?"

My pulse begins to race, and I take a quick, panicked breath. They know I haven't been here. They know I don't sail.

I don't know why I let it slip out.

"No," I reply. "I read up a little before I came." The words sound as false to me as they are, and I know they sound false to my mother too. If I were to glance at her right now, I'd see that troubled look on her face, the one I've seen a thousand times before. I learned early in life it bothered her, this strange ability of mine to sometimes know things I should not.

Jeff's phone rings and he turns the other way, while my mother walks ahead, frowning at the ground beneath her. "I hope they're going to water soon," she frets. "If it stays this dry, that carpet will be covered with dust by the time the ceremony starts."

She is right, unfortunately. I can see the soil shift loosely before me, the grass burned and threadbare beneath an unrelenting sun, all the way to the pavilion. If there were even the slightest breeze, we'd be choking on it right now.

We round the corner of the inn, and the lake comes into view, shimmering in the early July heat. It looks like any other lake, yet there's something about it that speaks to me. I stare, trying to place it, and as I do, my gaze is compelled upward, beyond its sapphire depths, to a cottage in the distance.

It's a tap, at first. A small tap between my shoulder blades, like a parent warning a child to pay attention. But then something shifts inside me, invisible anchors sinking into the ground, holding me in place. My stomach seems to drop as they go.

I know that house.

I want to look away. My heart is beating harder, and the fact that people are going to notice makes it beat harder still, but already a picture is forming in my head—a wide deck, a long, grassy slope leading to the water's edge.

"How can the grass be so dry with all this water around?" Abby asks, but her voice is growing dim beneath this sudden ringing in my ears.

And then, her words disappear entirely. There is no ground, no light, nothing to grab. I'm plummeting, and the fall is endless.

～

When my eyes open, I'm flat on my back. Soil clings to my skin and the sun is beating down so fiercely it drowns out all thought. I'm in some kind of field with a house in the distance, and a woman is leaning over me. Have I met her somewhere before? It feels like I have but I can't place her at all.

"Quinn!" she cries. "Oh, thank God. Are you okay?"

The light is too much. That drumming in my head turns into a gong. I need it to stop, so I squeeze my eyes shut. The smell of parched grass assaults me.

"Why am I here?" I whisper. The words are slurred, the voice barely my own. *God, my head hurts.*

"You fell," she says, "We're at the inn. For your wedding, remember?"

The woman is pleading with me as if I'm a child on the cusp of a tantrum, but nothing she says makes sense. *I* am already married. And since when did London get so *hot*? It's never like this here.

A man comes jogging toward us. His build is similar to Nick's —tall, muscular—but even from a distance, I know he's not Nick, not even close. My eyes flutter closed and for a moment, I feel like I'm with him again—watching the smile that starts slowly before it lifts high to one side, catching the faint scent of chlorine from his morning swim. Where is he? He was *right* next to me a second ago.

The man drops to the ground beside me, and the women scurry out of his way. "She must have tripped," one of them says, "and now she's really out of it. I think she may need to go to the hospital."

I'm not going anywhere with these people, but I feel that first burst of fear in my chest. The throbbing in my head is growing. What if they try to force me to leave with them? I don't even know that I'd be able to fight them off with my head like this.

"Where's Nick?" The words emerge wispy and insufficient, needy rather than commanding.

"The hotel manager is Mark," says another voice. "Maybe she means Mark?"

"Can you sit up?" the guy asks. "Come on, Quinn."

I squint, trying to see him better in the bright sun. *How does he know my name?* There's something familiar about him, but he also just has one of those faces. "Are you a doctor?"

His jaw sags open. "Babe, it's me. *Jeff.*"

What the hell is happening here? Why is this guy acting like we're old friends? I focus on him, trying to make sense of it.

"Your fiancé," he adds.

For a moment I just stare at him in horror. And then I begin scrambling backward, a useless attempt at escape. "No," I gasp, but even as I'm denying it, praying this is a nightmare, some part of my brain has begun to recognize him too, and remembers a different life, one in which Nick does not exist.

Nick does not exist.

I roll face down in the grass and begin to weep.

Buy Parallel here or read free in Kindle Unlimited.

ACKNOWLEDGMENTS

Thank you first to my amazing editor, Jennifer Roberts-Hall. You were the perfect sounding board for all things Olivia-related, and I don't know how I survived without you until now.

To Katie Foster Meyer, who basically determines right off the bat if a book gets published or goes in the trash. Thank you for reading and re-reading, for caring more than I do about NCAA compliance, liability, and keeping Olivia just on the right side of an assault conviction.

To Linda Russell at Sassy Sassy Fabulous PR for a million things. Thank you for holding my hand during the past two months, and for not laughing too hard at all my social media faux pas.

To my magnificent beta readers: Laura Ward Steuart (who, like Katie above, has to read a lot of my garbage to get to a keeper ... thanks for sticking with it!), Nancy Coleman, Amy Meyer, Karen Metcalf, Erin Thompson and Deanna Wolstenholme.

To Amy Meldrim Foster for answering all of my cross-country questions, and Kari March Designs for gorgeous teasers and cover.

Many thanks to my friends (you know who you are), my kids (but God forbid you ever read this), and my family for their unflagging support and encouragement.

Made in United States
Orlando, FL
08 June 2024

47643889R00185